THE
CRUELTY
OF LAMBS

THE
CRUELTY
OF LAMBS

ANGELENA BODEN

urbanepublications.com

First published in Great Britain in 2016 by Urbane Publications Ltd
Suite 3, Brown Europe House, 33/34 Gleaming Wood Drive, Chatham, Kent ME5 8RZ
Copyright ©Angelena Boden, 2016

A CIP catalogue record for this book is available from the British Library.

ISBN 978-1-911129-66-0
EPUB 978-1-911129-67-7
MOBI 978-1-911129-68-4

Design and Typeset by Julie Martin
Cover by Kevin Ancient

Printed in Great Britain by
CPI Group (UK) Ltd, Croydon, CR0 4YY

urbanepublications.com

The publisher supports the Forest Stewardship Council® (FSC®), the leading international forest-certification organisation. This
book is made from acid-free paper from an FSC®-certified provider. FSC is the only
forest-certification scheme supported by the leading environmental organisations, including Greenpeace.

For my daughters, Anousheh and Anisa

For Paul, who made it all possible

I will lift up mine eyes unto the hills,
from whence cometh my help.

Psalm 121

CHAPTER ONE

September 2014

Una Carrington felt the first rush of panic, not as a floaty, clammy sensation but as a deep groan in the colon which squirmed its way through the gut. It settled as a furry dryness in her mouth. She ran the tip of her tongue over her lips as she tried to force down the lump in her throat. Emptying her bag on the side of the washbasin, she plucked out a slim gold tube. There was only one way to relieve the sea-sick like feelings and that was a blood-red lipstick.

Other people flicked elastic bands on their wrists to scare away dark thoughts, no doubt suggested by their therapists, but Una had found her own way of getting control of the curl of anxiety in her gut.

In the dim light of the cloakroom, she leaned towards the faux-gilt mirror, stretching her narrow lips into a line. With the first dab of colour she waited for the tension to subside. It didn't. Tugging a paper towel from the dispenser she wiped it off and tried again with a similar colour from a different tube. She knew she was being irrational as she blotted the colour with a tissue, thinking that if anyone did a search of her house they would dig up lipsticks everywhere; in an old brown teapot, a ceramic dish from Portugal on the console table in the hall, bathrooms and even the garage.

Coat pockets would throw up the usual mishmash of coins,

tissues and tickets, but lurking in the depths the secret searcher would find a red lipstick.

Una spiked up her short, copper-tinted hair as she examined her pale skin pulled tightly across sharp cheekbones. A hint of shadow under dark blue eyes, a few fine lines around the mouth were the only signs of aging. The tips of her fingers smoothed in an expensive cream which she knew, deep down, could only deliver magic results to the hopeful or the deluded.

Three young women pushed open the door, arguing with each other for a place in front of the mirror. Una concentrated on stuffing down the spilled contents of her bag to avoid making eye contact.

'God, some people,' said the tall blonde shaking a mascara wand. 'That bloke is at least forty. Ancient.'

'He's from one of the banks. I've seen him in here before. Here, budge up a bit Zo.'

'I bet he's married.'

'Fit though. We can string him along. Get some drinks out of him.'

'What do you think of this tattoo Ali? I'm not sure I like it now. My mum went berserk.'

The door banged behind them leaving their strong Birmingham accents in their wake. Una to steadied herself against the basin. The lingering of their perfume assaulted her nostrils. Their youth and their words stung. She was almost forty. Half way through her life. The reality of it settled like an itchy blanket over her head. Taking slow deep breaths through her nose helped steady her nerves until she felt ready to return to her client.

'All this introspection is adding to your anxiety,' her doctor had told her as he printed off a prescription. 'You're too focused on yourself. Bring your children home from school, get a pet, have another baby.'

She'd slammed out of his surgery vowing never to go back yet the memory of that conversation played over like a scratched CD.

Jeff Archer was scrolling through his phone when she returned to the bar and did not acknowledge her immediately.

'There you are. I thought you'd slipped down the pan.' He laughed showing teeth yellowed from years of smoking.

Una curled her lip at his rough attempt at humour. She perched on the edge of the leather armchair to study him. His trousers strained around his bulging middle and she couldn't help noticing he wore socks of a different black. Why couldn't he have made an effort to look business-like she thought as he bent down to tie up his shoe-lace.

'Would you like to eat first?'

He pushed a sticky menu across an even stickier table. Una shook her head, lifting her empty glass for a refill. He'd chosen a good wine she conceded as the Sauvignon teased her tongue.

As he waited for his food, Jeff Archer explained his vision for a new hotel in inner city Birmingham. He spread out the plans, spilling drops of lager on the part marked Reception.

'We're trying to recreate the Japanese model of the capsule hotels you find in Tokyo. Have you been?'

Una nodded. She couldn't imagine the concept capturing the imagination of Birmingham.

'The difference is that part of the hotel will be traditional which is why we need staff but a third of it will be capsule rooms. They've not really taken off outside Japan but I think it's a great idea for the second city. Something a bit different.'

'Hmmm.' Una lifted her glass to her lips.

'I'm going to need you, or somebody, to recruit the staff, sort out the training, business planning, forecasting and marketing.'

Una winced as he over articulated the 'g' endings. So horribly Birmingham she thought.

'The usual sorts of things. I like the work you did with Dormez-vous last year. I see they've won an award for their customer service.'

He pushed the last few chips into his mouth and leaned back to assess her reaction.

Una felt on edge under his gaze. She ran a finger over her lips but stopped when she saw him smirking. She knew about men like Jeff Archway. He was the sort who would give her the contract but would want something other than the work in return. He'd be lucky she thought pulling out her iPad.

Straightening herself into a more formal pose she fired questions at him about schedules, fees, targets and budgets giving him no time to prevaricate.

'I'll get a proposal to you by tomorrow evening then I shall want to visit the site.'

Jeff tugged at his tie.

'There's not much to see at the moment. Give it a month.'

Swiping open her calendar Una glanced at the only free date for the following week.

'Next Wednesday at two.'

Her tone was expressionless, her lips set into a firm line. She stood up, gathered her briefcase and coat and held out her hand. Tall but slightly built, Una was aware she could be intimidating.

'It's that look,' Martha had said on many occasions. 'Those killer eyes.'

'Good to do business with you Jeff.'

His hand felt slimy against her cool skin. She shuddered as she pushed through a group of beer-stinking men towards the side door leading to Brindley Place. She chose to ignore the jibes about her flat chest. Being called a walking pencil wasn't worth challenging.

***

Una sat on a bench looking at, but not seeing, the moored narrow boats in their colourful livery. Some were operating as businesses serving coffee and snacks whilst another ferried those in need of retail therapy to the Mailbox complex. Birmingham was supposed to have more miles of canal than Venice but it was hard to draw a parallel under a grubby West Midlands sky.

A weariness came over her as she tied a silk scarf around her neck for a bit of extra protection from the cold breeze. She watched people going about their business but feeling as if she was trapped behind a large pane of glass. She felt part of the world, but not of it, as someone famous had once said. Una forced her mind back to the hotel contract, mentally calculating how much she could charge. Archer was a shrewd character so she would have to be careful.

Her phone rattled in her pocket.

'Hello Iain.'

'I've been trying to get hold of you since this morning. What time are you home? There's a chicken casserole on the go and some of that wine you love. I thought I might try my hand at a dessert. Any preference?'

Una felt a prickle of irritation.

'I don't know yet. I've still got things to do. You go ahead without me.'

'Oh. I see.'

She tried to ignore the fall of his voice.

'I can wait for you.'

Una bit down on the inside of her lip. Getting to her feet, she strode across the canal bridge towards the Convention Centre.

'As I said, Iain. I don't know my plans. I'll call you. OK?'

She flicked through some new emails before turning off her

phone. Her plan was to have a few drinks in a jazz bar tucked behind the banks and law offices in Colmore Row. It was a favourite haunt of Martha's who often went after work if the Blue Notes were playing. With the voice and looks of Lena Horne, Martha was a popular choice as a guest singer.

***

Dr. Iain Millar looked out onto the wet tarmac at the cars pulling into the neighbouring drives. Children were despatched from swimming or cubs, stomachs grumbling, he imagined, in anticipation of warming hotpots and fruit crumbles. With the twins away at school in Scotland, he felt the silence of the house fall like bag over his head. He couldn't remember the last time he and Una had sat down to a meal together and exchanged bits of news. She used to like him reading snippets from the Evening Mail especially when he picked out some particularly poorly written text.

Dunking bread into the remains of his meal, he tried to read bits of the paper but ended up slopping the sauce over somebody's obituary. Radio Three was on low in the background but he winced as the coloratura soprano ran, leapt and trilled her way over a piece Iain was not familiar with. It reminded him of the dentist's drill.

Shivering, he went in search of one of his shapeless cardigans which he'd rescued from one of Una's clearing out sessions. Their three storey Victorian house in Edgbaston had lost its warmth and eclectic cosiness over the years as Una had ripped out fireplaces, picture rails and any feature not fitting her view of Nordic minimalism. It now felt soulless.

The evening dragged on as Iain flicked between a rerun of a detective series and the news. He was alarmed at how the presenters seemed to take delight in making out Birmingham and other cities were on the verge of becoming some terrorist stronghold within a matter of days. Knocking his adopted city brought out his defences.

Whenever he heard a car pull up he assumed it was Una and went to the window to check. The clock of St. George's bonged the last chime of ten when he heard her key in the lock. She was muttering as she rifled through the post which she held in her hand as she stood in the doorway of his study.

'More bills.'

She waved them at him. Iain didn't miss the look of contempt in the coldness of her eyes. He struggled to get out of his chair, the muscles in his lower back pulling him back down. He hobbled after her into the kitchen where she poured some wine from the fridge despite having spent her evening alone in the bar. She knew she should have gone home instead of flirting with that smarmy twenty-three-year old from Central Point Recruitment.

'Have you eaten anything? Shall I warm this up for you?' He pointed to a bowl of chicken and rice.

She waved her hand in dismissal, emptying a bag of cashews into her mouth. Studying him through blurred eyes she noticed his hand shaking as he filled the kettle.

'What have you been doing all day?'

Iain flinched inwardly as he waved the cafetière in her direction.

'Do you want coffee?'

'You mean am I drunk? Suppose I am. It's all the pressure I'm under so are you surprised? I can't keep doing this on my own Iain. You're going to have to bring in some money soon.'

In an effort to keep his hand still, Iain focused on spooning coffee into Una's personalised mug. He placed it on the table with the sweetener capsule.

'I suppose you've been messing about with that bloody cello all day.' Una fought down the urge to have a go at him. It would only make her own headache worse. Slumped in the chair she moved the spoon around the mug with deliberate slowness.

Iain sat opposite her with his whisky.

'I've been practising, yes. We've got a concert coming up. I get paid for that. Good money in fact.'

She picked up a coaster and turned it round, tapping it on the table as she looked hard into his eyes.

'This won't do. A hundred quid here and there barely covers the food bills.' She paused. 'There's a new hotel opening up soon on the inner circle bus route. I'll be responsible for recruitment. You could do some of the cleaning. Twenty hours a week on minimum wage.'

Iain pushed his hands through his thinning hair. These were conversations he dreaded.

'I'm a musician Una. I don't know the first thing about hotels and cleaning contracts. I'm still looking for teaching work in the colleges but they've cut back on budgets. You know how bad it is at the moment.'

Una kicked back the chair and poured her coffee down the sink, slamming the cup on the draining board.

'Always some excuse with you. You've been unemployed now for over two years. You'll have to apply for Job Seekers or do some retraining course. It's what men do.'

Iain's jaw dropped a fraction. He tried to protest but the words were stuck like lumps of toffee on the roof of his mouth.

'I've never signed on in my life Una and I am not doing it now. Don't you think I've been humiliated enough?'

'There's no place for pride when it comes to money. It's your choice. Cleaning or dole money.'

She bent down to kiss his cheek.

'I'm sorry. It's just I'm so stressed all the time. I know it's not easy for you either. You coming to bed?'

She tried to pick up Beethoven, the sleeping cat, who hooked his stretched claws into her in protest and struggled free. Iain stared into his glass then out onto the wet streets as his thoughts waged war.

A nightmare jolted him from sleep in the early hours. His pyjama jacket was drenched with sweat as he thrashed about in the dark feeling for his glasses. It was the same terror. Girls pointing fingers at him, laughing, mocking and dancing around him. 'Dr. Millar is a pervert, Dr. Millar is a monster' they sang. Caricatured faces with bulging eyes and distorted mouths pressed onto the backs of his eyes.

'Shut up, SHUT UP,' he shouted to the empty room, struggling to his feet.

'What the hell's going on?' Una turned over to look at him. 'You're having a bad dream. There's no-one there. Go back to sleep.'

Leaning back on the pillows he sipped some water and picked up a strip of pink tablets. He examined them for a moment before pushing them back into the drawer. He would take Dr. Gordon's advice. Go downstairs and do something. Clean the kitchen floor, watch TV, play a game.

Una heard him close the door before turning on the bedside light. This was getting beyond a joke. She remembered the first time Iain had shouted out in the night. He'd smacked her across the face claiming afterwards he had no memory of it. Another time he'd called her a whore and a bitch but amnesia offered him a convenient way out. She'd researched night terrors resulting from traumatic memories and could only suppose that Iain had some unresolved issues.

Unable to sleep, she switched on her iPad and logged onto a game of Tetris to take the edge off her anxiety. At some level Iain's bizarre behaviour alarmed her because it was out of her control. He would be better if he was working she reasoned, logging out of the game and onto a search of potential jobs. By the time she was ready for sleep, she'd made a list for several possibilities she would present to him.

Iain sat at his desk adding a new line of music to his composition. It was a positive distraction which dragged his mind away from the distressing thoughts of those girls and back into sleep. Had it not been for the church clock alerting the good people of Edgbaston that they should have been at work fifteen minutes ago, he would have slept on. Stirring from his wing backed chair, he peered from behind the curtain to see the drive empty of his wife's BMW. His own car was out of road tax but he didn't feel he could ask Una to renew it.

A text message buzzed through on his old flip phone.

Pikuupin20F

Fergus you overgrown teenager, he thought fondly. At least learn to punctuate.

After a shower and shave Iain felt much calmer. He was scraping out the last blob of Dundee marmalade onto his toast when Fergus O'Neal pushed open the unlatched door.

'Where the feck are you?' His Birmingham accent was overridden with native Cork.

'Good heavens. What are you wearing?' Iain pointed to his friend's waistcoat splattered with a tapestry of flying pigs. Fergus had a reputation for ill-fitting shirts concealed by manic waistcoats.

'It's a new one. Freda found it online.' He grabbed a piece of toast and stuffed it in his mouth.

'You ready?' Crumbs flew out of his mouth onto his front. 'We've got to get to Aston and you know what the expressway is like. I always get lost.'

Iain locked his antique cello into its case, checked he had the relevant music, noticing the note on the edge of his desk. *Fill these in.* He flicked through the application forms for different jobs.

***

'You alright? You look knackered.'

Fergus pushed his way across a lane of traffic prompting a voluntary of horns.

'Didn't sleep that's all.'

'Maniac,' shouted Fergus raising a middle finger while Iain fiddled with the CD player.

They listened to a mediocre rendition of Handel's Water Music which Fergus criticised all the way to Aston Hall.

Most of the augmented orchestra had arrived and were either tuning up or nattering in low voices. As the musicians relaxed into their positions, Iain pushed away all thoughts that didn't involve Orlando Gibbons. Fergus took his place as first violinist, a button popping off his shirt as he leaned over to position his music.

'Feck,' he muttered as he struggled to fasten his jacket around his belly.

The charity concert in aid of the Children's Hospital was well attended. A nasty squeak from one of the oboes made Fergus scowl. 'That sounded like the slow release of a supressed fart,' he told the oboist who flushed to the eyebrows.

'That was a bit harsh. The young lad hasn't been playing

publicly for very long. You've probably traumatised him.' Iain loaded his cello into the car.

'He'll get over it. I can't be having noises like that popping out when least expected. God knows what the audience thought.'

Fergus chuntered on about musicians who couldn't control their instruments as they fought their way back down the A38, switching lanes with inches to spare. Iain closed his eyes and prayed they would live to play another day.

When they arrived back at Woodbourne House, Una was home. Iain's heart rolled down to his knees. He was hoping for a bit of time on his own to rest. His hand was aching from the awkward bowing action he'd had to adopt.

'Where've you been?'

He laid his cello carefully on the floor of the study before fishing out a crumpled programme from his pocket.

'Charity do for the children's hospital. I'm starving now.'

Una's eyes narrowed.

'Did you get paid?'

Iain averted his gaze.

'It was for charity Una. Not this time.'

'So who's going to fill the freezer this week? Me I suppose.'

Iain stood quietly by the kitchen sink watching a squirrel dart up an oak tree. He let her rant for a few minutes about his uselessness without uttering a word in his defence. It was pointless trying to make her see reason when she was in one of these moods.

When she paused to take a call he took his tea into the study and softly closed the door. The old sofa which had come from his mother's house gave him some comfort as he fingered the pulled threads and the familiar stain of spilt whisky.

Leaning back against its lumpy cushions he pulled open his tie with tired fingers. Holding out his right hand he observed the tremor which rippled from the wrist to the tip of his short nails. Morag would have made him go to the doctor's. In fact, she would have insisted on going with him. He thought back fondly to some of the happier times he had spent with his former wife. Had it not been for the madness of his late thirties he might be still in Scotland, teaching and composing.

He heard his wife's voice in the hallway. She was talking to someone called Abdi.

'Una?' he called.

A few minutes later the front door slammed hard and he listened to the crunch of tyres on the gravel. His scratch meal of cheese on toast triggered a severe heartburn. He bent over to relieve the worst of the pain, knowing that he should take a walk around the block. He promised himself he would after a nap. Beethoven pranced around his lap to find a comfortable spot, his tail knocking off Iain's glasses. Within minutes they were both asleep.

CHAPTER TWO

Iain sat at his oak desk tapping his fingers on the green inlay as he struggled to draft an advert for his tutorial business. The idea had come to him in a flash of inspiration as he mopped the kitchen floor. Some business guru on the radio was talking about the rise of self-employment amongst older people providing they had skills to offer and the right attitude.

With his father's Parker pen he sketched out some key words in a distinctive cursive script then stared out of the floor to ceiling sash windows onto the deserted street. A car was attempting a U turn watched by a ginger cat perched on the high wall protecting the primary school. A few amber leaves swirled down from an oak tree and settled on the wet verges.

Iain recalled memories of autumn being a lonely time of year. It brought an ending to his carefree summers and a return to the boarding school he hated. Bullies had mocked him because he preferred to play his cello rather than kick a football around. As he watched the tears of rain trickle down the window he tuned into those old feelings.

The trilling of the phone made him jump.

'Dr Millar? It's Tom O'Neal. Dad asked me to give you a call. How are you getting on with sorting out your social media stuff? If you're going into business you've got to have a strong on-line presence.'

Iain groaned inwardly.

'Still trying to formulate the wording. I'm not much good at this sort of thing.'

'I've got a couple of hours before college and I've got Mum's car. Shall I pop round and give you a hand?'

'Well that's very kind of you Tom. Thank you.'

Iain paused and tugged his beard.

'I can't pay you though Tom. Bit short at the moment.'

'No need. It's a favour.'

Iain went back to his task. It's funny how people can't write legibly anymore Iain thought idly, twiddling the fountain pen in his knotty fingers. He supposed it was because of the new technology. Even composers seem to prefer computer programmes instead of handcrafting their manuscripts. Fergus had shown him how to use notation software but Iain preferred the feel of placing the notes carefully on the stave with his special pen, transposing the beauty of the music he heard in his head.

He made an attempt to tidy up his study which was the only room in the house that had escaped Una's ruthless refurbishment. Rarely did he argue with her, knowing where it might lead, but he'd firmly said no to the slightest suggestion of redecoration. For weeks she'd ignored him, walking out of the room when he appeared, refusing his calls, maintaining a cold silence to his attempts at conversation.

While he waited for Tom, Iain made an effort to understand Twitter. He wanted to prove he wasn't a complete technophobe.

He mumbled to himself about the pointlessness of it all and who really cared if you were having the most delicious coffee at Paddington station. He followed the instructions to create an account @cellolessonBrum, finally managing to download a picture of a cello and post his first tweet. The 140 character limit stopped him mid word but with some creative editing he managed to compose something suitable. Before posting he wondered if twenty pounds for a thirty-minute tutorial was a reasonable fee. He could call Una for some advice but was wary about what she would say. Taking a slurp of his cold coffee he pressed the Tweet button, feeling a buzz of achievement. Old dogs can be taught new techy tricks he told himself.

Tom's wide grin pressed against the study window as he knocked gently to attract Iain's attention.

'We do have a door you know.' Iain smiled and ushered Tom into the study. It was a treat to have some young company. He was fond of Tom with his 'nothing is a problem' attitude.

'Coffee or something cold?'

'I don't suppose you have any hot chocolate?'

'Coming up. Make yourself comfortable at the desk.'

He set down the tray down on the edge of the desk before handing Tom a mug, annoyed that his hands were shaking a little.

'I've set up a Twitter account,' he said proudly.

'Great stuff. What's your handle name?'

Iain frowned.

'Your account name.'

'Ah.' Iain told him.

He watched with fascination as Tom's fingers flew across the keyboard.

'You've got a couple of followers already. See. Let's make it more interesting.'

Tom pushed a biscuit into his mouth until it half disappeared. He created a backdrop of musical scores and animated cellos pausing to ask Iain for some personal information.

'What's your USP?'

Iain laughed. 'You've got me there.'

'Sorry. What makes you special? Dad says you are really good teacher. You were at St. Hilda's weren't you? You taught one of my girlfriends.'

Iain felt a prickly heat rise from his neck. He blew out his breath as he grappled with the rising panic.

'Are you alright Dr. Millar? Sit down here. I'll fetch you some water.'

Iain leaned forward and took a few sips as the room zoomed back into focus.

'I'm fine. Just a spot of dizziness. I keep meaning to see the doctor but ... well ... it passes. Getting old I suppose.'

'Shall we stop there for today? I can do the rest at home. We need to create a Facebook page. Dad's got one so I can grab some pictures of the quartet.'

Iain mopped his temple with his sleeve.

'Fergus has a Facebook page?'

'It's the way to do business these days Dr. Millar. He has to reach as many punters as possible for the gigs.'

Tom scrolled through his laptop and logged onto the site.

'Here. It's quite an eye catcher isn't it? He's also got stuff on YouTube. I can film you while you play or give a mock lesson. Look, here's Dad's channel.'

Realising that he had hardly left the house other than for rehearsals and concerts, Iain felt detached from the real world. The virtual world was alien and made him feel uneasy. People would be able to search his name and track him down.

'Tom, isn't this dangerous? I mean couldn't I be stalked or something.'

He tried to keep the tremble out of his voice. He berated himself for sounding pathetic.

'You're not using your own name and there are privacy settings. Don't worry. I will make it as secure as I can. Sorry but I need to get to college now. Leave it with me.'

Iain saw him to the door.

'Don't people still put notices in shop windows these days? I thought I'd take these to the library and places later today.' He showed Tom some handwritten cards.

'Sure. There are loads in the newsagents in Bournville. Dog walking, window cleaning, that sort of thing.'

Watching him go, Iain mentally planned his route in the hope that some places would display his adverts at no cost. He set off, smiling at people as he wandered through the city centre streets, but received blank stares for his efforts. Feeling foolish like those naïve people who start up conversations on the tube, he kept his head down. He remembered Una telling him he acted like a child always looking for approval.

Birmingham had grown in cultural status over the years so he was hopeful he would find some adults wishing to indulge their dream of playing an instrument. This way he could go back to teaching on his terms and not need any police checks.

By the end of the week he'd received some email enquiries and his twitter account boasted over twenty followers. For the first time in two years Iain was getting up with enthusiasm, keen to further his marketing campaign. Now that Tom had helped him understand ways to avoid or deal with trolling, he was enjoying being part of the digital age.

Una had been leaving the house before daylight and returning late at night. He tried hard to accept that she was working so hard for their sake but was stabbed by guilt whenever her critical eyes met his.

One evening she'd startled him from his sleep on the sofa when she came back earlier than expected. Pulling himself into a sitting position, he flexed the cramp out of his right hand.

'Hello,' she said.

Iain smiled, registering the dull look on her face. He followed her into the kitchen with the aim of giving her a hug but she quickly turned away to lose herself in the vicious beating of eggs. He felt crushed.

'I'm making an omelette. Do you want something?'

'I'll have some hot water and ginger and one of your heartburn tablets please.'

Una passed him the packet as she rattled a knife across a sprig of parsley.

'Have you applied for those jobs? I left you the forms. I am sure you will get something. I've got a couple more leads for you. We can sit and do the forms together. I am sure I can push for an interview for this week.'

Iain hesitated, blowing on the boiling water in his mug. He wanted to tell her about his business, ask her for advice but above all he wanted some words of encouragement.

'Iain? Jobs?'

She swung round to face him, the knife pointing in his direction. She pushed back the short strands of hair from her damp cheeks.

Bracing himself he said, 'I've set up a business. Music lessons for adults. Mainly cello to start with but theory as well. Maybe composition later.'

He waited nervously for her reaction.

Una set her mouth in a line and flipped over the omelette. It broke in the middle. 'You? Business? What do you know about business?'

Iain twisted a few strands of his beard. The smell of food filled him with nausea. He tried to ignore the scorn in her voice.

'I've got a couple of students already. Tom O'Neal's been helping me with the marketing. He's a clever lad.'

'Really. How much are you charging? Where's the business plan?'

'The going rate for music lessons.' Iain knew he'd under sold himself but it didn't matter as long as it meant he could teach again.

'You can't make a business work as a one-man band.'

'I'm not a band,' he laughed, hoping she would yield to the humour.

Una pushed her plate away and sat iron- faced as he explained his ideas. Discouraged by her indifference he shut up.

'If you hadn't put us in this situation…'

'Please Una. Not again. We're both tired.'

Una stood up and slammed her plate on the table with such force it split in two.

'Well maybe I'm missing something here Iain. You got sacked for gross misconduct…'

'That's not true. I…'

'Shut up. You can't get another teaching job as a result. Which bit am I missing here?'

Iain flinched, pushing back his chair. Una's voice was morphing into those of his nightmares like a screech on the E string of a violin. Hands clapped to his ears he slowly counted down from ten: three, two, and one. When he opened his eyes, she'd disappeared.

Brooding over an untouched whisky, Iain let his thoughts wander back to when he and Una had fun together. They competed in the kitchen to see who could produce the most outlandish dishes whilst reading bits of the newspaper to each other. Una didn't understand music but she supported some of his concerts even if she left at the interval. She would wait for him in the bar, slipping her arm through his as they walked back through the deserted Edgbaston streets. Why had she become so cold and distant over the past two years?

Iain needed to know. He trod softly up the stairs and knocked on the bedroom door.

'Una? Can I come in?'

She opened it a fraction.

'What do you want now?'

She let the door slide open and went back to moisturising her skin. He watched her in the mirror. Once slim, she was now thin with pronounced collar bone and shoulders.

'Are you eating anything Una? You've lost so much weight.'

The genuine concern in his voice made her look up. She would have shared her fears about food with him at one time but now his enquiry was an invasion. It was nothing to do with him.

'I'm tired. What is it?'

Sitting on the bed he tried to explain how he was feeling but the words wouldn't come.

'Well?'

He slumped towards his knees. He'd turned fifty and should have been entertaining pleasant thoughts about retirement. Instead there were two children to educate, although the trust from his father took care of that for now, a millstone mortgage that Una was having to pay on her own and no real work. He needed to talk about it, to work through what they could do to change things.

'I know things are difficult but we could sell this house and buy something smaller. Maybe a bit out of town. A fresh start would help and take some pressure off.'

Una turned to him, tweezers still in her hand.

'I am not compromising my lifestyle because of you. If you want to move then go on your own.'

Iain felt close to roaring. Whatever he suggested she continued to stonewall.

'It's not all about you. We have to think about the twins. I know you don't rate me as a husband anymore but I am trying to do my best as a father.'

His voice shook as did his hand.

'Why won't you be reasonable?'

Una turned back to the mirror and rolled her eyes.

'I am being very reasonable. I am telling you that the way to sort this out is for you to get a job. Which bit of that don't you understand? Don't come up with any more crackpot ideas Iain. The answer is no.'

For an isolated second, Iain wanted to wrap his fingers around her throat and squeeze. The voices silently urged him on. Shocked to see himself flexing his fingers he bolted from the room and barricaded himself in his study for the night.

A few days later

Iain postponed a coffee-catch up with Fergus until he was able to lift his arm without pain.

'I'm going to have to bow out of the Sibelius,' he said quietly.

'Oh very clever.'

Fergus's eye locked onto the indigo bruising.

'I slipped and banged it on a window ledge. Nothing major.'

Iain took a sip of his coffee, pulled a face and added some sugar.

'Oh right. I see. Hmm. Like walking into a door? Did you lose your heart to a starship trooper as well?'

Iain stared into his mug aware that Fergus was shaking his head to show he didn't believe him.

'You need to get it checked out. It could have one of those hairline fractures and I can't do without my cellist.'

Fergus was about to say it wasn't the first time he'd noticed bruising on Iain's arms but clamped his lips shut and changed the subject.

Iain checked his watch. He needed to get home. Fergus eased his bulk from behind the table, knocking over someone's cappuccino. He grinned at the killer look from the woman who owned it.

'Una's treating me to dinner tonight and I promised to sort out a film. She said something about Netflix but I've no idea what she's talking about.'

Iain perched his frayed trilby on his thinning hair and pulling up his collar strode out as the rain eased off. He had to wait for over half an hour for the number nine bus which boasted an eight-minute service. Iain poured his coins into the slot while the driver showed as much courtesy as a slab of lard.

By the time he got to the house, the damp was seeping into his skin. His arm throbbed as he fumbled in the drawers for some painkillers. The convector heater in his study threw out enough heat to allow him to remove his jacket and sit at his desk. Dr. Gordon's number was programmed into the phone but as soon as it was answered, Iain hung up. Pulling up his sleeve, he gingerly touched the bruise which had taken the shape of a ragged map of Australia.

He was looking forward to the food from the new Persian restaurant around the corner and a good bottle of red. Una liked Bill Nighy so maybe they could watch the Exotic Marigold Hotel. She would know how to access it. He felt the heaviness in his chest evaporate as he anticipated the evening. An email pinged its arrival. A music group in Oxford wanted to buy one of his compositions. The sun popped into his world to say goodnight.

Iain was woken up by the sound of someone trying to break down the front door. Struggling to his feet he went into the porch to see Una slumped on the floor.

'Forgot the time,' she slurred, sliding her arms around his neck.

He helped her up and guided her into the living room. The church clock chimed two.

'If you'd not provoked me, I'd have come home earlier. You really need to behave better.'

As she kissed him hard, Iain recoiled from the stench of her breath. Giggling and stumbling she bit his lower lip until she drew blood. He unpicked her hands from his wrists, leaving her to slump back on the sofa.

CHAPTER THREE

Hammers banged away inside Una's head as she circled the car park for a suitable space for her car. The previous week she'd screamed at somebody from another office block who'd dared to take her space. Now she noticed Daryn's vintage Rover straddled across the white lines of a prime spot.

She thumped her fists on the steering wheel unable to articulate her rage. Who the hell did he think he was? Twenty-four, smug now that his remix for a famous American singer had received stunning reviews, Daryn summed up everything Una despised about the millennial generation; selfish, showy and anti-authority. She dampened down any ideas that she might be envious.

Seething at having to park in a side road, Una grabbed a lipstick from the glove compartment and dabbed on the soothing red with her fingertip before pulling her bags from the boot. She marched over to the building and up three flights of stairs to the offices of Aspire Ltd.

Una had built her training business since the early nineties, attracting huge sums of public sector money for the development of her Back to Work programmes. She'd focused on women returners who had lost their confidence after so many years at home raising children. She'd fenced passionately with her critics, blasted those who tried to copy her, earning her a fearsome reputation. Martha had once told her she could package elephant dung and sell it back to the safari parks, so persuasive were her arguments.

'Meeting in five everybody,' she called, poking her head round the door of the main office. 'Shelly, can you make coffee please.'

Spinning round to face Daryn, she said, 'You and I need to talk.'

Daryn tugged at his sapphire cufflinks to hide the burgeoning smirk on his lips.

The team of six gathered in the boardroom, mingling with some of the associates who had travelled into Birmingham for the meeting. Muted voices slipped in and out of awkward conversations whilst casting glances in Una's direction as she scrawled notes on the whiteboard.

Mike, the Health and Safety trainer was cracking his knuckles when Una spun round on her heels to glare at him.

'I hope she's not going to have one of her jelly throwing moments,' muttered Baljit to no-one in particular as she took her place.

'Quiet everyone.' Una rolled up the sleeves of her grey cashmere jumper.

'I want to start the meeting with the complaint from Delaney's restaurant. They are refusing to settle the invoice as they say the customer service training they had last month was too basic. The actual words from the HR Manager were, 'A pig on steroids would have injected more energy into the day. It didn't include anything on…' Una slipped on her red designer glasses to re-read the wording… *reputation management.*'

An awkward moment followed as eyes twizzled round to

Anita who had delivered the programme. Before speaking, she reached for her bottle of water.

'I went through the outline with them in advance as always and Amy from HR was happy with it. There were a couple of people on the graduate scheme who said they'd done it all before on their placement year. Maybe that's where it's come from.'

'Did you speak to them?'

'I put them in charge of an exercise and they seemed fine after that.'

A few seconds of menacing silence hovered over the room.

'You and I will discuss this with the manager and get it sorted out. We can't afford to be losing work when business is tough for everyone.'

Pushing back her chair, Una grabbed a couple of marker pens and handed them to Shelly, indicating the white board.

'Schedule for the next three months. Mike?'

'Hmm. Er… pretty full on for me. Most of it's ongoing work.'

'What about that meeting with Peglegs?'

'Peglegs?' Ann cut in.

'That new factory over Longbridge way. They make prosthetic limbs.'

'And they get away with calling it that?' Ann's jaw dropped in disgust. 'That's outrageous. They need some diversity training.'

She typed the company name into her tablet, harrumphing as the website sprung into shape.

'Let's not get bogged down in this. Is there potential for a new contract?'

Mike shifted in his seat. He tugged at a loose thread on his jumper, muttering it was early days and that the company wasn't really sure about what training it needed.

'They're talking to the college as well.'

The truth was that Peglegs had offered him a personal contract without wanting to involve Aspire. Una's laser eyes zapped him again.

'Is that so?' she said drily. 'I must get in touch with them myself.'

'What have you brought to the table Jo? Siobhan? Anybody?'

She tapped the end of a biro against her teeth. Only the whirr and clank of a copier in the next office rattled the silence.

'Baljit, how are your negotiations going with Restore? Surely they recognise your fluency in Punjabi as being an asset. Most of their staff don't speak much English.'

Baljit was about to respond when Ann said, through pinched lips, 'I don't think you are supposed to make comments like that.'

Baljit explained that the company were focusing on digital marketing training. 'We don't have anyone at the right level to do their training.'

'I hope you didn't tell them that. We have Carol.'

Una could feel her patience leaking through her pores. They didn't understand that the business badly needed new work as it was bleeding money. It seemed only she had the passion to make Aspire the most successful training business in the UK. Why didn't they share that vision? Her darkening mood was felt like a solar eclipse.

'Well while you've been sitting on your backsides, I've been working up a new contract with Restwell Hotels. We really need to shine at this one. Standards are slipping and we can't afford to let competitors sneak in through the back door.'

Una went on to give some details and spell out the expectations. As she spoke, she slipped her fingers around the lipstick barrel in her pocket. Towards the end of the meeting she caught Daryn playing on his new phablet.

'I'm assuming you've almost finished the changes to the website. You're overdue on this.'

Daryn didn't raise his eyes to deliver his unexpected strike.

'I'm leaving tomorrow and no I haven't finished. I put my notice on your desk last week.'

A collective 'what?' followed.

'You can't do that. You have a contract.'

'I don't have a written contract. You never sorted it out.'

The words strangled themselves in Una's throat. She wanted to leap across the desk and smack the smirk off his pouty lips. As if translating the ideas into actions, she knocked over the flipchart stand with all eyes watching it crash to the floor then swivel to Daryn who seemed unfazed by his boss's rising anger.

'I will sue you Daryn.'

'Oh dear. Time to go.'

Daryn flicked his dark fringe as he slowly made his move out of the room. He couldn't wait to tell Keith he'd finally done it. He'd be so proud and he could pack his stuff in those gorgeous powder pink and blue boxes he'd bought off eBay.

As he reached the door, he squared up to Una.

'I'm not going to be treated like a slug crawling over your keyboard anymore. I've got a big fat cheque coming my way.'

He sang a few bars of his new release, 'I don't need nobody,' sashaying out of the room.

'When your cheque runs out don't come back here whining. Pack your stuff and take your double negatives with you,' Una yelled not caring that her team were watching in fascinated horror. The atmosphere in the room was sulphurous with nobody daring to move. It was like one of those horrible moments when someone drops a fart and makes sure nobody thinks it was them.

As the adrenalin reduced to its simmer point, Una muttered a weak apology through tight red lips.

'Meeting over. Get working on some new contacts today. We need more business.'

She went back to her office and slumped in her chair for a while. Her thoughts bounced around from wanting to lay into somebody to needing to schmooze some clients. Iain's number came up on her phone but she dismissed the call. Maybe when he'd rearranged his brains she would speak to him. The denial over his sacking, his irresponsibility over helping with their finances and his constant fawning over her with his boring cooking made her shudder.

She picked over some bank statements hardly daring to look at the more recent ones as she scribbled computations and cash-flow options in her day book. Aspire was barely covering overheads and without more business she would be forced to approach the bank again. Or cut costs and that meant jobs.

She stretched over her desk to drag the landline towards her.

'Una Carrington. Have you had a chance to go through those figures Jeff? We're getting busy and I wanted to make sure we'd got your work booked in.'

'Good morning to you too. Yes, I have, but it's way over budget. You will need to cut by at least 25%. Oh and Wednesday isn't possible for the site visit. I'll be in touch shortly with a final decision.'

Una breathed in slowly.

'I've booked my time out already for that meeting.'

'You will have to unbook it and just so you don't make any more forward plans, we are talking to Ambitious People. I like the look of their ideas. Very fresh and innovative. I did say we couldn't commission without three quotes. It's all about best value as I am sure you understand.'

Una heard the emphasis on *you*. She felt paranoid. What did he mean? She was about to ask but he'd hung up.

Twiddling her pencil with such force until it snapped, a thought crossed her mind. Maybe Iain was behind this sudden downturn in business. His behaviour was becoming increasingly bizarre but he couldn't see it. He didn't remember things he'd done or said to her. She massaged her aching temples in an effort to clear her mind. She called in Carol who was mid conversation with Mike. Una studied their faces. She didn't trust either of them.

'Can we talk social media?'

Carol placed her coffee carefully on a coaster.

'Now Daryn's gone we need someone to pick up his work and you're good at this stuff. I don't think I am going to replace him just yet. We need to build a strong platform so … what do you think?'

Carol was Aspire's digital marketing trainer who had recently married an investment banker who worked in Hong Kong most of the year. He was desperate for her to join him but every time she tried to tell Una she felt her ribs collapse. Her resignation letter had lain crumpled at the bottom of her briefcase for days.

'And can you drum up some more business with your contacts in insurance? I will pay you commission.'

Carol shuffled in her seat re-running in her head some of the disparaging comments she'd heard about Una at a recent networking event. Vampire lips was one of them. She suppressed a smile.

'I'll see what I can do.' Tears threatened to spring from her pale green eyes as she hated herself for being such a people pleaser.

Mid October 2014

October half term was approaching. The twins needed collecting from Edinburgh but Una had no time to make the five hour drive north. Iain was slouching around at home so he would have to go but that meant taking her precious car.

'Damn him to hell,' she said out loud throwing her pen across the desk.

Iain did not answer her call straight away.

'Where have you been? I've called you three times in the past hour.'

Iain ignored her astringent tone as he told her with a burst of enthusiasm about his busy morning teaching.

'I'm up to seven students already and I've been paid,' he added, a triumphant grin on his face. He waited her for to say well done.

'The twins are not coming back this half term I've decided. I've no time and you've no transport. You'd better ring the school and tell them they will stay for the holiday programmes.'

Iain froze as an icy chill shot down the line.

'They were so looking forward to it. We'd planned a whole week of free stuff to do in Cannon Hill Park. It's the art and drama festival at the MAC.'

'I can't do anything about it. They'll understand.'

A line buzzed in his ear.

Una stared at the phone. Something felt off. His tone was cooler than usual. Was he still upset that she'd come home drunk and started the row over the disgusting state of the kitchen? Her mind was dragged back to that moment when she threw the Beef Wellington he'd made into the bin. Her cheeks burned. Had he really looked that stricken? He'd provoked her with all those sales particulars of cheap, nasty houses but she couldn't remember the exact feeling she'd had as she picked up the dish. At some level she realised she wanted to hurt him because he was so… fucking reasonable at times. She'd apologised later and tried to give him a hug but he'd pushed her away with such force she'd fallen against the door jamb. It was his blank stare, followed by the hollow laugh that had left her off balance.

Una now stared out of the window, stroking the site of the cut on her elbow. Later that day Iain spoke to his children, explaining how much he missed them and that he'd set up a music teaching business. When it came to telling them it was best they stayed at school for the holiday he felt his gut smoulder.

'That's great news Dad,' said James keeping his voice light but Iain detected the hidden disappointment. 'You're a brilliant teacher. It'll soon be Christmas anyway.'

Iain pushed his finger under his glasses to rub his eye. He drew on his son's strength.

'Daddy, we want to go to day school and live at home. We don't want to be up here anymore.'

'Jo, shut up,' hissed her twin. 'We agreed.'

Iain felt his heart swell. He would endure any row or worse with Una just to have the twins back home. He was careful not to promise anything however.

'We'll talk about it during the Christmas holidays. You be good both of you. Love you.'

He sat at his desk quietly thinking back over the years he'd been without his family in the sprawling house which spoke coldly to him. Its sinister rooms were ripped of any comfort and safety and it wasn't solely as a result of Una's redesign.

It used to be such a welcoming place, a port in a storm but now he felt unsafe anywhere other than in his study with its heavy oak furniture from his family home. It was as if the love was polished into the wood and stitched into the fabrics and tartans of his clan.

The twins hadn't been planned. Una wanted to sue the pill manufacturer, the doctors and even Iain for conning her into having children she didn't want. In that first year of exhaustion and depression, she had accused him of plotting to screw up her carefully planned life but as they became talkative toddlers she softened and seemed determined to give them all the material things she'd never had.

She'd told him about her ex-husband Rick – a useless prick she'd called him who had cleared off to Saudi to teach English. They had screamed at each other as the coffin lid was screwed down on their marriage, his parting words being he'd sooner chop his own hand off than live with the Screaming Furies. He remembered the night she had told him the story over a takeaway curry, a few drinks and some tender if unimaginative lovemaking.

Iain puffed out his cheeks and sighed deeply. He needed to practice the Bach Two Part Invention but his fingers felt too stiff although the tremor seemed to have settled down. A violin and cello duet played with Fergus was his idea of paradise. Iain once told him that he felt they were twin souls when they played together. Fergus had given him a colourful mouthful.

Later that evening Una appeared at his door nibbling the edges of a rice cake.

'Did you speak to the twins?'

Iain nodded, not able to face her. He felt his chest fill with anger.

'What about this trust fund business? Can we access it?'

'I don't know much about it. It's a mixed portfolio or something. Why is this so important to you? We can't use it to pay down debt Una.'

Una leaned back and sipped her wine. He was hiding something. She could tell from the way his eyes seem to dart around the room.

'Well you had better find a way of accessing some of it. Ring them tomorrow then meet me for lunch.'

She reached into the fruit bowl for a pear watching his expression. He knew damn well how the trust fund worked.

'Well?'

Iain turned his back on her and stood rigid. He turned the word no around in his mouth for a while before it slipped out of his control.

'What do you mean no? We're supposed to share everything so what's with the sudden what's mine is mine attitude? We're married. We're supposed to share everything.'

Tossing the rest of the pear in the bin she touched his arm.

'It's just to get us out of a temporary hole. We can pay it back after Christmas when things pick up.'

'I said no. That trust fund is for the children and I promised my father…'

Una gave a rough slap on his chest. The mention of his sanctimonious father made her see red. The pain of the first blow across his face sent Iain reeling backwards. He put out his hands to stop him from falling as she continued to slap his head.

'For God's sake Una. Stop. Calm down.' Iain pleaded as his wife picked up the wok from the draining board and brandished it in the air. He grabbed her wrist to knock it out of her hand but she pulled away in such a manner that her wrist turned awkwardly.

'Look at what you've done,' she screamed. 'You've broken it.'

'Let me see.' He examined her wrist. 'It's just twisted.'

She pulled it away shrieking in pain.

'You're a freak. A mental case. You can't see what you're doing. I could have you up for abuse. It's a good job the twins aren't here to witness your madness.'

Iain's jaw dropped.

'You were the one who attacked me and was going to bash my brains out with that wok. Have you been drinking again?'

'That's rich coming from you. Have you counted up the number of whisky bottles in the recycling lately? That plus those pills must be giving you amnesia. You're the one who provokes these fights. I just defend myself.'

Una picked up an almost empty wine bottle and slurped the contents. Wiping her mouth with the back of her hand she said calmly and deliberately, 'Don't come near me Iain or I shall report you for assault. You don't exactly have a clean record so I suggest you think carefully about what that might mean.'

For the next two weeks, she ignored all his efforts to communicate with her. When he went into the kitchen for food, she went out. Some nights she didn't go home, preferring to hang about the bars. Nothing Iain tried would break the deadlock. He left Una notes of apology and small gifts which he later found in the bin.

When he wasn't teaching or rehearsing he tramped the streets, hat pulled down, scarf covering his face, listening to music through his headphones. At times of utter desperation, only Elgar could soothe him.

Looking out at the driving rain one evening, he watched her car swing into the leaf-sodden driveway. She paused to make a phone call. Outside a Jack Russell was walking its owner. In the darkness he heard someone talking to him.

'She's home early,' said the voice. 'She's caught you out. Look at that food she's bought, injected with the poison that is going to kill you.'

Iain rammed his hands over his ears.

'Go away please. Please,' he begged. The hectoring noise evaporated as quickly as it had come.

'I'm home,' she called as she emptied her bags of chicken, salad, cheesecake and wine. 'I thought I'd make us a special dinner tonight. I met Martha in town. There might be a chance of doing some work with her.'

Iain was wandering about the hallway muttering to himself. A whooshing sound filled his ears as he watched her approach him with a glass of wine. He froze as she slid her arms around his neck and kissed him gently on the lips.

'I'm glad you're back to normal,' she said, slipping her hand inside his shirt.

Iain stepped back quickly and the cat yelped. He searched his wife's gaunt face looking for a sign, of what, he didn't know. Her cheek bones seem to morph into daggers. The wine in her hand turned to blood. Reality slid from his grasp as he stumbled into the downstairs bathroom to be violently sick.

CHAPTER FOUR

A warm glow lit up the front bedroom at number five across the road. Bill Simmons had a prostate problem which got him up several times a night. On his way back from the bathroom, his habit was to pull back the curtain for no reason other than to acquaint himself with the night. This time it was different. Straining his eyes he saw a vague shape of a man slumped against a tree.

Mary woke up, shielding her eyes from the sodium lights lining the road.

'What is it Bill? You ok?'

'I think Iain Millar's out cold in his front garden,' he muttered. 'Not like him to get into such a state.'

Mary got up to look.

'Don't let him see us. It looks as if he's bashed his head. Do you think we should see if he's alright or ask him in?'

Mary thought back to a time when she heard Una shouting some terrible things at him. It had been a hot summer so all the windows had been thrown open. She'd watched Iain stagger out of the house and sit on the bench under the oak tree for hours.

'He won't want us both seeing him in this state. I'll get dressed and see if he wants anything. You go back to bed.'

'It's terrible… being thrown out of your own house like that.'

'We can't make those sort of assumptions,' said Bill wobbling as he pulled on his trousers.

'I know he's had a rough patch what with those wicked girls saying those things about him and him losing his job as a result but...' Mary tidied up the newspapers they'd been reading.

'Tabloid hype, my love. I'll go and see if he's okay.'

Mary followed him down to the kitchen where she emptied the dishwasher whilst waiting for the kettle to boil.

'He says he's ok. Fell over in the garage and banged his head then locked himself out.'

Bill hung his jacket up and rubbed his hands.

'It's cold enough to freeze a bull's...'

'Bill. Language.'

They sat in the warm glow of their 1970's kitchen, raising mugs to their lips in unison.

'Do you believe him?' Mary had her doubts.

Bill sighed accepting a mug of weak tea.

'It's not our business. I invited him back here but he just wanted to go back to his own bed. He seemed a bit out of it. He was talking about some man told him to do something or other. He wasn't making much sense.'

A final glance out of the window told him that Iain had gone indoors.

He didn't believe that the cut on Iain's head was from a fall; more likely some sort of blunt object but it was pure speculation. Bill was unable to go back to sleep. The gaudy red numbers on the clock showed 5.08. Thank goodness he wasn't expected anywhere.

He went downstairs to let Mitch, their dachshund, out into the garden while he hatched a plan to invite Iain to the Rutter Requiem at Coventry Cathedral. Bill was a tenor in the Cathedral choir so such an idea wouldn't seem contrived. He didn't know what he hoped to achieve by it other than improving neighbourly relationships.

Hearing voices in the garden, Una came downstairs and opened the door, her hair standing up like bare twigs.

'What the hell's going on? Come inside before the curtain twitchers wake up. You must have been sleepwalking.'

Una examined the deep gash on Iain's temple and shook her head.

'How've you done this? You need to see Dr. Gordon about your clumsiness Iain. I've seen how your nerves twitch. It could be something serious. You'd better clean that up.'

Iain went in search of the first aid box and wincing, dabbed some antiseptic on the wound. He tried to block Una's grating voice which was competing with the others in his head.

'SHUT UP Una. My man is trying to tell me something. GO AWAY.' He turned to face her. 'For your own safety, please go away.'

Una clenched a fist and punched it into her open palm. She felt a muscle snap in her neck.

'What are you talking about Iain? What man? There's no one here.'

'Stop pretending. You're on their side. I don't know what your plan is but I've got my man helping me.'

Iain mumbled as he paced around the kitchen leaving Una to watch his manic gesturing in a bemused silence. She vowed to speak to Dr. Gordon as soon as the surgery opened.

'Has my husband been to see you recently?'

'I'm sorry I can't tell you that. It's patient confidentiality Miss Carrington. You need to talk to Iain yourself.'

Una bit her lip to block the flow of sarcasm.

'He won't talk to me but he's behaving like someone who's lost his mind. Talking about his man giving him instructions. I know he's under stress but this is beyond me. You have to do something.'

Dr. Gordon was scrolling through Iain's notes as he waited for Una to finish her rant.

'I can call him in for a routine WellMan check but I still can't disclose anything discussed. I'm sure you understand that.'

'No I bloody well don't. I'm the one who's stressed all the time and his behaviour is so bizarre it's making it worse. You need to come over. See for yourself.'

Her tone softened.

'I am really concerned about him.'

A few days later

As she stirred her coffee in the kitchen, unable to concentrate on the meeting she had yet to prepare for, Una heard the sound of furniture being moved directly above.

Iain appeared with the wooden base and headboard of an old single bed from the top floor. He pushed open the door of his music room and propped the bits against the wall before fetching his tool box.

'What are you doing?' Una rested her hands on her hips.

As he assembled the frame, Iain whistled, ignoring her rapid fire of questions.

'Iain, what's going on?' She pulled the hammer from his hand. Sighing in a way an exasperated parent might, he held out his hand for its return.

'Answer me first or I will call 999. You're clearly not well Iain.'

'All I am doing is setting up a bed so I can have some peace.'

Iain banged the slats into place then heaved on the mattress together with some bedding that had been in storage. Una recognised the duvet cover as the one they had shared in her tiny London flat. She swallowed hard.

'You don't come in here anymore. This is my room. With my things.'

Una saw his eyes contract into the size of a tiny drill bit which bored through her skull. She smelt her own fear as he backed her towards the door. She watched as he fitted brass bolts to the door, trying to find some words which would trigger him back into reality. He pushed past her in search of a kettle, tea and coffee, long life milk and a packet of biscuits which he placed ritualistically on a table by the window. He moved the kettle so the spout pointed to the window and the mug handles were turned towards him all the while muttering.

'You're mad, insane, do you know that?' Her voice shook as she dug her hand in her pocket for her lipstick which she applied blind.

'You are, aren't you?' he mirrored back. 'I'm glad you see it now. Maybe you will see the good doctor. Hmm?'

'Stop it now. This is crazy behaviour.' Una slumped on a stool like a candle melting.

'I'm just protecting my assets. You know all about assets don't you? Mrs. Business Woman.'

'You mean that bloody cello.'

Una leapt up and gave the case a hard kick. He held back from kicking her.

'Don't touch that. Don't. Ever. Touch. My. Cello. Again.'

'Why are you doing this? Tell me what's in that messed up head of yours?'

'I don't want any more arguments with you Una. I care about you a lot but we are both under a lot of pressure. Now, please will you leave me alone to do my work?'

Una grasped clumps of her hair and let out a deep moan.

'You are Jekyll and Hyde. I never know who I am going to get when I come through that door. Trying to get through to you is like swimming the Channel in a fat suit.'

She ran upstairs shouting out her frustrations, pushing Beethoven out of the way. Grabbing her bags down from the wardrobe she began throwing in some clothes. Fifteen minutes later she reappeared.

'I'm going away to give you time to come to your senses.' The door slammed behind her leaving Iain to contemplate his next move. His DIY skills were limited. He planned to call a locksmith to secure his room and provide a new window lock for his own use. One of the tall cupboards would provide space for his clothes, he decided, as he spent the rest of the day organising what he'd renamed the Den. He realised he would have to tell the twins something to explain what he'd done without alarming them.

A penetrating chill sneaked through the hallway but with the Tiffany lamps, pictures of the twins and his older son Stuart on his travels and his music scores, his space was cosy and comforting. Above all it felt safe.

He spread out his lesson plan templates and as he pondered how best to teach the B flat major scale, he was interrupted by the phone. His inclination was to ignore it but it Tom had said every call could mean a prospective student.

'Iain Millar.'

'Dr. Gordon. Iain, I'm running a WellMan surgery for the over 50s. I would like you to come.'

Iain frowned as he ignored a voice telling him it was a trick.

'Wouldn't your receptionist be sending out a letter or something?'

'Oh dear. Rumbled. Yes, she would but I wanted to speak to you myself.'

'Is Una involved in this plot?'

Dr. Gordon drew in a deep breath and watched a squirrel on the lawn watching him.

'She's concerned about you. Says you've not been yourself. Obviously I can't discuss your welfare...'

'I'm fine. No worries at all.'

'She's emailed me a picture.'

'Oh?'

'Look, come and see me and we can have a proper chat.'

Reluctantly Iain agreed to make an appointment but only because he needed to see who had been taking pictures of him. A text message announced its arrival with an angry beep. Una was on her way to Amsterdam. The idea of having the house to himself was like slipping into a warm bath on a wintry night. Sitting back in his chair with the music of Handel low in the background, he closed his eyes and savoured the respite. Tomorrow he would go shopping.

Birmingham City centre could be intimidating at the weekends. Hundreds of thousands poured into the iconic structure of the Bull Ring from as far away as Cardiff. Didn't they have shopping in Wales? The multi-million pound bronze bull statue seemed to be a central meeting point for people or an opportunity to practice rodeo skills. Iain ran his hand over the beast's fine head as he passed squashing the urge to copy the teenagers who were trying to climb on its back.

During the week it was calmer and easier to move around the small city centre. People who didn't know Birmingham often commented on how compact it was. Hands thrust deep into torn pockets, Iain went in search of household goods he'd never had to buy. Now he wanted luminous pinks and lime green things for his den even if they were neither use nor ornament as his mother used to say. The more outrageous the better he thought with a grin. He found a bright orange tea pot with white polka dots, a lime green vase complete with white silk flowers and his favourite purchase of all – a cushion with musical print.

After a couple of hours Iain looked for somewhere to rest his throbbing ankles. An offer for coffee and scone caught his attention. The International Convention Centre building was a good place to stop especially since it housed Symphony Hall. He might just treat himself to a CD. Dropping his carrier bags onto a leather sofa he heard someone call his name.

'Iain! What are you doing here?'

He twisted his head round to see where the soft, Scottish voice was coming from.

'Morag! I thought you'd gone back up to Scotland.'

'I've been visiting Sheena McEwan. Can I join you for a coffee or are you waiting for someone?'

'No-one. Just taking a breather. What can I get you?'

'A skinny latte please. Thank you.'

Morag tugged off her scarf and gloves folding them neatly on top of her bag.

'Will you have the special? I'm going to. The scones are freshly made.'

There was a fluffy argument about payment for a few seconds which ended in laughter.

Iain hadn't seen his ex-wife for over a year. They emailed occasionally to share news of their son and relations had always been cordial, even during the divorce. Morag had been surprisingly understanding about his midlife crisis which resulted in his marriage to Una. He gingerly carried the tray back to the squishy sofas, the sort that once you were down, you had to perform an undignified scissoring of legs to get back up.

'Anyway, how are you?' she asked, lightly buttering a scone.

'Mustn't grumble and all those clichés. I've set up a small tutoring business and I'm writing music for the string ensemble. You remember Fergus don't you?'

'How could I forget?' she laughed. 'Do you remember that time he fell off the stage when he conducted some performance or other at the Barbican? His arms spun like windmills.'

'Oh yes, then he took a leap backwards into the arms of the front row.'

More laughter. Iain felt the tension ease from his shoulders.

'He's managed to get us some good gigs over the past few years. Won't take no for an answer.'

Morag knocked some crumbs from her cashmere cardigan, her rings catching the sun's pale light.

'I was really sorry to hear about Ken. He couldn't have been very old.' Iain found himself slipping back into a soft Edinburgh accent.

'Aye, just fifty-three. He was planning on an early retirement.'

She removed her gold framed glasses to give them a wipe on a linen handkerchief.

'Selling up, buying the cottage... it was all very difficult Iain but now I love it. It was a tough move and the weather's not so brilliant but just to get out into the Highlands and over to Skye … the dogs love it too …'

They exchanged bits of news but Iain was careful not to stray into Una-related territory. Stuart's travels, his hope for the twins' return to Birmingham, their shared love of teaching were safer topics.

'I'm really sorry too about that bad business at St. Hilda's. How can girls do that sort of thing to their teachers for heaven's sake? And for the school to get the police involved.'

Iain wiped his clammy hands on a serviette. Any mention of St. Hilda's set off a wave of nausea. Her nodded woodenly, stirring additional sugar into his coffee. It helped him rebalance.

'It's over now. They withdrew their statements – said it was a bit of fun. Not for me it wasn't. Problem is, although I've got my clean police check back, schools are reluctant to take me on.'

'It's a couple of years ago. Things do blow over Iain. Try again.'

Morag broke the pregnant silence which sat between them like an uninvited guest by asking about Una.

'She's fine. Away on business.'

Morag watched him carefully. He couldn't or wouldn't meet her eyes.

'It must be hard for her keep ahead of competition,' Morag sighed, dabbing her forefinger in some stray crumbs on the plate.

Iain focused on slathering more jam on his scone. The knife slipped and fell onto his trousers.

'Damn it. Always clumsy these days,' he grimaced.

Morag laid a hand on his arm.

'Stuart would really like you to go out to visit him. He's in Vietnam now I think.'

She scanned the dark smudges around his eyes not missing the cuts and bruises on his temple and lower arms. Iain couldn't tell her that he would have to ask Una for the money since he had no access to the main accounts.

'I'll see what we can arrange if it comes up. Look, I must take this stuff back home then get ready for my students. Keep in touch won't you?'

He kissed her cheek briefly, taking in her signature fragrance of roses.

'If you can't make Asia then there's always an invite to Inverness. You know that,' Morag said.

As he walked out of town to the Edgbaston border, his spirits felt lifted. Una wouldn't be home. He could use the whole house if he wanted instead of creeping around like some tolerated guest. The idea of inviting some of the ensemble round for a musical supper gave wings to his step as he made a note to mention it to Fergus. He could play his music as loud as he wanted and wash it down with the best red wine he'd been saving. As he turned onto his street he wanted to sing something jolly in his rich baritone but waited until he got in through the front door.

Iain made himself one of Una's energy drinks strong enough to reenergise a dead battery. He had a student due in an hour whose Grade 4 exam was looming. His aural work was not up to standard and Iain had mulled over different ways of helping him. As he dropped in the bags in his den he noticed his desk had been disturbed. A drawer was not properly shut as a bunch of papers seemed caught in the hinges.

The window was closed and there was no sign of a break-in. Maybe he'd done it in his hurry to reorganise his stuff. Further investigation showed that the drawer where he kept some of his compositions had been forced open, the broken lock on the floor. Who had been looking for what?

'I know you're in here,' he called out. 'You're watching me.

Everywhere I go you follow me. I know what you are doing but you won't fool me. Wait till I've set up the camera. Ha. Then I will catch you.'

The clanging of the doorbell made his nerves leap. Iain picked up his bow; creeping into the hallway he brandished it at the door. A young man, frozen with shock, his cello case in one hand, a music bag in another, slipped backwards and fell onto a stone plant pot.

CHAPTER FIVE

The flight from Birmingham International to Amsterdam was delayed by over an hour. Una snapped at the check in assistant. She had broken the speed limits to get to the airport, the tension of the forthcoming meeting fuelling her impatience to get away. Another of her team had resigned saying she couldn't work under the current conditions (whatever that meant) and the bank were on her back to discuss her loan. She recognised she'd never been blessed with the virtue of patience and that sometimes the smallest pebble in her way could trigger an explosive outburst.

Martha had spouted some rubbish about the planets being in hard aspect in her natal chart but as she came through security and settled down with a glass of wine and her iPad she had to admit it felt as if the universe was conspiring against her.

She called the office, boiling when the line wasn't answered straight away.

'Why isn't this line answered in three rings for hell's sake? You know that's the rule.'

'It's Anita. I thought you'd be on your way by now?'

'Don't change the subject. Make it clear that everyone must be answering this phone and emails according to the service standards. No wonder we are losing business.'

Una bristled as she heard her senior trainer sigh.

'What happened with Armaggio's? Are they renewing?'

Anita formulated a diplomatic reply in her head before responding.

'They like the ideas but everything has to go to Head Office. The budget's being cut down to essentials.' Anita held her breath. 'I'm sure it will be fine.'

'Training is bloody essential and that place needs it. Their staff are lazy and don't know the first thing about customer service.'

'I can only pass on what they said.'

'I want you available while I am in Amsterdam. If I ask for a document to be emailed you do it straight away.'

'Ok.'

Una's guts recoiled. If they didn't renew she was going to lose a lot of money and this was making her anxious. A couple of years ago the mortgage and business debts had been no scarier than a bit of dandruff. She knew she should have started cutting back costs when Iain lost his salary and there seemed to be a reining in of training budgets but felt unable to face reality. Her mother had been the same when she found herself a single parent. She'd spent more than ever on frippery as her father called it instead of food and heating.

Una bashed out an email just as her flight was being called. Jeff Archer was playing cute so she would have to do the same and say Aspire was involved in a major overseas contract, but if he committed in the next few days they would be able to fit in his work. An out of office reply came back.

'For fuck's sake,' she spat, heading towards the gate. She caught the eye of a woman with children giving her a disapproving look but didn't care.

By the time Una got the train into Amsterdam it was dark. Her hotel was just off Rembrandtplein. Normally she felt invigorated by this bustling touristy area of nightlife, bars and adult shows but not this time. Instead she felt a trepidation as if someone was following her, yet whenever she turned round there was no-one. A dab of lipstick helped to shore up the panic she felt as a tingling in her fingers. Things were beginning to feel unreal. All she wanted was to get into her room, order some food and sleep. After her morning run she needed to prepare for her presentation to the board of Lovetotravel.com. She really needed this work couldn't appear too keen. This had never been a problem when work had poured in like liquid honey. She was queen bee but her worker bees had started sniffing around another hive.

Their interest was developing an international coaching programme for over 5,000 staff. Online access was the brief. If she could pull this off it would solve everything and perhaps her and Iain could go away somewhere together, if she could get him away from that bloody cello. She was so sick of hearing that depressing whine.

Slipping into the rose-scented bath she called the home number. She let it ring out for a minute before trying Iain's mobile knowing it would be turned off. Unable to relax in the deep pink water, she grabbed a towel and padded through to the bedroom where a salad and soup in a flask waited for her.

Dunking some bread into the soup, she tried Iain again and again. A scream followed by a crash as her phone hit the TV screen brought a knock to the door.

'Is everything alright in here?'

'Yes. Go away,' she snapped.

Her sleep was disturbed throughout the night, partly because of a couple shouting at each other outside her window but more because of a lucid dream in which Iain was accusing her in court of breaking his neck. She'd been unable to speak in defence. It was bizarre, terrifying but so real. She leapt from the bed and splashed cold water on her face but nothing would wash away the sight of Iain's stricken face. By the time morning came she was exhausted.

Smoothing an overpriced concealer under her eyes, she stared hard at herself in the mirror. A grey ghostlike reflection stared back unblinking. It appeared like a shadow side of herself, unpleasant, cold, and cruel, but Una put her imaginings down to lack of sleep. Get a grip she told herself putting the finishing touches to her face.

Running alongside the Prinsengracht canal to the meeting, Una had to stop to rub her heels, raw from the new shoes. Dodging the surge of bicycles coming her way she almost fell into the road. Tears spurted into the corner of her eyes. She was going to be late.

Six members of senior management were lined up at the breakfast buffet chatting in Dutch. Una knew enough to exchange pleasantries and offer an apology. As Una presented her ideas the nods of appreciation and the positive questioning showed a genuine interest in her proposal. She smiled and thanked everyone for their attention, believing that it was just a question of battening down the fine detail hopefully over a drink.

'I am not happy about these costs, Miss Carrington. We are talking about 5,252 staff and your proposal is not viable per person.'

Una was prepared for this and talked confidently about other approaches which focused on sustainability, taking ownership and return on investment.

'We are very familiar with the jargon,' said the Finance Director, shuffling through his paperwork, 'but I want an alternative costing before taking this forward. Cut back by 40% and we might have a deal.'

Una narrowed her eyes as she searched his face. Could he be serious?

'At this point I think we should tell you we are meeting with two other potential providers. One is local, the other is in Singapore. We like your ideas and feel they fit well with our ethos but cost is a significant factor. If you would work up a couple of alternatives we can talk again. Maybe a conference call next week?'

Una knew when she was in a corner. This had not happened in her ten years of business. The staff had called her Miss Midas. If she was to win this prestigious contract and make it financially viable for her she was going to have to make cuts in Birmingham.

'Of course. Thank you for your time.'

The tinge of sarcasm in her tone didn't go unnoticed by Henk de Vries, the Training Director she'd had a brief fling with some years previously when he worked for another company. He raised an eyebrow in response.

Stunned, Una stomped towards Kalverstraat, Amsterdam's main shopping street. She had booked three nights in the city, convinced she would be spending time talking to staff, indulging in some corporate entertainment and packing a signed contract in her briefcase. She felt tired and old. Discarded. Lunch in her favourite bar didn't do anything for her mood. Over coffee she struggled to think of a valid reason to call Henk but desperation was such a bad look. Going back over her presentation she couldn't hope to make such severe cuts without compromising the quality. The technology alone was going to costs thousands.

A tall man with dirty blonde hair asked if he could sit at her table. She nodded, sizing him up to be in his early thirties. They smiled awkwardly at each other.

'I'm Brian.' He held out his hand.

'Business?'

'Couple of days. Last trip though. I'm escaping and I can't wait.'

Una put down her lipstick holder.

'Escaping from what exactly?'

'Work, the rat race and the rats.'

Una half laughed.

'What do you do that's so bad?'

'Investment banker. I hate it. I wanted to study art but my folks made me go into the city.'

'I bet you've made a fortune though.' A sudden thought sprang to life in Una's brain.

'You listen to too many rumours.' Brian ordered a burger and beer. 'I've got a nice little place in Hove and a bit put by as my Dad would say. I'm going Florence to study art.'

Una watched him dip some fries into a pot of mayonnaise as she weighed him up. Maybe the trip wasn't a waste of time she mused. It's a long time since I pulled anyone this cute.

They exchanged bits and pieces about themselves, the changing nature of the market place, her business, his dream.

'Do you have to go back to work this afternoon?' Una twirled a finger in her hair, wishing she'd not had such a severe cut.

''Fraid so,' he said, dabbing his mouth with a paper napkin.

'What about after work, since we are both on our own…'

Brian stood up and smiled.

'I don't think my wife would be too happy about it.'

Raising his hand he stepped out into the street, narrowly avoiding an oncoming tram. For a fraction of a second, Una wished it had hit him. By the time she got back to her hotel room she was shaking with humiliation. She called up Martha on Skype.

'Hey girl. Where are you?' Martha's face appeared on the screen.

'Amsterdam and before you ask, no it didn't go well. Big egos compensating for small appendages.'

'I take it money was the problem. Honestly Una you are losing your grip on the market. Better to have 50% of something than 100% of nothing. It's the name of today's game but I don't think you've rung me to talk business. What have you done?'

Una told her the story, clapping her hands to her flaming cheeks.

'Forget it. We all do stupid stuff like that but you are a bit old for it. Look at that time I went back to Nevis and flirted with that waiter. He turned out to be some third cousin of my auntie. She wacked my backside with her handbag. I was twenty-four.'

Una breathed out, as her muscles relaxed.

'You need to chill out. You're like a coiled cobra waiting to spring all the time. Come with me to a mindfulness class. Get your sense of proportion back. Hey, look at this.' Martha held up a mindfulness colouring book. 'Get one of these. They're great for de-stressing. By the way, did you report that black eye?'

'What?' Una raised the palms of her hands.

'You said Iain had laid into you again. You've got to do something about this.'

Una dismissed it by saying Iain hadn't been well and things were fine. The truth was she didn't really know what Martha was talking about. The need to defend Iain was strong when the attack came from outside.

'Honey, I have to go. I've got a big marketing event tonight. Don't be a stranger.'

While Una tried to get an earlier flight home, Iain was praising himself for not responding to his wife's demanding calls. He wasn't a game player but he was relishing the time on his own. Fergus and Tom had been round for a pot luck supper and had complimented him on the lamb shanks in a red wine and shallot sauce. Fergus had brought round a couple of ukuleles he'd picked up in a charity shop and they had fun picking out tunes with Tom playing an improvised drum.

'This is great,' Iain said as he strummed the chords to *Here Comes the Sun.*

Fergus boomed out the words, his stomach bulging through his red jumper, his hands tugging up his trousers. Hours later, exhausted and thirsty they flopped on the sofa like tired little boys.

A bubbling headache forced Iain awake before it was light. He was feeling rough despite having such an entertaining evening and put it down to the amount of alcohol they'd consumed. As he sat at his desk with a mug of black coffee, a scribbled note reminded him to get a new prescription for his blood pressure. He was aware that he was a candidate for another minor stroke. He didn't want a consultation with Alex Gordon. Maybe he could slide in to see the nurse.

As he sat in the waiting room, anxiously flicking through a

Stop Drinking Now magazine he heard his name being called to go to Room two. Knocking before pushing open the door he heard Dr. Gordon's voice.

'Is this a trick?' Iain was not pleased.

'No trick. I needed to see you. Let's get the routine stuff out of the way first.'

Iain pushed up his sleeve as instructed for the cuff. He tensed as the pressure strengthened. The doctor told him to relax but he wanted it over and to get out of the stuffy room. His arm was lifted, prodded and pressed.

'I don't like the look of this Iain. I want you go have it X-rayed.'

'It's fine.' Iain pulled down his sleeve and slipped into his jacket.

'And this head wound. How did this happen?'

'Nothing. Getting clumsy in old age. Prescription please?'

As the printer whirred into life, Alex Gordon pushed a finger over his eyebrows, deep in thought. He turned to his patient.

'Iain. You can fool yourself but I've been in this business a long time. I've seen it all. I can't make you tell me anything but I can give you the name of a counsellor who might be able to help. Martin Goldman. Here's his card.'

Iain pushed it into his pocket, planning to forget all about it.

'If you are thinking that Una's attacking me then you are wrong. Absolutely wrong. She's not the calmest of people as you know but she wouldn't hurt anyone.'

Dr. Gordon pulled a sheet of paper from a folder. It was a

photograph of a woman with a thin face and short copper hair. A dark bruise clung to her eye.

Iain leant forward, his hands spread on his knees. He struggled to push the breath through his lungs.

'Head down. Breathe into this paper bag.'

A few minutes later Iain felt the colour return to his face. The room seemed to swim in and out of focus as he stood up.

'You're telling me that Una sent you this saying I am responsible?' Iain snorted making for the door. 'If you believe that then you are both crazy.'

He stamped his way through the city centre with the doctor's words zinging in his head. They were educated, civilised people who didn't go around wielding fists because they couldn't control themselves. Yes, they were going through a bad patch and he was partly to blame because he couldn't get another job but it wasn't his fault. Righteous indignation burned his ears. He was still suffering from the shock of unfair dismissal but the idea of resorting to physical violence was preposterous. Bloody psychobabble.

Deep in thought he crossed Centenary Square where a small crowd had gathered by a bronze sculpture which had attracted a lot of controversy. Depicting an ordinary family but one without a male figure had drawn an angry man from New Father's for Justice to preach about loss of rights after divorce.

'This hatred of men is screwing up society,' he shouted in his distressed voice. 'Women are fabricating lies so they can kick the fathers of their children out of the house and live with their boyfriends and the courts collude in this.'

He regaled his audience with tales of his ex-wife hitting herself with a hammer and then calling the police and blaming him. Some of the gathered women shouted abuse at him. The few men listened quietly.

'We are reviled in the media and made to look useless and worthless and they do this in front of children.' The man's voice broke. 'They are misogynists,' he yelled, playing to the gallery.

'Misandrists,' Iain muttered as he walked towards the library, a pulse hammering in his temple.

CHAPTER SIX

November 2014

The Christmas market was in full swing. It had grown extensively over the past decade, now stretching down New Street, across Victoria Square, spilling its wares as far as the new library. German beers, pretzels and wooden handicrafts attracted people from all over the country. The buzz, the colours, the crowds were both tantalising and overpowering.

Iain skirted round a bulge of people busy biting off the ends of hot sausages or swilling beer from tankards. He was tempted to join them in a glass of gluhwein but knew he would be unfocused for his students.

The market came every year from Frankfurt, Birmingham's twin city, from mid-November to a few days before Christmas so there was plenty of time. He felt growing excitement at the thought of taking the twins skating or feeding them with popcorn despite Una's protestations.

He was pleased that the city had dropped the nonsense of Happy Holidays for the sake of political correctness. Iain was not a religious person but empathised with his non-Christian friends who didn't want to be singled out for special treatment.

Iain would have protested through letters to the editor of the Evening Mail at one time but his passion for local politics had waned. Everyone seemed to have an agenda which revolved around self. What had happened to people to make them so egocentric. Me, me and me he thought miserably as he got a mouthful of abuse from a young woman pushing her double buggy through the crowd. She'd rammed it into his ankles causing him to yelp in pain.

The three girls in his year group must have had an agenda he told himself as he edged his way through the throng. Una had said at the time they'd wanted a bit of a laugh. They'd argued about it with Iain wanting her to understand how deeply hurt and humiliated he'd felt. Being accused of something he hadn't done left him powerless. Making his way to a bench in front of the Council House he flushed as he batted away some of the things they'd said about him.

'Tried to kiss me,' said one. Iain was flabbergasted. Una had called him asexual because his kissing technique was so full of teenage angst.

'Made improper suggestions,' said another. He couldn't recall a single example of that and the girl in question had pursed her lips saying it was too upsetting to quote what he'd said.

'Touched me,' said a third. Iain felt his breath coming in burning waves. He couldn't have a panic attack here. He felt his scarf tightening around his throat as he tried to untangle it, knocking off his glasses in the process. Yes, he was friendly with all the students especially when he had to demonstrate the bowing action for the two violinists. It was innocent. He was being helpful.

'They're all lies,' he said out loud.

'No they're not.'

'Who is that? Who are you?'

Iain swung round to see where the voice had come from. He was in a pugnacious mood, his fists clenched, his jaw set. There was no-one there. He sat down feeling foolish. The words of the deputy head came back to him.

'Dr. Millar you do understand we have to investigate these allegations don't you? We have a duty of care. Blah and blah.'

He understood that. What had upset him most was that she suggested he got in touch with the union rep. He hadn't done anything he wanted to shout at her.

Dave Green knew his stuff. He'd dealt with similar cases across the city. It was a sad state of affairs he told Iain.

'So you'll be able to sort it? I want to go back to work. I need to go back to work for my sanity.'

'We've got to go through procedure. Let's hope those girls' parents don't involve solicitors. They've got money and the clout. Don't discuss this with anyone and whatever you do stay away from them. I've known some teachers go to their homes to reason with them.'

He felt sorry for Iain. His frayed jacket with its leather elbow protectors, his tousled hair and hang-dog look made him a prime target for teenage spite.

'I'll do my best Iain but I can't promise. These things can get tricky with so much media and social media focus. The Savile affair has made everyone paranoid. You know how it is.'

Iain didn't. All he knew was he wasn't guilty and shouldn't be put through this torment. The head had promised a glowing reference but suggested he tried colleges and adult education institutes. In other words, stay away from vulnerable teenagers for your own sake. He'd been smouldering with the injustice of it all and as he clicked through those kaleidoscopic events those feelings returned.

'You alright mate? You look a bit peaky.'

Iain looked up to see a youngish man in a suit, open collar shirt and a pink tie hanging around his neck.

'I'm fine thanks. Had a bit of a turn as they say.'

'I'll fetch you a coffee. Hang on there.'

Iain checked his watch. He felt guilty hanging around town when there was stuff to do but his legs felt as if someone had strapped weights to them. He'd asked Una for some money for a new bow but she'd ignored him. It still rankled. After a few weeks of unthrown vases he thought they'd started a more positive chapter in their marriage but she'd put him back in cold storage like a piece of meat she no longer fancied cooking.

'Here you go. Sugars?'

Iain took the cardboard cup with its corrugated holder with a smile of thanks. There were some kind people in the world he thought.

'I'm Ed by the way.'

'Iain.'

'Gets you down doesn't it?'

Iain blew on the insipid looking liquid and frowned.

'Christmas. All this madness. Getting into debt to buy stuff for people they don't really want. Most of it ends up on eBay.'

Ed jiggled his knee as he lit a cigarette.

'My kids are in California with their mother and stepfather so I won't be seeing them. Can't afford it.'

'I'm sorry.' Iain felt badly for him.

'Thank goodness for Skype eh? What about you?'

'My twins will be home from school. I haven't seen them since September.'

'Tough isn't it? I took my ex-wife to court over access so many times but it seems men don't have any rights. It's all geared towards the mothers even though I am living in a bedsit and busting my backside to send her money.'

The cold air was filled with his bitterness. Iain, not comfortable with his own emotions, felt awkward. He struggled to find something to say but instead pulled out a couple of Christmas concert tickets and handed them to Ed.

'This might not be your thing but I find music gets me out of my head.'

Ed pushed them into his top pocket with a perfunctory thanks.

'I'd better get back to the sweatshop.'

Iain gathered up his things and made his way to Corporation

Street for the bus. The number nine pulled in just as he strode through Pigeon Park, the popular name given to St. Philip's Cathedral graveyard. He had to ask a woman to move her bags from a seat so he could sit down. She cursed loudly then pointedly ignored him. As he stood up to get off he heard her say, 'posh git.' Iain felt a surge of annoyance. What had he done other than politely ask he if could sit down? He had a mind to go back and speak to her but people were pushing him to get on the bus.

'You getting off mate or you planning on spending Christmas here?'

As he sauntered home, he wondered what had changed in the last ten years to make people so antagonistic. They'd become like coiled springs ready to explode at the slightest provocation. Memories of his childhood in Scotland soothed him as he thought about the calm nature of his parents. His mother ruled the household and was strict but he couldn't remember her raising his voice to anyone never mind his father. Their respect for each other was mutual. His father doffed his cap when in the presence of women and always insisted on walking on the outside of the pavement. Even when his father had taken up rock and roll in his forties his mother would say, 'He's going through his crisis. We'll leave him to get on with it.'

Iain had done the same. Looked for adventure while Morag had focused on Stuart, leaving him to work things through. Their marriage had become a wilderness from which Una had rescued him and pushed back the need for him to face his mortality.

A fresh deluge of leaves covered the driveway reminding Iain he'd promised to clear them up but he couldn't summon the energy. The garden, devoid of colour and life, reflected back how he felt inside. A blast of cold air hit him as he entered the house. Thankfully Una was out. Turning on the convector heater in his den, or the Man Cave as Fergus called it, he heated up some soup and leafed through the post. He left two brown envelopes addressed to Una in a prominent place.

As he dunked some dry bread into his bowl, he reflected on how he'd been as a husband. Not the most demonstrative but faithful and loyal. He'd never shared his domestic problems with anyone else, not even the astute Dr. Gordon. He made a pact with himself that he would show more interest in his wife's life as he felt her slipping away into a place he felt he would not be able to enter.

Shuffling through the contents of the fridge he found some salmon and a tub of chive sauce. With wine, candles and a bit of Andy Hamilton in the background, he hoped to recover a little of the intimacy they had once shared. He'd even show willing about the cleaning contract she'd talked about.

His afternoon was enjoyable and easy. One of his older students commented on the delicious aromas from the kitchen.

'A man of many talents,' she said, lightly brushing his arm.

Iain leapt back as if burnt from her touch, knocking over the music stand.

'Ooops, steady. Let me help you.'

Iain felt an electrical sensation zip through his body. He felt somebody had climbed into his chest and was dismantling his ribs one by one.

'No, no. Thank you.' He adjusted his glasses and made for the door. 'Practise that adagio for next week. It needs to be lighter. My wife will be home soon so… see you next week.'

Iain all but pushed her out of the front door. He leaned against its peeling paint and closed his eyes. He couldn't have young women in the house again he decided. Not without an escort. Maybe he could pay Tom or ask Fergus to come over and work in the snug room.

Una was home early, looking as pale as an apparition. The rain had turned her hair into a copper skull cap.

'What's that smell?' she asked, rubbing her head with a towel from the downstairs bathroom.

'Something special. Dinner a deux. Time for a shower then a glass of Merlot. Let me look after you.'

Una raised an eyebrow as if to say, 'what have you been up to?' She pulled off her boots and tossed her wet coat over the radiator. As she went up the stairs she picked up the letters.

Iain heard her cursing and his heart sank as he went to turn on the hob. Once Una was riled it took a long time for her to calm down. His hands began to shake as he chopped up the salad. He heard her bang the bathroom door with such force he felt its reverberation downstairs. Wishing he'd had the foresight to hide the letters until the next day he prayed she would appreciate he was trying to help. It was an hour later when she came downstairs.

'Shall I heat this up for you?' Being with Una in this mood was like walking round an unexploded bomb. His nerves were twanging.

'I can't eat anything. Pour me a drink.'

Iain scrabbled around for the right words to soothe her, testing them like an unfamiliar sweet in his mouth.

'Please tell me what's upsetting you. I can't help if you don't talk to me.' Iain was almost whispering for fear of igniting her very short fuse.

Una sneered. 'What can you do? I'll tell you what's wrong shall I? The tax people are after me for over ten grand. I haven't got it. I used that money to pay your legal expenses if you remember.'

Iain's blood began to cool until his fingers were stiff and colourless. Any mention of money made him feel inadequate and useless as he did right now. He reached out for her hand which lay like an object pulled from a petrifying well.

'I know and I'm sorry I seem to have got us into this mess. I don't know what else to say. Can't we find a way forward?'

He didn't feel very manly as he waited for her to soothe him and say it would be alright. He felt continually punished by her refusing to see things through his tired eyes. As the gloom of the evening seeped into the cold kitchen where even the appliances seemed to be judging him, he tried another tack.

'Did you get the hotel contract? I would do some work if there was anything you felt I was suitable for. I have got another few hours teaching. I think I could build it into a proper tutorial school if you would help me.'

He sensed the volley of sarcasm was coming before she opened her mouth. He winced as her words slashed him. The set of her mouth set off his survival alarm.

'That'll help with the massive debt that's piling up. The mortgage, the loans and now this bloody bill.' She refilled her glass and swallowed deeply.

'Here, look at it. LOOK.'

Grabbing his hair, she forced his face down onto the papers so that his nose was pressed onto the table. The figures loomed large on his retina. The clock sung the half hour in the heavy silence as his heart banged against his breast bone. He tried to peel her fingers away from his neck when suddenly she let go. He pulled himself up, rubbing the spot where her nails had dug into his skin. Turning the paper round in his stiff fingers he tried to speak but the words wouldn't come.

'How much is in the school fund?' Una towered over him, arms akimbo.

'I've told you. We can't use that money for your business debts Una. We can find another way. Sell this house. It's far too big for us now.'

In the fog of his anxiety, Iain fantasied about a cosy cottage in the Worcestershire countryside with a log fire and Una asleep on his shoulder. Beethoven would be out chasing voles and maybe he'd get a little dog to keep him company.

Iain watched her grab the dishes and slam them into the sink. He was afraid of what she was going to do and how he would respond. Things got out of hand so quickly between them sometimes. He told himself to leave the room, lock himself in his den but was unable to give the command to his brain. As Una leapt towards him, grabbing his shirt collar, he smelt the stale alcohol on her clothes.

'You bastard,' was all she could manage through the dragon heat of her breath. 'You're a waste of space. I've carried you for years while you've scraped away on that bloody cello of yours instead of being out in the real world like a man. One of these days…'

'Una, I…'

'Shut the fuck up and get out of my sight.'

Iain knew that whatever he said now would inflame her more.

Slamming down the lid of her laptop she kicked her way through the house, leaving him to clean up the broken shards of glass from his mother's rose bowl.

As he bent to brush them onto some newspaper, Iain felt very alone.

CHAPTER SEVEN

Bacchus was heaving with the usual after work girly-crowd, couples who didn't officially belong to each other and cougars on the prowl. Una avoided eye contact with those with whom she'd had a brief fling in the past. She squirmed as fragments of a memory floated past. Edging her way sideways through the crowd to the door marked Mesdames, illustrated with a large brimmed hat in case anyone had missed that particular French lesson.

The basement bar was so dimly lit it, it warranted a safety inspection she thought. The intimate king and queen booths for two were usually taken but Martha had managed to grab and cling onto one, pushing her carrier bags onto the empty chair. As she stood up to catch Una's attention, she risked bursting out of her tangerine dress.

'Hey girl!'

'Hi.' Una dumped her brief case on the floor as they hugged warmly.

'It's been ages. How's things?'

Martha poured a second glass of wine and pushed it across the table.

'Same, same. Business is tough. Maybe I should go into the wine bar trade. I've never known this place so busy.'

Martha tugged her dress into place as she looked around.

'Drowning sorrows most likely. You heard about Global Network going bust? That's a big blow for Brum.'

Una shook her head and sat back in her chair. She took a liberal swig from her glass and settled in for the gossip. Being with Martha was like lying on white sand under the Caribbean skies. She also knew everything and everyone in the business district.

'Announced a couple of days ago. An American firm is taking it over but all jobs are dead. It's going virtual. Sign of the times.'

'But that's over five hundred jobs. I'm glad I didn't have a contract with them.'

A young girl with a pin in her lip brought some nibbles to the table. She handed them menus, rattling off the specials as if she was giving a train announcement.

'Where do they get them from?' muttered Una, as she checked her phone again.

'See that bloke over there. The very tall miserable one with the bandaged hand.'

'What about him?'

'Rumour has it his wife lamped him one when he told her he'd been made redundant. He'd been out on the pop and picked up some prozzie on Hagley Road.'

While Martha dipped into the crisps and nuts, Una felt a mild discomfort in her intestines. She drank some water in the hope it would go away. The room was stuffy making her palms clammy. As Martha continued her story she felt a frisson of guilt creep around her throat. She pulled off her scarf and abruptly changed the subject.

'How's the marketing business doing? I want to talk to you about doing a campaign for Aspire. We need to be repositioned.'

'We're out for the night. No business talk. Text me a date to meet up but please let's just chill.'

The arrival of food interrupted conversation for a while as they focused on making sure the linguine reached their mouths without being hi-jacked enroute. Una didn't like people seeing her eat and tried to avoid it but she needed to fill the hollow space in her stomach. She twirled the pasta round on her fork.

'Oohhh that was so good.' Martha pressed a hand to her stomach. 'I shall probably suffer for it though.'

She pointed to Una's plate.

'You've hardly touched yours.' Martha pulled out the soft folds of her dress.

'How's Iain doing? I saw him in town the other day, not to speak to. He looked a bit down.'

'He needs a job but isn't putting in much effort. I've tried to suggest things but he explodes at the idea of having to get his hands dirty.' Una explained about Iain's tutorial school realising she was being harsh about his efforts to set up a business.

'He spends so much time locked away in his study I've no idea what he's up to. In fact,' Una paused wondering if she should be sharing so much with her friend, 'he's moved his bed in there.'

Martha was distracted by one of her clients who leant down to hug her. 'Great campaign,' he said. 'Ring me. I've got another job for you.'

The green beast sprung before Una's eyes. Why was Martha raking in so much work when she was struggling? She worked just as hard and was damn good at her job.

'I don't know what to say Una. Maybe he's not well and doesn't want to trouble you.'

Una folded her arms and looked away.

'Look Una. I know how difficult it's been for you having to bail Iain out but you're going to have to let it go. He needs support. It's a two-way street these days. Time to spit the lemon.'

'Hello Ladies. Can we join you?'

Una glared at the two suited men with ties hanging around their necks. She told them to piss off but when one of them called her a scrawny bitch she leapt to her feet to square up to him. Martha pulled her back down but Una shrugged off her hand.

'What's got into you lately? You're like a lion on heat. The slightest thing seems to set you off. Are you premenopausal or something?'

Una stiffened as she exuded hostile vibes towards the two bankers. She felt the fight leave her as she slumped into her chair.

'It's not me. Iain's behaving weirdly. I've seen him talking to someone that only he can see. He cocks his ear like this every so often to concentrate on some voice he says is guiding him.'

Una realised she sounded ridiculous as soon as she voiced her concerns.

'Woah, hold it right there lady. You must be imagining that.'

Una snapped.

'No I am not.' She rolled up her sleeve. 'Am I imagining this too?'

Martha stared at an atlas of different coloured bruises. She'd seen a lot of this in her own family.

'If you're saying Iain's done this to you in a fit of … whatever… then you should report it. It's a police matter. It's domestic violence.'

Una closed her eyes. Things were becoming foggy and vague in her memory.

'He even threw me out in the middle of the night and the neighbours came to see if I was ok.' Una heard her voice coming from a long way away.

Martha stood up, grabbed her bags and struggled into her coat.

'Let's go to Crazy Ladies and have a bit of fun. You need to chill out girl.'

***

Iain was enjoying an extra-large mug of hazelnut coffee with Fergus after string practice. It was the one thing he loved about Christmas; being able to indulge a little. The Canal Side was his favourite haunt for people watching and scanning the free papers. Sometimes he pulled out a scrap of manuscript paper and jotted down a few bars that came into his head. He'd been advised to keep his mind busy and to take the tablets prescribed but as soon as the side effects kicked in he'd flushed them away.

'My back's aching,' Iain said as he wrestled out the aches from his neck and shoulders.

'I'm not surprised. You've been slumping over that music stand like the proverbial hunchback. You can't get maximum use of energy if you don't sit properly. That second movement needs a lot more work if you are going to perform for the Malvern concert.'

'I'm not up to it this year to be honest. Let Bill do it.'

Iain felt disappointed that he wouldn't be performing the most wonderful cello concerto in the Elgar country but his mind couldn't focus for long to put in the work. Fergus argued with him until a woman sitting close by told him to keep his voice down.

'Maybe you need a check-up. One of those WellMan things. Feck it Iain. Even I had to go.'

Iain threw him a baleful look.

'I hope he told you to lose some weight. That waistcoat is about explode those pigs off the fabric.'

Iain took a last satisfying gulp of his drink, dabbed his beard which he'd trimmed earlier and smiled broadly as Fergus' indignant expression.

Out on the canal, one of the narrow boats had been decked out in baubles and coloured lanterns which reflected on the dark waters which twitched gently as the rain fell.

'I'm a couple of Barbican tickets short. I gave one to a bloke I met in town. We got talking and he seemed really down about not seeing his children over the holiday. Sad really.'

'Well I don't think Sibelius will do much for his mood. It makes me want to lob myself over the canal bridge sometimes.'

Iain mulled over what it must be like to be without family. The twins were at school but he knew he could fly up to Edinburgh to see them and they always came home for holidays. Nearly always he corrected himself. He'd been upset with Una over her unilateral decision not to collect them for half term but without transport or money what could he have done? He felt some of that resentment creeping back.

'The twins want to come back to Birmingham to live. I'm going to contact the grammar schools to see what the situation is about the eleven plus.'

'I can't believe you said that. Bloody elitism on a stick. The council should have got rid of them years ago. Nothing wrong with the comps.'

Iain knew the signs precipitating Fergus working himself into a lather if it involved some socialist principles. Iain was too exhausted to defend his corner as all he wanted was the best for his children. He sighed with contained happiness at the thought of them being together for the holiday but when he thought of Una the gas went out of his balloon.

Iain went to the counter to order more drinks. The thought of going home made his blood cool. Two women in sharp business suits pushed past him to get to the front of the queue. The tray in his hand slipped, the paper cups and their accompanying mince pies slid to the floor. Slack-jawed Fergus watched as one of them stuck her boot in them.

'Excuse me,' he called loudly.

'You're excused,' smirked the shorter one, kicking his violin case to the side.

'That's my instrument,' he shrieked, swivelling his eyes from the crushed tart on the floor to the tanned one in front of him.

'Most men keep it in their trousers,' she sniggered. 'And don't talk to me in that tone. Who do you think you are?'

Iain thought of Fergus, a well-built man with a surgical tongue, well able to hold his own. But his bluster seemed to evaporate at that moment. The woman was watching him, her mug handle angled towards him. She was one of those sent to spy on him and that was the signal. It was time for him to get out of there and into fresh air.

'What is wrong with people these days,' grumbled Fergus, grabbing his precious Stradivarius and examining the case for damage. 'No bloody manners.'

He joined Iain on the towpath where he was hoovering up gulps of ice cold air.

'Get off home and have a rest Iain. I'll give Bill a ring later.

On my new Smart Phone.' He pulled his new toy from his pocket. 'Early present from Freda. It's not a mobile phone it's a mobile moment engager the sales bloke told her. What a load of bollocks.'

Iain couldn't be bothered to wait for one of the buses which passed down his road so set off into the driving rain. Men losing their children because of divorce was weighing on his mind. Suppose Una decided she'd had enough and threatened to take the twins away somewhere. He had no money for a court battle even if there was a chance of him winning. How could he look after his children and find work? Why was the system so biased against fathers? Was it just a myth perpetuated by action groups? He'd read about parent alienation syndrome in the paper but none of this horrible stuff applied to him, to them, to his family. Did it? The thoughts whirred around in his head like a computer sub-routine with no off button.

Iain turned round and caught the approaching bus back into town. He had to see Una so he could be sure that she wasn't planning anything like that. He rarely went to her offices in the Custard Factory. He found Digbeth to be dirty and menacing having been mugged late one night getting off a coach.

He caught sight of Anita hurrying to her car with a box of stuff. A photograph wobbled on top of the pile. She noticed him but kept her head down. Iain saw she'd been crying. Taking the lift to the third floor he pondered on what excuse he was going to give. Now he'd arrived, he felt a bit stupid. Shoulders back, he strode down the corridor looking for the distinctive purple sign.

The door was half open. He peered in to find an office in the throes of being emptied and packed up. Una looked up and tilted her head as if to say, what the hell are you doing here?

'What's happening? Are you moving?'

'Looks like it doesn't it?' She went back to ticking off her list. 'What do you want?'

He assessed the situation and feigned calm.

'Can I help in anyway?'

Without missing a beat, she said, 'You can leave us to get on with it. OK?'

He wasn't going to allow her to dismiss him like a small boy who had transgressed some unwritten rule.

'What's going on Una? I've a right to know.' His voice was low as he closed the door. Damn right I have a right to know he told himself firmly. 'We're a couple, a family. This impacts on all of us.'

'I can't afford these premises anymore by order of the bank. I've been telling you this for months but your mind wanders off into the wild blue yonder.'

This isn't true. How many times have I asked you to sit down and talk but you got angry and defensive. There is always a solution to a problem but you have to want to solve it. Sometimes I don't think you do.'

Una rolled her eyes and shook her head.

'Iain go back to fiddling your strings or whatever it is you do. Some of us don't have the luxury of hobbies. This is grown up work.'

He felt the stinging words like an open handed face slap. He sensed the people behind the partition were lapping up every word.

'I'll leave you to it. I assume you're moving the office back to the house?'

She taped up a box, her mouth set resolutely in a no comment line.

'There was a call for you from the VAT people. I said you were away.'

'Thank you,' she murmured. 'You can get something in for dinner if you want to be helpful and Martha wants to take some clients to your Malvern concert so some reduced price tickets would be good.'

Swivelling open the tube of a new poppy red lipstick she looked down on the carpark as she waited for Iain to leave.

He flagged down a black cab, a luxury that cost the price of a single music lesson, and told the driver he was in a hurry. He needed his room, his sanctuary, away from the people who were suffocating him, watching him, laughing at him. The driver, in broken English, tried to strike up a conversation but soon fell silent as he caught sight of Iain's closed eyelids.

Pushing open the door he could smell gas. Remembering not to turn on the lights, he sniffed his way through the house but couldn't source anything. Out of the corner of his eye he saw a shadow pass through the kitchen.

'Hey you. Come here.'

Iain flung open the back door, almost falling onto Beethoven who sauntered back inside looking for food. Smashing down the shrubs with a stick in search of the intruder, he crept round the side of the conservatory, hell bent on finding who had dared disturb his refuge. Slipping on the icy side path leading to a back walkway, he called out again. Unblinking eyes bored into him from the shadowy bushes. A cold wind and a few flakes of snow responded to his shouts. Fear filled his nostrils as he felt his mind taken over by a plutonic force determined to drag him into the underworld.

As he locked the back door, he noticed some wet leaves on the floor by the pantry which seemed to have formed a significant pattern. He bent down to examine them. Convinced it was a message he fumbled with his phone to find the camera and took a picture. It would be evidence he thought gleefully.

Ignoring the ringing house phone, he locked himself in his room. He stared at his trembling fingers as if they were strangers. Hidden behind the heavy curtains he checked on the crepuscular activities on the road, studying every movement like the subtle shifting of frames in a film. Satisfied, he double checked the window locks and after pulling the curtains tight, he poured a slug of neat whisky. He opened the box containing the new security camera, scanned the instructions and put it back. He'd have to find someone to fix it up.

A CD of the Elgar Cello Concerto lay open on his desk. He slotted it into his outdated player and while waiting for it start he opened the score. The opening bars triggered a quiet anguish which mounted as the music rose and fell in its dramatic unfolding. Iain closed his eyes as he locked into the deep despair; the angst and disillusionment of Elgar after the war. He too shared the deep introspection of the composer's death and mortality. Iain felt all these things deep in his core.

He felt his life had become worthless. Fergus was right he thought. His playing had lost its verve and brilliance in the fog of his mind and the uncontrollable spasms of his fingers.

He felt scared to leave the room. He sat in a puddle of silence, listening to his heart in the belief that someone was manually winding it up in readiness for an explosion.

The shrilling of the phone made him drop the tumbler. He made a clumsy attempt to mop up the liquid, shouting at the caller to go away. It stopped then rang again with insistence. Iain didn't answer but on checking found the caller had withheld their number.

CHAPTER EIGHT

Una sat at her desk on the top floor of the house playing a game of Solitaire on the computer. Huddled into the depths of her dressing gown, she kept telling herself another five minutes then she would get dressed and start work but her head felt as if was stuffed with a pack of wire wool pads.

Feeling uneasy with the silence which was soaking in her bones she turned the radio on low. An email flashed on her screen. On opening it she felt her heart tighten. Her mother, who had been in a nursing home in Scarborough was very unwell and could she call them as soon as possible.

Turning her face to the stinging hot needles from the shower, she closed her eyes and tried to dig up some happy scenes with her but either they slipped out of her mind or they never existed. She remembered the crying and the meltdowns when she got frustrated over the slightest thing; the time when the postman delivered a book to an address up the road, the day she got her eleven plus results and she'd failed. She'd been stopped from going on the school trip to London as a punishment.

Una smiled to herself when a good memory finally clawed its way out of the negative ones. They'd shared a chocolate sundae with nuts and strawberry sauce in a café overlooking Scarborough's North Bay. Maybe that was why Isla had refused to go anywhere other than the North Yorkshire resort for her final days. Una stepped out of the shower and towelled her thin legs and arms before wrapping a towel around her hair.

They'd never really talked about things that mattered; love, relationships, how to be a woman. Homework, not messing with boys, getting a good education so she didn't have to rely on a man were the things that absorbed Isla Carrington.

She pulled on leggings, a T shirt topped with a thick black polo neck which she tightened with a gold belt. Letting her hair dry naturally, she sat back down at her desk and checked her work emails. A new contract had been agreed with one of the theatres providing Una delivered the training personally. She felt light with relief. This way she could maintain the quality control and keep the fee for herself. She fired off a reply, saying she was away working for a couple of days but could set up a meeting the following week.

Stretching her arms over her head she eased the tension from her shoulders. The feeling was sweet.

When she finally got round to calling The Seashells, that feeling had turned to a cold glue.

'Your Mum's contracted pneumonia,' someone called Sharon told her.

Una felt a coppery taste in her mouth. Contracted? Had her mother signed an agreement with a company called Pneumonia? Bloody stupid word.

'You mean my mother has caught pneumonia?' Even that sounded ridiculous, like catching a thief or a ball. Una was well aware that when she was annoyed with someone she would challenge their use of language and fill her own with as many long words as she could muster.

'She's very poorly, Miss Carrington. I think she would really like to see you. She calls for you in the night.'

Una felt herself melt like a marshmallow on a barbecue. She hadn't visited her mother for several months, making the occasional phone call to keep a connection. Isla Carrington had almost lost the power of speech, her condition being a Pick's Disease type dementia. Una knew that her own bubbling frustration with her made her agitated and distressed yet the guilt of not doing more was starting to add to her wobbly pile of stresses.

'I'll come up later today,' she told the nurse, trying to stop her voice shivering.

She threw some clothes in a bag together with her gadgets and went in search of her husband.

'Bloody typical of him,' she said to the cat who turned his back and buried himself deeper in his basket. 'Never here when needed.'

Iain appeared from his den, a pen in his ear, a scarf muffling his ears. He raised an eyebrow.

'Mum's very sick. I have to go to up north.'

'Oh. I can't come with you. I've got a concert tonight.'

'I'm not asking you to come. Mum won't recognise me so since you've seen her twice since we've been married she's hardly going to know you.'

Una saw his face change.

'Don't put on the hurt look for god's sake. I've got enough on my plate without having to worry about your sensitivities.'

Iain said nothing as he watched her struggle to pull on her black boots.

'Shall I make you a flask of coffee or something?'

'No thank you. I'll stop at a service station. Enjoy your concert.'

Iain reached out to give her a comforting hug but dropped his arms as they met with her resistance. Una hated being touched when anxious. She felt it like hot tongs on her upended nerves. She opened her mouth to tell him how she was feeling but stopped. There was no longer any point.

He stood on the step watching an occasional snowflake settle on her coat or float to the ground melting into nothing. It was as if it never existed. Snowflakes represent our lives thought Iain. Unique, briefly lived then gone without a trace. As he closed the door he recited the few words he remembered from one of Auden's poems. 'In headaches and in worry.' Iain picked up Beethoven and addressed him personally. 'Vaguely life leaks away.' The cat stretched as if asking to be released. 'Ok, Ok. Go back to sleep.' He made himself some coffee muttering the last couple of lines. 'And time will have its fancy, tomorrow or today.' He thought about writing some music to go with the poem.

***

The M1 was at a standstill owing to an accident. Una felt a mini explosion going off in her head, like a Catherine wheel sparking out in all directions. She wished she'd not wasted time buying more gloves for her mother's collection. It was madness to indulge this obsession which she'd had since Una was a child.

Gloves of all colours, materials, designs were hidden all over the house, even behind bricks in the fireplace, away from her father's eyes. Isla only ever wore the soft black leather ones he'd bought her, not allowing Una to even touch them after he'd left the house for good. They'd become a sort of memento mori even though he was living the high life in Bali.

Una didn't like being still as it meant she had time to brood. Banging her hands on the steering wheel, the traffic news burst in on the radio.

'About bloody time,' she said out loud as the cars in front inched forward.

'Move your arse,' she yelled as she pushed into the outside lane, leaning on the horn.

Not bothering to pull into the services, she arrived into Scarborough late afternoon. The sinister merging of the dark sky and sea made Una shiver. She didn't like what she couldn't see clearly. A wind shook the car as she drove along the sea front to the north shore. Dog walkers were out in packs, parka hoods up, battling against the rain which lashed the boarded up huts. Strings of Christmas lights swung dangerously overhead, casting a pale reflection on the water.

Dropping down a gear, she peered out at the side streets trying to find the turn which would take her to the nursing home. As she parked, Una slumped into her seat and closed her eyes until the buzz of a text announced its arrival. Iain was checking she was alright. She knew she should reply but something told her to make him wait. It was like a perverse force that invaded her mind which she was unable to resist.

The entrance to the nursing home was softly lit with Christmas tree lights and a warm smell of vanilla candles. Una slipped off her coat, turned off her phone and waited for a nurse to register her presence.

'Mum's asleep at the moment. Can I get you a cup of tea? I know you've come a long way.'

Nurse Sharon spoke softly, her blue eyes sparkling with a peace Una didn't feel. She led her to a side room where Isla Carrington lay like a tired sparrow in a bed with a Christmassy coverlet. Una pulled up a chair and sat motionless listening to her mother's light breathing. Her tea grew cold but her hands even colder. Emotions were unspooling in her head but felt blocked from reaching a full expression in her heart. She knew she was angry with this woman who had yielded to a living death after Una's father had left for a new life with some Indonesian woman young enough to be his daughter, yet the feeling remained at a distance as did the sadness at seeing a ghost of a figure who had once loved her. She wanted to shake her and comfort in equal measure.

Una pulled out the parcel of gloves and laid them on the bed. Closing the door, she began to talk to her mother not knowing whether she could hear or understand.

'Mum, it's Una.'

There was no response.

'Remember the fight we had about my name? You wanted me to spell it the Irish way – Oonagh – but I hated it. You said it meant lamb. You told me I was like a lamb skipping around, curious about everything and always staying close to you.' Una's voice cracked. She paused, looking around the room to battle away the threat of tears. 'Well I'm close to you now. I'm right here Mum and I've brought you a present.'

Una thought she saw a slight movement of her mother's hand as if to say, I know you've brought me gloves.

'James and Joanna send their love. They're doing really well at school. Maybe I can bring them to see you during their holidays. It's been a long time but you've been so unwell. Iain's busy with his music as usual. He's set up his own little business. You don't need to worry about us. We will be fine.'

Una wrapped her hands around her mother's and held it tight, unable to speak anymore. She didn't believe what she was saying. She didn't know if they would be fine or not.

Isla Carrington slowly opened her eyes and a smile fluttered across her thin mouth.

'Mum?' Una stood up and kissed her papery cheek. She helped her sit up, fussing with the pillows. She offered a cup of water to her lips, watching as she sipped with birdlike movements dribbling a little onto her nightgown.

'Oonagh?' Her voice was barely audible.

Una busied herself with the parcels, helping her mother to tear the paper and tease out the pairs of gloves in orange kid-leather, soft brown wool, purple and pink magi-gloves. Their eyes met in a shared joy rather than the old furious resentments. Una helped her mother try them on making admiring noises as she spread out her fingers to show them off.

'Box. Bed.'

Una frowned.

Her mother waved her orange hands and repeated. 'Box. Bed. Box. Bed.' getting upset when Una didn't respond. She began to cough, falling back onto the bed with exhaustion.

'Ah. Box under the bed?'

Una scrambled under the bed and pulled out three large colourful boxes. She lifted one onto the bed and slid off the lid. Her mother's rheumy eyes lit up as she carefully lifted tissue wrapped gloves and laid them in rows on her lap. Una watched helplessly as Isla babbled nonsense as she picked them up and kissed them. 'Baby,' she said, handing a pair to Una.

A sob caught in Una's throat. Someone had stolen her Mum and replaced her with this alien.

'Gloves. They're gloves,' snapped Una, pushing them back in the box. She felt as if, like a building with a stick of dynamite buried deep in its core, she was going to explode into dust and rubble. A huge gaping hole would be left where her heart now was thumping.

Her mother began to cry silently, turning her back on Una as the dry, hacking cough took hold. A nurse pushed open the door and tended to her patient. She took in the untidy pile of gloves sliding from their protective wrappings onto the floor.

'Maybe if you took a break now. Are you staying in a hotel?'

Una swallowed her hurt.

'I'd planned to drive back to Birmingham tonight.'

'The weather's really bad. There's quite a wind getting up. There's a bed and breakfast round the corner, The Sanctuary. The owners are used to visitors here turning up at odd hours for a bed. Try them. You look exhausted. Hopefully your Mum will be a bit better tomorrow.'

Una rang the bell of the guest house and was immediately shown a warm room and brought a bowl of soup and sandwiches. Her coat was taken from her for drying. She felt grateful for the lack of small talk and questions. Too tired to even soak in the bath, Una texted Iain to say she was fine. She lay back against the pillows and closed her eyes. She tried to feel something but it was if she'd disengaged from anything emotional. A therapist had told her she was traumatised and needed to reconnect with herself. Una had told her she was talking psychobabble and had walked out. She went back over that conversation feeling the pain of the truth fill her chest.

Sleep turned its back on Una in the squashy bed like a sulky partner. She lay awake as the grey band tightened around her forehead. All she wanted to do was shut the world out forever. By the time morning came she had the sick feeling of jet lag. Encouraged to eat an English breakfast, she thanked her reserved hosts and went back to the nursing home.

'Mum isn't well enough today to see anyone. I'm really sorry but she is distressed.'

'Are you saying this is my fault? You asked me to come.'

'No no. Of course not. It's the gloves we think. She insisted on wearing the black pair she keeps under her pillow and has thrown the others all around the room. I am so sorry but she needs time to calm down. Pop in and see her for a few minutes but please, no gloves.' The nurse smiled but her manner was firm.

Una peered through the window into her mother's room. She was sitting up staring at the television and giggling behind a gloved hand. Una slipped inside and gently gave her a kiss.

'I've got to go now Mum but I'll be back soon.' She was about to say take care but realised how trite it sounded. Her mother was on the gangplank to oblivion not recovering from a bout of flu.

Isla turned her face to her daughter and beamed.

'You did so well at university, winning that award for education. I wish I'd had a career.' Her mother turned away to stare at something in the corner of the room.

Una clasped her throat and staggered to her feet. Sharon saw her sobbing by the coffee stand. She laid a hand on her shoulder.

'It's like she was my mother again,' Una said dragging a tissue over her sore eyelids.

'It's normal. An odd moment of lucidity but then it's gone. I'll call you. Drive safely.'

Birmingham City was snarled up with Christmas shoppers. An accident on the Aston Expressway had caused a long tailback which meant Una had to cancel a business meeting. She was hungry, cold and irritable. She called Iain and told him to prepare some food and crank up the heating.

Iain was finishing up with a married couple who had chosen to learn the cello after retirement. They were keen but had no ear for music. They had money and he had the patience so they'd agreed to keep trying. He put some chicken and wine in a pan, chopped up some vegetables and put it on the hob. Mildly irritated by being told rather than being asked to prepare lunch when he had to go to rehearsals later that day and needed to practice, he chuntered to Beethoven about how next time he would come back as a cat.

Una threw her bags on the porch floor and walked into the kitchen.

'How was your mother?' he asked adding more water to the casserole. He noticed the dark circles under her eyes.

'Not good. She's talking rubbish.'

'She has dementia. That's how it goes.'

'Well thanks for the support Iain.' Una threw her coat over the banister.

Iain tried to find a suitable response that wouldn't push his wife into a meltdown but just said, 'Oh dear. I am sorry. Sit down and have this. I'll make you some coffee. Maybe you should have a sleep this afternoon. I have to go out.'

'I could do with you here,' she said, spooning some chicken into her mouth.

'I would do but we've got rehearsals. It's the Christmas concert season next week. You know how it is.'

'No I bloody well don't. When I need some backup you're never here. You've no idea what I'm having to deal with.'

'Una please. I'll be back in few hours then you can tell me what's happening with your mother. I will do what I can to help, you know that.'

Una pushed her food away and looked at him. A tsunami of fear and pain threatened to engulf her. She wanted him to feel it with her. As the red mist of unreason descended, she picked up the dish and threw it at his chest.

'There are times I think I could kill you,' she said coldly.

Without a word, Iain turned and walked out of the room. She listened to his heavy footsteps on the stairs as the hand of guilt slapped her across the face.

CHAPTER NINE

Iain lay on his narrow bed in the den trying to hold back the urge to vomit as a jumble of memories turned over like clothes clanging against the drum of a dryer. Una had avoided him since the incident of the flying chicken dinner and he nursed a hope that she felt some remorse. He put his hand over his eyes as he steadied himself to his feet. Checking his diary, he was dismayed to see a booking for two students later that day. He bent over with a groan, as the pain in his stomach took away his breath.

The Sibelius hadn't gone well despite Fergus saying the cello solo was moving. Iain knew he hadn't put in the practice on the arpeggios and felt that his interpretation came across as impersonal. He was finding it difficult to connect with anything and likened it to looking at life through a bus window. He'd mentioned this to Fergus when trying to explain how he'd felt on the night of the concert.

'If you're talking about West Midland transport then that means through the glass very darkly.' Fergus chuckled as he flicked through the Evening Mail for the reviews. 'You're being too hard on yourself, so you are. Freda said she was close to tears. Mind you that might have been because my shirt buttons were not done up properly.'

Fergus thought back over Iain's unexpected confession as he marked some scores for the French horns, pausing every so often to look up at his wife as she beat some mixture for a cake.

'I'm worried about him,' he said voicing his thoughts out loud. 'He's withdrawing into his shell. He was right about that solo. It lacked spark.'

His wife handed him a mug of tea and put her arms around his thick shoulders. She loved him so much it choked her sometimes. Yes, he could be annoying at times, especially when he was so lost in his music that he forgot she was there but no doubt she irritated him too.

They had choreographed their own quick step for almost twenty-five years and apart from a tricky passage through midlife like many couples they'd slowed down to a companionable waltz. He squeezed her warm hands, fragrant from washing up liquid and allowed her a quick ruffle of what remained of his hair.

'This ring looks a bit tight.' He slipped his glasses down his nose to examine the thin gold band.

'It could do with expanding if there's anyone in the jewellery quarter still doing that sort of thing.'

'What about a new one? For Christmas?'

She leaned over and kissed his bald patch.

'No way. This is much too special.'

'I love you,' he said gently, pulling her into a deep hug, 'but now I've got to go over to Woodbourne House.'

'Be careful on the roads. The weather is dreadful. Look at that fog. Why don't you bring Iain back here for supper? '

He stepped out into the bitter cold feeling deeply troubled.

He'd believed Iain's explanations about falling or cutting himself too many times. A recent bruised eye and ribs which the A&E doctor had said was caused by a forceful kick or something similar couldn't be dismissed so easily. Iain had become defensive when Fergus mentioned it. Fergus knew that his star cellist was worried about the tremor in his hands and wondered if there was some neurological explanation. What he didn't understand was why Una seemed to blame him for being clumsy instead of encouraging him to get some tests.

Fergus felt distinctly ill at ease in Una's presence. Rarely acknowledging him, she could often be heard crashing about in the room above Iain's den like a poltergeist determined to drive them out. It was like she gave off a bad aura but that was New Age nonsense he told himself.

As he turned the corner on the Edgbaston Road he saw two sets of flashing blue lights. Two police cars were parked on Iain's drive watched by a huddle of mothers and whining children. Fergus cursed as he pushed past their spacecraft like pushchairs which took up the whole pavement. Una was on the steps, her lips pulled into a post-box like slit.

'I might have known you'd turn up. We don't need you poking your nose in. You're part of the bloody problem.'

A WPC put out her arm as a barrier as Una lunged towards him.

'You've been feeding him lies about me. Look at what he's done this time.' She pulled off her coat and showed him the deep gash on her hand. Even to the untrained eye it looked broken.

He threw me against the desk. Says I'm part of a conspiracy. He's mad. Absolutely barking.'

'Mrs Millar, Come inside. This isn't helping your case.'

Una fired the young police officer a dark look.

'My case? What are you talking about?'

'Are you a relative Sir?'

'I'm here to see Dr. Millar. I'm as good as family. Where is he?'

Fergus' eyes scanned the scenery and saw Iain hunched in the back of a patrol car.

'What the hell is he doing in there?' His voice shot up half an octave. 'He's ill. He should be in hospital. This is outrageous.'

Fergus strode towards the house, clasping his chest as he climbed the steps.

'Sorry Sir but you can't go in there. I suggest you go home and call this number later.'

'No I damn well won't. You'd better tell me what the hell is going on.'

Fergus argued loudly, dancing around like Rumpelstiltskin but took the card anyway, pushing it angrily into his pocket. No-one would answer any questions. He watched in disbelief as Iain was driven away and Una bundled into another patrol car with the WPC. Jeremy Kyle's ratings must be dropping he thought if the number of people settling down to watch this local drama unfold was anything to go by.

Feeling the adrenalin rush subside, Fergus got back in his

car wishing he still smoked. He took the back roads home to Bournville, pausing by the barely visible duck pond to gulp in some air. It was raw in his throat. When he arrived home, his stomach growled in appreciation of the beef casserole Freda had brought out of the oven. She sensed his mood immediately and served the food into white bowls with hunks of home-made olive bread. Eventually he found his voice.

'The police were there when I arrived. That woman told them that Iain had attacked her in a blind rage.' He tore off a piece of bread and dunked it into the rich sauce. 'Her hand is injured but I don't believe Iain has it in him to do anything like that to his worst enemy. The woman's mad.' Fergus injected indignation into his voice to hide his upset. Freda poured him some wine.

'I don't know what the hell's going on,' he sighed, pushing away his empty bowl. 'That was so good. Thank you.'

'I guess we don't really know anybody unless we live with them. We're a bit like prisms, showing different sides to different people.' Her voice trailed away as she stared out into the sodden garden. It was just after 4pm and so dark and miserable. She heard Tom come in and go upstairs.

Fergus poured a drop more wine and stared into the glass. He'd known Iain a long time. He was one of those people who were simply too nice for their own good.

'Shall I wash up?' he asked as she cleared the table.

'You go and sit in front of the fire. You look all in. I'll bring you some tea.'

She gathered up the dishes and filled the kettle. She felt men couldn't always see what was under their noses but other people's marriages were not their business. Tom sloped into the kitchen looking for food. Freda indicated the dish she'd put aside for him.

'Is Dad alright?' he asked, through a mouthful of bread.

'He's tired with all these rehearsals and concerts. You know how it is at Christmas. Why don't you sit with him for a bit?'

The phone rang and Tom answered it while waiting for the microwave to ping.

'Dad, it's for you. It's Dr. Millar.'

Fergus grabbed the handset and went into his snug.

'What happened? Where are you?'

'I'm ok. Back home. Una withdrew the charges.'

Fergus rubbed his temple.

'What charges? I don't understand.'

'We had a disagreement about the twins and who was going to collect them. I don't remember what happened exactly but I think she tripped and banged her arm on the edge of my desk. It's all so vague. She said I'd hit her.' Iain's voice cracked. 'Fergus, I would never do anything like that. It was all a misunderstanding which led to an accident I told the police. In the end they let me go.'

'Where is Una now?'

'She's gone to stay with a friend. The police said one of us had to leave the house to calm down.'

'You should have come here. You still can. Don't think you've got nowhere to go Iain. In fact, Freda's making faces at me now indicating there's plenty of her beef special with your name on it. I'll pick you up. '

'That's kind of her but I don't feel up to socialising tonight. Ask her to freeze me a portion though.' Iain paused for a moment. 'I'm flying up to Scotland on Saturday to collect the twins and maybe we'll go onto Inverness for a couple of days to see Morag.'

'Ok. I'll get Bill to play for the hospice do.'

'Damn, I completely forgot. Sorry.'

As Iain sat back to watch the news and the latest terrorist atrocities, he felt he was letting Fergus down. It plucked the strings of his conscience. Musicians were a team, each element down to the last triangle needing to be in harmony with each other. He was compromising that by being so out of harmony with himself. He owed Fergus so much. If he hadn't given him a place in the string quartet and ensemble his life would have slid down a manhole without trace.

His stomach felt out of sorts. Feeling hungry but unable to face food, he nibbled on some of Una's rice cakes, pulling a face at the cardboard taste in his mouth. Peering into the street he saw shadows dance in the trees, their hooded eyes staring back at him. The harder he looked, the more solid their form. One, two, six… they were everywhere, spreading themselves over the window like black blood clots. Iain fell back onto the bed clutching his chest.

'Please go away,' he begged, feeling cold beads of sweat form on his upper lip.

'You're evil,' said the voices. 'You're useless. She's going to kill you because that's what you deserve you dirty pervert. Hell is being prepared for you. Disgusting.'

'Noooooooooooooo!'

Iain pulled a pillow over his head. Like a child he made himself believe that if he couldn't hear them, they didn't exist. The words faded into a manic laughter then disappeared. Iain's shirt was soaked with sweat and the whisky he'd tipped down him. Fear clawed at his throat as he lay shivering under the duvet. He swallowed a couple of his tablets Dr. Gordon had prescribed. As the torment lessened he buried his face in the pillow wishing he could die.

***

A couple of days later when he felt more like himself he picked up an email from Stuart asking him to go on Skype on Friday night. He wanted to talk about plans for Christmas. Iain was fearful of inviting him to spend it with them remembering how Una had purposely ignored him the previous year.

He called Morag.

'I'm coming tomorrow night if that's still convenient.'

'Of course it's convenient. We can do an early Hogmanay if you can stay a couple of nights. The twins can feed the new horses in the field opposite.' Morag paused and tugged on her pearls. 'Will Una be alright with that?'

Iain gritted his teeth. He didn't care whether she was or not. He was going to Inverness. He longed for a normal family celebration, tension free, where he didn't have to walk on eggshells or be on guard for her microscopic shifts in mood. Morag had always embraced Christmas, filling the house with friends, good food and music. They'd fought with the turkey to get it in the oven, played endless games of Ludo and Draughts and taken Stuart and a friend to a pantomime or two.

A knock on the door prompted him to end his conversation. He needed to pack and tidy up the house. Maybe if Una came back to a tree and some coloured lights she might soften into being ... what? He didn't know what he wanted to say. Homely? Motherly? Loving? Normal?

Iain took in the sight of a woman in tight turquoise trousers wrapped around an ample backside and matching eye shadow.

'Martha?'

'Sorry for dropping in without an invitation but I can't get hold of Una. I thought she might be here.'

'Come in. It's freezing out there.'

'I got a frantic call from her saying she's in the police station. She wasn't making much sense. What's going on?'

Iain sidestepped the question.

'She's gone away for a couple of days. I thought she might be stopping with you.'

He made some coffee and cut a generous slice of ginger cake, apologising as it broke into pieces on the plate.

'No. Her phone is going to voicemail. I know she's freaking out over these threats she been getting against Aspire.'

'Threats? What do you mean?'

Martha swallowed the dry cake and began to choke. She waved her hand towards the sink in a request for water.

'I don't know. You have to ask her. She plays her hand close when it comes to business. The last time we spoke it was about a campaign to get the company back on track. It's a tough market out there.'

Iain glanced quickly at the clock. He'd got a lot to do but wanted to try a couple of places he thought Una might be.

'She could have gone out to Dubai to see this Abdi bloke. He's one of her investors.'

Martha stopped speaking as soon as she realised Iain had no idea what she was talking about.

'Bugger. I've put my big toe in my even bigger gob haven't I? Look I can see you're busy. I'll get off.'

As he rolled up some warm clothes into a carry on holdall he thought about how different Una's life was from his own. A quick trip to Dubai for her when he could barely muster the energy to get his tux on for a concert a few miles away. He felt exhausted trying to make sense of Martha's speculations.

He caught the train to the airport and by the time he had battled through the heightened security he felt drained. The flight to Edinburgh was delayed owing to bad weather which added to Iain's growing anxiety. He felt it like a grinding of pestle and mortar in his lower gut. He paced the departure lounge, leafing through newspapers, picking up his coffee cup then putting it down. He rubbed his hands, checked his passport and boarding card, Martha's words tumbling round. Who was this Abdi person? It gnawed away as he hovered around the departure gate willing the flight to be called.

Finally, the Edinburgh flight was announced. Iain was first in the queue. As he handed over his documents, his phone vibrated to the irritation of the people behind him. Without his glasses he couldn't see who was calling but assumed it was Morag again.

'I knew there was a hidden agenda. You were so desperate to go up to Scotland to see your ex-wife and using my children as the excuse.'

Iain stopped in his tracks.

'Sir, please will you turn off your phone and board the aircraft.'

'Where are you? Martha came looking for you.'

'You'd better not get any ideas about staying up there for Christmas. I've made plans Iain. I'm warning you.'

He felt the disconnection as a thump in the groin.

'Sir. Please.'

Fighting down the urge to turn round and go back home, he forced himself to keep walking down the gangway and onto the plane.

CHAPTER TEN

Iain shuffled in his window seat, the lower part of his back sore, unable to find any comfort in the knowledge he would soon be on home soil. Even the soft burr of Edinburgh accents around him failed to lift his mood. Una's veiled threats whirled around in his head.

He snapped at the flight attendant who offered him refreshments then apologised before turning to stare down at the frayed ribbons of cloud. His neighbour tried to engage him in conversation but Iain wasn't in the mood to talk so kept his eyes firmly on his paper.

'Sir, would you please fasten your seatbelt for landing.'

Iain heard the voice in the distance but was too preoccupied with a competing noise in his head. He snapped the buckle into place impatient to land and be released from the stuffy cabin. The airport was teeming with travellers holding tightly onto festive carrier bags. Whoops of delight, bear hugs and a few tears greeted the fortunate ones entering the arrivals lounge. Iain turned away quickly. He felt like a voyeur, spying on a private party.

As soon as he collected his bags and went to collect his hire car, Iain felt the tension melt from his shoulders. Home, he breathed, pulling out into the light traffic on the Glasgow Road which led into the city centre.

He so wanted to see the twins. They were his family who would stretch out their arms and dig for presents. It had been months since he had seen them and whilst Johanna was always very tactile, James had been pulling away of late. They were growing up so quickly which made him proud and sad. Sending them away to school meant missing the joy of watching them change.

Iain was so deep in thought about his children and how he could make things right for them that he almost missed the turn for St. Mungo's Academy. A few miles out of Edinburgh, in a semi-rural location, stood the grand Victorian buildings which made up the small boarding school of just eighty children. It was Iain's old prep school.

The terms of his father's trust determined where the twins were to be educated up the age of 11. What he did with the money after that was up to him. James had won a small maths scholarship which was a bonus.

He cast his mind back to the conversation about the investment. No way was she going to have access that money. Una had only shown a cursory interest in the school when they first visited four years ago. Now they wanted to come home she responded with a defensiveness which frightened him.

'You're doing this to punish me,' she'd said. 'You know I can't look after them at home.'

'They don't need looking after. Besides I am at home so what difference does it make?'

Una had looked at him suspiciously. He remembered how her eyes had taken on a particular brightness.

'Does this mean we can use some of the money to settle with

the bank? Maybe they could come back and board weekly. Somewhere local. It would be cheaper.'

They did more circling of the argument than a plane looking for a slot to land at Heathrow. Una had shouted and thrown around threats when he'd stood his ground.

Navigating the twisty roads, lined with skeletal trees, Iain travelled back to the day they took James and Johanna for their first term. Johanna clinging onto him sobbing whilst stoic James shook hands before slipping a proprietorial arm around his sister as they followed their form teacher into the cavernous hall. Una had kissed them briefly on the cheek, ushering Iain away saying he was making it harder for them all.

As he swung his hire car into the imposing driveway, Iain watched the sea of petrol blue blazers, grey trousers and blue and yellow kilts emerge from the Great Hall.

Without locking the large estate car, he went into the foyer where trunks and cases were piled up ready for collection. Miss Kennedy, the twins' form teacher was standing by the oak reception desk. Her large frame was too big for the tweed jacket she wore but it was her coffee brown eyes Iain noticed more than her figure. Warm and sincere, they enveloped everyone she spoke to.

Iain noticed she had a way of laying a light hand on the arm of a pupil before speaking to them. It was the gesture of someone who cared about children in their care. That was all he had ever done with the pupils at St. Hilda's yet it had been so misinterpreted. He could feel his heart begin to thud. Mustering a bright smile he stretched out his hand and introduced himself.

'So glad to meet you once again. You missed a wonderful carol service,' said Miss Kennedy with a faint Highland accent. 'I wonder if you could spare a few moments before you collect the twins. There's something I'd like to talk to you about.'

In her office, walls lined with books, a small window onto the tennis courts, she offered him freshly made coffee and shortbread. Tugging her long corduroy skirt as she sat down she watched him carefully.

'Dr. Millar, I understand from James and Johanna that you are taking them out of school at the end of the year.'

Iain took a sip of his coffee before replying.

'I know the twins want to be nearer home for their secondary education then maybe back up to Scotland for university. James has his heart set on St. Andrews. Nothing is final yet.'

Miss Kennedy lifted her cup to her lips before responding.

'They have both been unsettled for a while here,' she said carefully choosing her words. 'I don't believe it's to do with school but Johanna in particular is anxious about you and her mother. Forgive me. It's not my place to pry but when a child is anxious about their home life it does reflect on their overall wellbeing here.'

'Yes I understand that. My wife runs a very successful business which means she has to travel a lot. I run a tutorial business from home so it makes sense for the twins to return to Birmingham at this age so they can make new friends.'

'I understand. As you know the school needs two terms' notice. We would be sorry to see them go. If it's a question of finance…'

Iain stood up, pushed his glasses onto his forehead and walked to the coffee stand to replace his cup. He fought to maintain his composure. Money, money, money. He fought to maintain his patience.

'No Miss Kennedy. It's not a question of money. Now if you would arrange for me to collect the children we will be on our way. The weather doesn't look too canny and we've a long drive.'

Within minutes, James and his sister were standing in the foyer with its Nordic Pine tree, their suitcases and sports kit ready to be loaded up. Johanna hurtled into her father's arms while James stood back looking embarrassed. Iain put his arms around their shoulders and ushered them out to the car. A porter followed with the luggage.

'Hungry?' he asked, a knowing twinkle in his eyes.

'Starvaysherous!' they chorused.

After much sparring over who was to sit in the front passenger seat for the first part of the journey, they settled down and began to shoot questions at their father.

'Why have you come today when they said it would be tomorrow? How was the flight? Are we flying back? Can we get burgers?' Finally, they asked about their mother.

Iain danced around the questions. Spotting a brightly lit gastro pub with a Christmas tree reaching the ceiling, he pulled into the car park and grabbed the map and satnav.

'Let me do it Dad please. Shall I just put in Birmingham?'

Johanna was fighting with herself whether to have burger and chips, something never on the Eat for Life menu at St Mungo's, or the chocolate and mint cheesecake.

'Let me do the food order first then we'll talk about it. I've got a bit of a surprise for you both.'

Several agonising minutes later the twins made their choices leaving Iain to put in the order at the bar. His own appetite was sharpened when he saw the size of the steak and stout pie being carried over to another table.

'What's the surprise Daddy? Is Mummy here and you're hiding her somewhere?'

Iain put his daughter's innocent face between his hands and shook his head.

'We are going up to Inverness to see Stuart's mother for a couple of days.'

Johanna groaned.

'Not Morag? But why? I want to go home to see Mum.'

For a moment Iain felt irritated with his daughter. He hoped she wasn't going to whine until they got back to Birmingham.

'Well we will be going soon enough. Inverness is so beautiful and she's got two new puppies. Skye terriers called Hamish and Hadar. They wear little tartan coats.'

Johanna sulked throughout the meal. She wouldn't answer Iain's questions about school except to say she wasn't going back after the summer holiday. James was more diplomatic in his explanations as to why St Mungo's wasn't the best place for him and his sister anymore.

'So many of our friends are leaving to go to school nearer home. I've researched the King Edward Schools and they are very high in the league tables. If we can't afford to go there then maybe the Grammar schools. I don't mind a comprehensive. I will work hard Dad wherever I go. You don't need to worry.'

Iain looked at his son with pride. James was quiet and thoughtful in his approach to life's problems. Johanna on the other hand seemed to be becoming volatile and emotionally charged when things didn't go her way.

'How do you feel about it Jo,' he asked gently.

She stabbed a fat chip with her fork and chewed it slowly before replying.

'I want to leave as well. I want to be near Mum. She hardly ever calls us and when she does she seems really unhappy. I think she's missing us.'

Iain poured himself some tea from the big white pot. He wondered what she did feel about her children not being at home. She rarely talked about them other than after the weekly phone call and letter. The school upheld the tradition of hand written letters to parents. Iain struggled to read what was behind her cold expression. It was as if she had no feelings at all sometimes.

'Of course she does,' was all he could find to say.

'Please Daddy, can't we go back home instead of up to Inverness. I don't feel very well.'

'Stuffed your face with chips that's why,' said James under his breath and received a whack on the arm.

'Johanna! Stop that.' Iain was appalled at her behaviour. 'Apologise to your brother.'

Johanna set her face like a stone.

'Sorreeee,' she muttered.

'We are going for a couple of days then we will go back home. Now get your coats. We need to be on our way before it gets dark. It will take us about three hours.'

In the back of the car, Johanna pulled the tartan car rug over her face and pretended to sleep. Iain thought he heard her crying but thought it best to leave her alone. He was worried that she was becoming too attention seeking.

As they drove into the Highlands he wondered if he was doing the right thing after all. Morag's offer was generous and sincere. He was so pleased that they had stayed friends after the divorce but then Morag was not given to irrational outpourings. They'd agreed that Stuart needed to see them as positive role models and although Iain took full responsibility for the breakdown of their marriage, Morag wanted no one to be blamed. 'It happens,' she had said nonchalantly. 'Let's make the best of it.'

Her calm, rational approach to life was what he liked most about her. He was looking forward to seeing her again.

It was after ten when he finally pulled up outside her double fronted cottage between Inverness and Loch Ness. He could see the black waters of the loch ahead and made a mental note to take the children to the visitor centre the next day.

Colourful lanterns twinkled in the windows where the white puppies in their tartan collars were sitting in anticipation of seeing a cat saunter by. The children made a dive for the warmth of the fire from the wood burner. The tang of the smoked apple wood caught in Iain's throat as he knelt before the flames to warm his hands. The terriers barked, snuffled and jumped around.

'Och, push them off m'dear,' Morag told Johanna. 'Naughty boys they are. Showing off for you.'

As Morag handed him a drink she noticed his hands shaking.

'Are you cold?' she asked, putting another log on the fire.

James was looking wide eyed through the window at the deer whilst his sister sat on a corner chair, still in her coat and woollen hat. Her sullen expression was purposely ignored but Iain was increasingly more frustrated with his daughter's behaviour. She had always been the compliant one of the two but something had changed.

'Right everyone, we have a choice of lamb stew and crusty bread or something simpler like ham, cheese and pickles. Home-made scones with raspberry jam for those who can manage it.'

James looked at his father before requesting the stew and the scones.

'Come into the kitchen then I can serve you. I know it's a bit late but you won't sleep well on an empty stomach.'

Johanna reluctantly followed them into the old-fashioned kitchen with its green range cooker and blue and yellow crockery on the oak dresser. An old black cat with a white collar was asleep on some blankets.

'She's called Tam,' Morag said. 'She likes little girls who will let her sleep on the bed.'

Johanna's eyes lit up. 'I will!'

'After you've eaten something,' Iain said into her ear.

Gentle murmurings of approval between mouthfuls of food and glances over to the sleeping cat were interrupted by Iain's phone announcing an incoming text message. Iain excused himself and went into the hallway. It was the latest text message from Una, threatening to call the police and report them all missing if he didn't call her back.

The clock in the hall chimed 11pm. He texted back to say he would call tomorrow morning and they were staying in Scotland for a couple of days. Anxiety crept through his veins but he was determined not to let Una spoil these special moments. She had no case for the police. He was with his own children and he'd let her know what was happening. Empty threats that's all he told himself. Being away from her made him feel stronger he realised.

It was gone midnight when the children finally settled into the attic bedroom. The experience of sleeping under blankets and fresh cotton sheets was a novelty. Homemade patchwork counterpanes stretched across the foot of the beds for extra warmth.

Morag was sitting in the snug room with a cup of tea when Iain came down to say goodnight.

'I thought we might take the twins to Loch Ness tomorrow,' she said.

'Reading my mind again. I was just about to say the same. It's a long time since I've been there.'

A heavy tiredness swamped him. Much as he wanted to talk to Morag his eyes were dragging him to bed.

'We've got all tomorrow to catch up,' she said as she began her locking up routine. 'Goodnight Iain. It's really good to have you here.' She squeezed his arm as she passed him a hot water bottle.

'You'll need it,' she laughed.

Iain couldn't sleep. He tried to read. Radio 3 didn't soothe him as it usually did. Una's words tumbled around in his head intertwining with his rekindled feelings for Morag which he dampened down immediately. He worried about Johanna's moodiness and rude behaviour, pushing away the thoughts that she was beginning to sound a bit like her mother.

A gnawing in his gut reminded him that Una would make him

pay for not returning straight to Birmingham. He felt fearful for them all but had no idea what to do about it.

CHAPTER ELEVEN

Una dug her sharp, red nails deep into her hair. Tearing at her scalp gave her some relief from having to deal with the terror rising from her gut. More tears of rage burst from under her sore eyelids as she paced the kitchen floor, furiously kicking anything in her way.

Empty bottles rolled languidly around the recycle box. Una resisted the urge to throw them through the window. Instead she opened the fridge and pulled out a half empty bottle of white wine and sloshed some into a cup. It was 10.30 am but she didn't care. Somewhere in the world it was after six.

The police had been disinterested in her story. She'd felt treated like some hysterical teenager.

'You've said they are away with their father. Is that correct?'

'He went to collect them from school and hasn't come back.'

'There's nothing we can do. No abduction has taken place. I'm sure they'll be back soon.'

'You're not bloody listening are you?' Her balled fists thumped the table. 'My husband is unbalanced and dangerous. Who knows what he's capable of. Check your records.'

Encouraged by a deep swallow of wine, which tasted sour in her dry mouth, Una continued to berate the police for their negligence. The experience of standing outside herself, looking on, was surreal. She saw a woman, angular and angry, with a bright red mouth, and empty eyes screaming out of control while two bemused uniformed officers looked on.

'Miss Carrington, will you please calm down. This isn't helping anyone. I suggest you call us back in 24 hours if you've not made contact although I am not sure what we can do at this point. Is your husband likely to visit anyone in Scotland?'

Una pursed her lips and ignored their question. She knew where they had probably gone but that wasn't the point. Iain had defied her and she believed he wasn't coming back. The police exchanged a brief glance before seeing themselves out.

Through a film of unshed tears, she tapped out Martha's number on her smartphone but it went to voicemail.

'Call me. I need to talk to you.'

She tried Iain's number yet again but the number wasn't recognised. She didn't stop to think that he might not have reception, preferring to believe that he had changed his sim card so he couldn't be tracked.

Una went in search of something to prise open the door to Iain's den, the keys of which were always with him. She was convinced that she would find something to prove he had been planning to kidnap the twins. All she could find was a trowel which snapped as she attempted to jimmy the lock.

'I'll kill you for putting me through this,' she said through clenched teeth, as a sharp pain cut through her shoulder.

Una dragged the curtains across her bedroom window pulling one of them from the track. Throwing the sleeping cat off the unmade bed, she rained curses into the pillows. An image of her thirteen-year old self floated through her head.

As she worked out the frustration, a crazy idea of getting in her car and driving up to Edinburgh buzzed around in her head. Anything to do be doing something. Her mobile vibrated somewhere on the bed. She tugged at the duvet and pillows to find it. This had better be Iain she thought.

'It's Martha. What's going on? I've been ringing and emailing for the past hour. Where are you?

'At home. Iain's taken the children.'

'What? That's crazy.'

Una slumped onto the floor, her head resting against the wall. Her white shirt was stained with coffee, her right heel bleeding from where her boot had rubbed against it. She didn't care. Her hatred of Iain was overriding everything.

'How dare he do this to me? He's been planning something for months. He's been secretive, acting like a psycho to make me think he's sick or something. He's a cunning bastard and not the person you seem to think he is.'

Martha looked at the clock. She was due at the hairdressers but it would have to wait.

'I'm on my way. Don't go anywhere. I will be twenty minutes.'

Tugging off her clothes, Una stepped into the shower. She tried to rationalise her thoughts. Iain wasn't going crazy she'd decided. He was being cunning. He'd taken her children back to his dumpy ex-wife and they would all live happily ever after.

NOT she said aloud pulling on some thick tights.

An idea came to her as she pulled on a grey cashmere tunic. She could ring the school. Iain would have told somebody his plans. All she had to do was say she was very worried about her children. They would cooperate. They wouldn't want any adverse publicity.

'St. Mungo's Academy is now closed for the Christmas Holidays.'

The strangled noise which left Una's throat alarmed Martha as she walked up to the front door. A fluffy white coat over a dress that looked as if it had done several rounds with an ink bottle was tossed to the side as Martha pulled her friend into her arms.

'You poor baby,' she soothed, her eyes scanning the mess and the empty bottles. She knew Una liked her drink but this was worrying.

'You have to pull yourself together. When did you last look in a mirror? I've been through tough times with my husbands but I didn't let myself get into this state.'

'He's been planning this all along,' Una sobbed. 'I knew there was something going on. My babies.'

Martha busied herself in the kitchen while Una moaned like a wounded animal.

'Stop blubbing. You're being a drama queen. There will be a reasonable explanation for him not getting in touch. Anyway, I've gotta say this Una but you're hardly a model mummy.

You sent them away cos you said they got on your nerves. Remember?'

'Don't come here pointing the finger at me. It was Iain who said they had to go to boarding school.'

Martha handed her a mug of strong black coffee and sat with her on the stairs.

'You need to calm down girl. You're like a bag of bones dancing on hot sand.'

'Thanks for the support.'

Una curled her lip as she tore off bits of tissue.

'I've told you. Iain's not the person you think he is. He's abusive when he can't get his own way. I could have reported him a number of times. I had the evidence but where would that leave us? I can't afford a divorce. He earns pin money and I can't see that changing. Everything falls on my shoulders.'

Martha pulled her friend close and gave her a long, silent hug.

'You in debt?'

'No, no. The business has stalled so there's a cash flow problem. No matter how many contracts we pitch for there seems to be somebody out there determined to sabotage us.'

'Ambitious People,' they said in dry harmony.

'Yeah they've tried to steal one of our campaigns,' said Martha draining her cup.

'I wonder if Anita was feeding them stuff. She's gone to work for them now.' Una went off on another rant.

'Twang your thong back into place and think positive. Iain told you he was staying in Scotland for a couple of days and it's nothing more sinister than that. He probably needed a break with his children. Business will pick up next year. I don't know what's got into you these days. You're becoming obsessive.'

Martha did not thrive well in negative environments. She tried to change the subject.

'What's the plan for Christmas? I thought we might all go ice skating at some point.'

Una let out a heavy sigh as she picked at a scab on her arm.

'Christmas is cancelled. If and when they get back, I am going to take the kids to Spain for the holiday and he can spend it on his own. See how it feels.'

Martha groaned deeply. Her cheeks fell into her hands.

'The UN would be at a loss to sort this out.'

She stood up to go. Out of the window she could see thick flakes of snow settling on the trees. Tugging on her boots, Martha lost her balance and fell over laughing. It sounded like a blast of unexpected percussion in a library.

'At least I can see the funny side of things Una. That's what you need to do. Chill out. Go and buy yourself some handmade chocolates and for heaven's sake, cut down on the drink. You'll end up with skin like a snake's armpit.'

***

'This is a real Nessie fest,' said James as he examined all the different souvenirs on offer to retail hungry visitors. He picked up a large monster in purple felt and pushed it into his sister's face who yelped like stung puppy.

James' eyes sparkled as they wandered through the exhibition which took the visitors through seven themed areas to show the history of the loch and its alleged monster. Lasers, special effects and the latest multimedia gadgetry had prompted question after question.

'Look at that ancient diving suit, Dad. It's so weird. What's the helmet made of?'

'Brass I guess. See the lead boots? I would suffocate to death in that gear.'

Whilst he chatted to Morag about his life saving classes at school, Iain took Johanna to one side. She'd been scowling all morning. The trip to Loch Ness was to be a treat but she showed no enthusiasm, neither on the boat trip across the loch or in the exhibition centre.

'What's wrong?' he asked quietly.

She turned her face away, trying to hold back tears.

'Do you want to ring your mother? We are going home tomorrow. A quick flight down to Birmingham then you can catch up with your friends. Come on, give her a call then we'll go and have lunch in the Loch Ness café.'

'Morag's trying to act like she's my mum and she's not. You're not going to go off with her are you?'

Johanna sniffed and clung on to her father's arm.

'Of course not!' Iain felt uncomfortable. He had toyed with such thoughts but placed them firmly back in their box.

'Here's my phone. Ring your Mum and tell her we are on the three o'clock from Inverness. Maybe she would like to pick us up from the airport. I'm going to leave most of the luggage with Morag and she'll take it back to school after the holidays.'

Iain watched her crumpled expression as she ended the conversation. He'd heard Una's raised voice and his heart plummeted. Lunch was a subdued affair. James munched thoughtfully on his sandwich, whilst making sketches of the Nessie in his notebook. Morag sipped her tea, gazing into the mid distance across the loch. 'Mummy's angry,' Johanna said suddenly. 'She said that you never told her we were stopping with Morag.'

'I did tell her we were spending a couple of days in Scotland after school.'

'She called the police,' said Johanna, noisily drawing the last of her milk shake through the straw.

Iain felt as if a hundred snakes had woken up in his stomach and were writhing and spitting their venom. He couldn't face his soup.

'Don't worry Jo. It will all be fine when we get back. It's Christmas next week.'

Morag and Iain exchanged glances. Although he had said nothing about Una except that she was under a lot of stress he knew that his ex-wife was very intuitive. He wrestled with loyalty to Una and a need to unburden himself.

Later that day, when the twins had gone out on an organised pony trek, Iain slumped into the wing backed chair by the log fire, a crystal tumbler of whisky untouched on the table. He closed his eyes. Morag sat opposite, her current tapestry resting on her lap. She watched discreetly the tremor in his hands and feet.

'Do you want to talk about it?' she asked gently.

Iain looked into his glass, took a sip before telling her about the allegations of sexual harassment at the school and how he'd been asked to resign to save face. He went on to say how he'd become a leper within the educational system and no-one would risk employing him.

'They've even said as much. Oh we know you were innocent and girls will be girls sort of thing but we have to think of the parents.'

'That must have been so difficult for you. For both of you.'

Iain turned the amber liquid round in the glass.

'I don't think Una fully believed there was nothing in it. Oh she paid the legal fees and backed me up in public but …it's warm by this fire,' he said, slipping off his jacket and rolling up his sleeves.

Morag caught sight of the red marks on Iain's arm. They seemed like small burns in different stages of healing running in a zig -zag from his wrist to his elbow. Catching her eye, he tugged down his sleeve and fastened it at the cuff.

'Stuart has emailed by the way. He's met up with some friends and decided to go to some beach party in Thailand over Christmas and New Year. I hope he's going to be sensible,' Morag said, deftly weaving her green wool in and out of the tiny squares.

Iain had drifted away, barely hearing her.

'Och, he's young and needs to get this out of his system especially since he's going to be starting work soon,' she continued.

Iain thought about the last time they'd had a holiday as a family. He could do with some sun. Alex Gordon had said if he could put it in a prescription he would be a billionaire. The dark, cold nights were dragging down his mood. He knew it was his fault that they didn't have any money for luxuries. He blushed when he remembered asking Una for money for a new pair of trousers. She'd made him beg. He refused.

In twenty-four hours' time he would be back in Woodbourne House, away from the tranquillity of this restful cottage. He knew what to expect from Una and he was eaten up with anxiety. Maybe he should phone her now just to get the ranting over with.

He slipped into the kitchen where the dogs were asleep and punched in her number.

It went straight to voicemail. He didn't leave a message but managed to send a properly written text. He wouldn't give in to text speak.

Within two minutes she called him back. Waiting for the verbal onslaught, he was knocked off his feet when she said,

'I've been really worried about you,' with a tenderness in her voice Iain hadn't heard for a long time. 'Jo called me to say you're back tomorrow. I really wished you'd told me your plans. I'll be at the airport to pick you up. Let's try to sort things out Iain over the holidays. Love you.'

He stared at his phone in stunned silence.

CHAPTER TWELVE

Una's sleep had been disturbed for most of the night. She punched the pillows, got up to make camomile tea and watched a re-run of Dragon's den on her iPad but nothing would shift the recycling of negative thoughts. Iain. Children. Business. Abdi. Iain, Abdi, Business, Debt.

It was still dark when Una pulled on her trainers and went out into the crisp morning. A dog walker greeted her as she ran past, her breath burning in her chest. Determined to push herself along the streets, despite the pain in her hips and knees, Una found some relief from the mental torture. Maybe this is what I should do every day she thought as she rounded the corner to the house, feeling less tense.

She noticed how messy the house was. An overflowing bin, a table littered with papers, dirty dishes and overturned cat food made her heave. Swigging from a bottle of sparkling water, she pulled on some latex gloves and did battle with the dirt.

The thud of letters on the mat triggered an attack of indigestion. Brown government envelopes were arriving daily but ended up unopened in the recycling bin. The meeting with the new solicitor had been a waste of time. Una recalled his smug face when he reiterated her responsibilities as a company director. She'd wanted to smack it. She needed help not criticism.

Una scrubbed the counter tops, the microwave and mopped the floor with strong bleach. It was a strong, cleansing smell which made her feel in control. Her mother swore by bleach to get rid of germs. Poor Mum, she thought. A cleanaholic and now doesn't know what time of day it is.

She sat at her desk for while catching up on emails but avoiding checking the bank accounts. A couple of new contracts had been agreed thanks to Siobhan with her contacts in Northern Ireland and some positive reviews posted on their website. Una felt encouraged. Maybe Martha was right. Things would pick up next year.

She pulled on an oversized black jumper and glanced at the church clock as it chimed the hour. The flight from Inverness would be leaving in a couple of hours. Blue icicle lights which snaked around the fascias of the big houses in the street threw a mocking reflection onto the dead trees of Woodbourne House.

Una finished the packing and secured the holdalls with a strap, making a mental note to buy travel cosmetics at the airport. The weather forecast for southern Spain promised sunshine. It would be good to get away. Una knew she shouldn't be taking the children away nor spending money they couldn't afford but she had to make her stand.

She sat in her car waiting for the engine to warm up, scowling at the memory of being told to sell it before it was repossessed by the bailiffs.

It was three days before Christmas, a time Una hated and feared. Her childhood Christmases had been destroyed by trees pulled to the floor in rage, her mother 'forgetting' to buy presents and food for the dinner. Una put her hand to her mouth as she remembered going to Mr. Ali's on Christmas day. He'd been so kind. A box of chocolates for her and a cake for the family had been his gift. She'd spent the day under the blankets reading a book and praying for it all to be over.

Her phone trilled as she navigated the tail gaiting traffic out of the city. Una switched to loudspeaker.

'It's Martha. I'm at the NEC later. Shall I pick up Iain and the children? Saves you coming out in this weather.'

'Thanks but I promised to be there,' Una said stonily.

'You still mad with me?'

'No. Why should I be? I've got to go.'

'You're a frosty cow sometimes.'

The flight had arrived early despite the weather. Iain called her over from the coffee bar where Johanna was licking the whipped cream from her hot chocolate. Una saw her and made a pledge not to give her daughter anymore fattening stuff. She was looking pudgy.

'Mum!' she called, getting up for a hug. 'I've missed you soooo much. James has been a beast.'

'I've missed you too my darling.' Una fired a filthy look at Iain who was carrying over a tray. He gave a nod of apology to someone who bumped his elbow.

'James?' Una tilted her head on one side waiting for her son to acknowledge her.

'Mum.' He held back looking to Iain for permission.

The twins sat at a corner table, silently watching their parents as they sipped their drinks.

'So you've been to see Morag have you? How was she?'

'Fine. She's settled in Inverness so we popped up to see her.'

Iain tried to sound nonchalant. He sipped his tea urging Una to try her cappuccino.

'Well you've had your fun so it's my turn.'

Iain's stomach lurched. Una's calm unnerved him more than her outbursts of temper.

'I'm taking them away for Christmas,' she continued, tightening the belt of her coat.

Iain felt his hands go clammy. He carefully laid down the cup.

'You can't. We've made plans. You agreed…'

She pressed her face towards his and hissed,

'I can do what I bloody well like. You've no idea what I went through when you disappeared like that. I was crawling the walls.'

'But I told you. I sent you a text.'

'Stop playing games Iain. I called the police because I thought you'd decided to abscond with them. I wouldn't put it past you.'

'Don't be silly. Of course I wouldn't do that. I'd got plans for an old fashioned Christmas this year. Simple things like we had as children.'

Una froze.

'You have no idea what my Christmas's were like as a child.'

A muscle twitched at the corner of her mouth. She slid a lipstick over it.

'Now I suggest you say goodbye to the twins and I will explain what's happening.'

Iain sat motionless and pale like a mannequin in a shop window. He felt the pain of abandonment under his ribs. He leaned forward to ease his breathing. James saw him and ran over.

'Dad. What's the matter? Don't worry. I'm not going with Mum. I've told her I am staying with you.'

Iain felt his son's arms around his waist and closed his eyes as he savoured the precious moment. He knew he could insist that the twins stayed at home but the fight had drained out of him. The confusion in the boy's eyes pushed him into being selfless.

'No you must go. It's a lovely idea,' he managed. 'We can do something special when you come back.'

He steadied himself as he got up from the chair and turned to Una.

'Let's go home and open some of the presents. We can have family dinner with crackers. When you are going?'

'Now. The 7 o'clock to Malaga. The bags are in the car.'

Iain's jaw felt tight as if trapped in a vice.

'I see,' was all he could manage.

He hugged the twins, one under each arm, with such an intensity he thought he would break them. Pulling out a handkerchief he made a show of cleaning his steamed up glasses whilst scanning the departure boards.

Una felt a twinge of guilt. Somewhere deep in her core she didn't want it to be like this but Iain had to learn he couldn't put her through any more torment.

They looked at each other, a deep pain in his eyes, a vague look of triumph in hers before Una shepherded them out of the airport.

She'd been clever, Iain thought, choosing a public place to drop such a bombshell on him. Quiet, unassuming Iain, wouldn't want a fuss. He wanted to spit.

'Can I take your cases sir,' asked the young taxi driver. He was so polite that Iain let him help into the back of the black cab.

'Where to sir? Are you alright? There's a bottle of water on the seat.'

Iain shook his head and asked him to take the quickest route back. Kindness was too much to process at that moment. He rested his throbbing head back on the seat and closed his eyes.

As he stumbled out of the cab, the driver took his arm and helped him into the house.

'This is my number sir. Please call me if you need anything.'

He needed his children but no-one could magic that for him except his wife. If she had any compassion she would come home he thought, unlocking the door to his den. He poured a measure of whisky which he promptly emptied back into the decanter. Alex Gordon was right. He needed to cut back on the stuff.

Iain sat in the dark for a long time, staring out of the window. The street was quiet apart from a giggling young couple pushing each other off the pavement and next door's cat meowing to go inside. He wished he was a cat. He would be fed, could sit undisturbed in front of a roaring fire and dream of whatever cats dreamed of. He would be stroked and loved and wanted instead of rejected.

Beethoven strolled in and rubbed his back around Iain's legs. He bent to pick him up. They sat together in the blackness listening to the boiler going through its motions.

'She's left you. I told you she'd leave you in the end. It's punishment.'

'What? Who's that?'

As Iain jumped up, the cat fell to his feet with a yelp. A paperweight in his hand, he moved stealthily towards the curtain.

'Come out and say that. Coward. Say it to my face.'

He swung round, brandishing the weapon above his head as he tip-toed to the bookcase. With huge effort he pulled it to the floor, books and photographs crashing over the desk. Stumbling out of the room, he kicked Beethoven out of the way to reach the panic button in the hall. Just as he was about to press it, the house phone rang out. Iain stared at it as if it was a grenade.

At that same moment the doorbell rang. Sweating and swearing he stared in horror at the outline of the person peering through the stained glass.

'Iain, it's me. Fergus. Open up. Let me in.'

'You're not Fergus. Who sent you?'

'Fecking hell,' muttered Fergus as he banged on the door.

'Don't be ridiculous. Look through the spyhole.'

Iain saw the distorted figure of a man wearing a bow tie imprinted with musical notes. Something in his brain clicked.

'Come on Iain. I'm as cold as a tit in Greenland.'

It took Iain some time to unlock the door and draw back the bolts. The two men looked at each other, deep concern etched on Fergus's face, a shadow of terror on Iain's.

Fergus followed him into the den, littered with torn manuscript paper, spilled CD boxes and crockery.

'What a stink.'

'I've not had time to tidy up. They've been after my compositions.'

'Eh? What are you on about?'

Fergus bent down to retrieve some of the manuscript paper. He couldn't make sense of it. It was a jumble of notes on the wrong stave and in a mix of keys. He didn't say anything but laid down some containers of hot food from the local Chinese.

'Come on. Chow Mein and prawn fried rice.'

Fergus handed him some plastic cutlery and piled up the prawn crackers. He stuffed a couple in his mouth, blowing out flakes as he spoke.

'I'm not hungry,' said Iain thinking the food was some sort of trick.

'Well you can watch me then. I've been out at boring meetings all day. These funding committees seem to think musicians are angels. Don't need to eat and pay the gas bill.'

Iain tentatively dug his fork into the noodles and put them in his mouth. He was hungry. Very hungry. He took another mouthful, some rice and prawns, sighing as the food slid down into the void of his stomach.

Nothing more was said until they'd slurped every noodle and beheaded every prawn.

Fergus belched and undid the belt of his trousers.

'Why are you here so late anyway?'

'Must be missing you. I could do with a cuppa. Have you got any of that stuff that looks like cat pee?'

'You mean camomile.'

Iain busied himself with the drinks, talking non-stop about some new string quartet in Birmingham.

'They're not even out of nappies,' he said with a bitter laugh. 'Not much chance for us wrinklies.'

'Iain. Stop. Listen to me. Una rang the house and spoke to Freda. Some rambling story about you being drunk at the airport and in no fit state to be around the twins. She said and

I quote, 'he went mental at the airport and tried to restrain me from leaving. Please get him to see a doctor. There's something seriously wrong.'

Iain picked up a manuscript and began to hum.

'I'm not sure about this bit. What do you think? The timing's not right.'

Fergus took the music gently from his hand.

'What I think is that you should come and stay with us over Christmas. In fact Freda says I won't be let back in the house without you. Whatever is going on between you and Una won't be resolved by you sitting here alone in your cups every night. Go and pack your stuff. Bring your cello. I'll tidy up a bit in here.'

Iain was on the verge of telling Fergus not to move anything but closed his mouth.

'I can't leave the house.'

'Don't be daft. There's nothing stopping you unless you've fixed a date with the Grim Reaper tonight.' Fergus groaned as he realised what he'd said.

'They might ring.'

'Una's got our number. Maybe when she's let the steam out of her ears she'll change her mind and come back. She's building skyscrapers out of bog paper. Come on.'

Fergus took the rubbish into the kitchen along with the dirty crockery. He resurrected the bookcase and made a stab at putting back its contents. It was the best he could do in the time. They could come back and sort it out later. He needed to get Iain out of the house and into somewhere safe. Freda's cooking and the warmth of the cottage would soon restore Iain's equilibrium. He wasn't making much sense at the moment he sighed, locking the back doors and turning off the lights.

As Iain came down the stairs with some bags, Fergus picked up his cello.

'Leave that. Nobody must touch it. Fingerprints,' Iain said, touching his nose.

Desperate to distract him, Fergus pointed to his throat.

'Hey listen to this.' He pressed something on his bow tie triggering a tinny rendition of Slade's Merry Christmas.

Iain forced a smile and tugged on his scarf. He followed Fergus out to the car. The landline rang. Fergus shot back inside and picked it up.

'Iain? Iain? Damn you. Answer me.'

'Not fecking likely Mrs. Millar,' he muttered, pulling the line from its socket.

CHAPTER THIRTEEN

December 24th

Andalucía was experiencing an unusually cold spell with forecasts of heavy rain. Driving to the hotel along a windswept bay, James stared out at the empty beach. The wind was whipping up the grey froth of the waves pausing to smash them against the rocks which stuck out like rotting eye teeth.

In good English the driver lamented Spain's economic difficulties with heavy sighs in between shouting at other road users swerving in front of him with an inch to spare.

'Pero que hace? Idiota!'

Pulling in his head he continued his monologue.

'The British and Germans like to come here in the winter to escape the snow and rain but look at this weather. So bad for us.'

Whilst Una was too tired to feign much interest, James put together some halting sentences in Spanish.

'So you learn Spanish in school. Very good. Here in Andalucía we eat our words. Drop the final 's' and the 'd' so if you want to sound like a local you say, supermerca'o and mucha gracia.' He laughed as he twisted the car down a narrow alleyway, avoiding the overflowing potholes, to the hotel entrance.

'Aqui estamo. Here we are.'

Una climbed out of the back seat, cursing as she slipped on the wet pavement. She pointed to the luggage and walked ahead into the foyer towards reception, her heels tapping on the wooden floor. James pulled out some euros and handed them to Pedro with an embarrassed smile.

'Good evening Mrs. Carrington. Welcome.'

The receptionist scanned the computer screen and frowned. Una tapped her fingers on the counter, telling the twins to sit down and be quiet. A noisy crowd were coming up from the restaurant, two of the women giggling as they waved to the dark haired manager who was picking up a red bauble that had fallen off the enormous Christmas tree.

'We are putting you in a smaller room than requested just for tonight as your room isn't ready. There was a small leak which is being repaired. To compensate we offer you a free dinner in the restaurant this evening.'

Una set her face in readiness for a fight.

'This isn't good enough,' she snapped. 'My children are tired. We don't want to keep packing and unpacking. You will upgrade us to a suite. Thank you.'

'Mrs. Carrington, please do not shout. You will upset our guests.'

'It's Miss Carrington. Get this sorted out or we find something else.'

Una threw a challenging glare at a couple who had stopped to eavesdrop.

The duty manager poked his head round the door of the back office. Taking one look at the tall woman with the stone eyes he quietly told his bemused receptionist that he would deal with the matter.

'If you would like to follow me into the conservatory please Miss Carrington. Jose, drinks menu please.'

Calmly but firmly he explained the situation but said if she wanted to find somewhere else then he would be happy to cancel their reservation with no penalty.

He stayed quiet, watching the muscle twitching in her cheek.

Una grabbed the menu and selected drinks and snacks.

'I assume this is on the house?'

He gave her a small, tight smile and inclined his head.

Una huffed, feeling cornered. The children were slouched across the sofas, James playing with some electronic gadget and Johanna almost asleep.

'I suppose I have no choice. I will be making a formal complaint.' Una took the keys for the room and ushered the twins none too gently towards the lift.

The buttermilk room was small but brightly decorated with crimson bedding and bold abstracts. A TV and DVD player with a selection of English films for children together with a well-stocked tea tray helped take the edge of her frayed nerves. She sat on the edge of the bed wondering what the hell she'd done. Rain lashed mercilessly against the windows as the wind pushed its way under the window frame. Una felt drained of colour. Leaning across to the mini bar she pulled out a small gin and tonic mix. She needed to blot out Johanna's whining and the irritating noise of her son's Gameboy.

'Johanna get into bed will you and read a book or something.'

Kicking off her shoes, her daughter slid under the duvet fully clothed and turned her back on her mother.

'You're horrible,' she said between sobs. 'I hate you.'

'I can live with it. Put your pyjamas on and clean your teeth. Do things without being asked.'

Una nursed her head as a pain shot across her eyes. If this was mothering then she could do without it she thought. Her children seemed like aliens, so poor was her understanding of them these days. She remembered her mother saying something similar about her. Una wanted to be relaxed and fun around them but felt stupid and out of control. Fun wasn't in her nature.

'I'm still hungry Mum. Can we order room service?'

'James you've eaten a load of chocolate and crisps, so nothing more tonight. You make sure you clean your teeth properly as well.'

She'd been shocked at how much rubbish they'd both eaten since boarding the flight. She felt it showed a lack of self-control and made a note to speak to the school about what they were teaching them.

With a large glass of wine at her side she logged onto her emails. Iain popped up on Skype so she changed her status to invisible. The ghostly look on his face as they walked away from him at the airport now preyed on her mind. If he hadn't looked so pathetic and stood up for himself she might have been impressed enough to change her mind.

Her hand hovered over the Skype button as she wrestled with a decision to call him or let him sweat it out. If she gave in, then it would pave a sticky path for the future. No, Iain had lost the right to equality. He's simply getting back what he did to me she argued with herself as she drained the last of the wine.

As she undressed, she glanced at the sleeping twins, feeling their need for her as an entrapment. Ideas of bringing them home to Birmingham so she could access some funds both fascinated and horrified her.

James lay still in his bed until he was sure Una was asleep. He'd chosen the bed nearest the door to make it easier to slip on some shoes and slide out into the corridor. Feeling in his pocket for his mobile phone, he rang Iain's number hoping he would have enough money to have a quick word. It went through to voicemail. Fighting down his disappointment he left a message to say he missed him and hoped he was alright. He didn't know what else to day. When he crept back into the room, Una's eyes flew open.

'Where've you been? What's that you're hiding?'

'I felt hot and couldn't sleep.'

Una pushed back the duvet and held out her hand.

'Give me that phone.'

James pushed back his shoulders and looked his mother in the eye. For the first time Una noticed how tall he was.

'No. It's mine. Dad bought it for me.'

'Yeah with my money. Give. Now.'

She raised her hand then lowered it quickly, shocked as she realised she was about to slap her son across the face. She put her hand over her mouth to calm her breathing.

'You'll get it back when I say. Your father had no business buying you a phone. If he's too weak to discipline you then be sure that I am not.'

'NO, He's NOT. Don't talk about him like that,' James shouted through his tears.

The noise woke Johanna.

'Where are we? Where's Daddy? Why are you all shouting?'

Wide-eyed and shivering, she climbed onto Una's bed.

'Mummy?' Why are you crying?'

She put her arms around her mother's neck and tried to sit on her knee.

Una grabbed her arms and pushed her away roughly.

'Get off me, for heaven's sake.'

Johanna began to cry loudly.

'You're scaring us Mum.' James put his arm protectively around his sister. He glared at her accusingly.

'Why can't you both be quiet? Get back into bed.'

Una disappeared in the bathroom and stared at her reflection in the small mirror. She saw a crazed glint in her eyes which seemed to protrude from their dark sockets. She splashed her pale face with water in an attempt to regain control.

'Look. I'm sorry. I shouldn't take it out on you. I came here to give Daddy some space. He's not been feeling well.'

James frowned.

'He was fine in Scotland. He was always laughing and making silly jokes.'

Una sat on the edge of his bed.

'I shouldn't be telling you this but your Dad has a problem with his mind. It's sort of broken. You can't see it like a broken bone but it means he doesn't think normally sometimes. He sees and hears things that aren't there. And…' she paused to pick at a loose thread on the coverlet, 'he does bad things but forgets about them.'

'Like what?' Johanna's tear stained face filled with horror.

'Well, he tells people that I sometimes attack him. He's called the police and shown them bruises that he's done to himself.'

Fresh sobs broke from Johanna as she locked herself in the bathroom.

'He's not ill Mum,' said James 'You're wrong. He's a normal person but he's very sad. We shouldn't have come here, leaving him on his own.'

Una felt a little bit afraid of her son who she knew in a couple of years would tower over her and over whom she would have no sway. She pressed her fingers into her forehead.

'This is grownup stuff and nothing to do with children. I shouldn't have expected you to understand.'

***

The bad weather warnings for the week meant the need for a hire car. A number of indoor activities were close by including a water park with giant slides.

Una showed the twins the leaflet but James pointed out that it was closed. Much to her frustration they shrugged when she asked what they wanted to do. She wanted to shake James as he kicked against the table leg over breakfast, his face screwed into a ball of misery.

She watched Johanna dip churros, one after the other, into thick chocolate, smearing it over her face and hands. She was fed up watching her cram so much rubbish into her mouth. Una checked to see if other guests had seen this disgusting display of gluttony.

'That's enough,' she snapped,' dragging the bowl away from her. 'God knows what state your teeth are in.'

'We could go to Bio Parc. It's open on Christmas Day.'

James pulled a leaflet out of the tourist rack in the foyer.

'I don't agree with zoos,' Una told him firmly.

Christmas day was a non-event. The rain lashed against the hotel windows as disgruntled families sipped liqueur coffees for want of anything better to do. Reading material balanced on their knees as they stared unbelievingly towards the sodden courtyard and covered swimming pool.

Una kicked herself for forgetting to bring some of the small presents. In an effort to placate them she suggested they went on a drive into the hills to see the donkeys and have a picnic in the car.

A young Spanish woman in a red skirt and jacket was handing out mince pies and drinks. She stopped to chat to Johanna who was curled up in the corner of a sofa, arms over her head.

'This is such bad weather for you. I am so sorry. Maybe the sun will shine later chica.'

She handed Una a leaflet whilst rattling off the programme of events in the hotel, receiving a tight smile for her efforts. The day dragged on. A beach walk broke the tension once the rain had turned to a light drizzle. Una blew up the beach ball and tried to engage the twins in a game which lasted no more than ten minutes.

Johanna walked by the edge of the water, hood up, head down while her brother skimmed stones into the distance. Una sat on a rack tapping her foot. 'They've been spoilt stupid,' she thought as she batted away any idea that maybe their behaviour was to do with not having a mother around.

As she watched them play languidly for a while Una felt she was locked behind a glass panel. She felt no connection to these two children who she'd adored when they were younger. Memories of tea parties, trips to the animal farm at Cannon Hill Park, kite flying and boat trips, were a jumble of jigsaw pieces. She'd tried to join their world but it was like she was a visitor without a pass. Una felt as miserable as they looked.

She strolled down by the edge of the sea, hands thrust deep into the pockets of her trench coat. Maybe taking them away from Iain to teach him a lesson was backfiring. She pictured him not at home alone in a cold, empty cellar of a house but chuckling over whisky and cake with Fergus and that frumpy housewife of his. A pang of envy poked her in the ribs. She tussled with the idea of booking a return flight as soon as possible but how would she do it without seeming to cave in?

Pulling out her smartphone she checked the airline. There were three remaining seats available for the next day.

'I want to go home,' said Johanna in a small voice. 'This is horrible. Why did you bring us here?'

'You ungrateful little madam. How did I know it was going to tip it down like this? It was your Christmas treat, but if you want to go home I would rather do that than listening to you whining.'

'Can we phone Dad to wish him Merry Christmas?' James clenched his hands as he waited for his mother to explode. She handed him her phone.

'Five minutes that's all. It costs money.'

Johanna perked up and skipped behind her brother to a sheltered place away from the wind. After several attempts they were able to get through.

'This is a lovely surprise,' said Iain, clearly delighted to hear their voices. 'How's Spain? I bet it's hot and sunny. We've got snow.'

Jo began to cry again and pushed James when he dug her in the ribs.

'Stop it,' he hissed.

'It's been raining since we got here. What are you doing?'

'Oh I'm sitting in Tom's living room with his Dad, having bacon sandwiches and watching the snow. I've got a new musical bow tie. Listen.'

'Send us a selfie.'

'A what?'

'Take us a picture of yourself and send it to us, Daddy,' called Jo over her brother's shoulder.

James was trying so hard to be grown up and matter of fact that his throat felt scorched. He heard Una calling time. She snatched the phone from him.

'I suppose you've been telling him how miserable you are. If you hate it that much we can fly back tomorrow morning. I have to book the seats now so make up your mind.'

'Are you happy here Mum? You could put us on a flight back and ask Dad to collect us then we wouldn't be in your way when you meet that man for drinks when you think we are asleep.'

She grabbed his collar and marched him back to the hotel.

'Don't you ever speak to me like that again,' she hissed,

glaring through the window at the duty manager who was watching.

'This is child abuse. I could report you,' he said, trying to get free of her grip.

Una spun him round to face her.

'Who's been giving you these ideas? You need proper discipline and manners. So do you Johanna. You eat like a pig. I'm going to pull you out of that school and keep you in Birmingham where I can keep my eye on you. You need splitting up.'

James wanted to cartwheel on the wet sand. He never expected his mother to say that but he knew he couldn't look too keen.

'You can't do that,' he protested as she pushed him up the hotel drive.

'Oh can't I? Watch me.'

Once the seats back to Birmingham were secured, everyone brightened up. Una looked around at the tired hotel with its dated furniture, gaudy decorations and was relieved to be getting out of such a dump. The children joined some others in the entertainment lounge to watch Aladdin while she ordered a large cocktail and asked to speak to the manager. She wanted a refund.

'I'm sorry señora but you signed the no refund policy when you booked and you can take me and the whole of Spain to court if you so wish.'

Watching Una stomp away he was relieved she was leaving. He didn't want professional complainers in his hotel.

The twins threw themselves into all the activities, pausing only to grab some snacks from the buffet. Una got slowly drunk, feasting on crisps to soak up the gin. It was late when she threw their clothes back into a bag and booked an alarm call and taxi. She'd let Iain know and he would have to come back home. Before climbing into bed she dialled a number in Scotland. The answering machine clicked in. Una tapped her phone against her palm as she thought about the message she would leave.

'Stay away from my husband Morag. He doesn't want to see you again.'

CHAPTER FOURTEEN

The flight back was delayed by heavy snow. Woodbourne House was damp and dismal. Una got a strange feeling that the house begrudged her return. She went through the rooms turning on lamps, telling James to fetch some logs from the shed. It was too late to go shopping so she searched the freezer for a couple of quiches, snapping at Johanna when she turned up her nose.

Without taking off her coat, Una walked into the family room, hands thrust deep into her pockets. The room was cold. Her fingers had turned white, the colour of the Swedish leather sofas, pristine but no longer inviting. She paced the length of the huge space, peering at pictures she couldn't remember buying and gazing at a solitary photograph of the twins in their uniforms. A carefully placed piece of porcelain on the piano was covered in a film of dust. Una ran her finger over it realising that it was a long time since they'd used this room.

Lifting the lid of the piano she skimmed her long fingers over the keys quelling a sudden urge to be able to play. She could see Iain sitting on the stool, flexing his fingers in readiness for his party piece, 'The Flight of the Bumblebee.' The twins would say, 'Again Daddy. Play it again.' They'd never been in awe of her as they were of their father. She doubted they even liked her very much. She heard them outside arguing.

'Get your coats. We're going to collect your father.'

'Yay!' they chorused. 'Can we put up the plastic tree and open our presents then?'

'I suppose so. Hurry up Johanna or I'll leave you here.'

***

Freda came to the door, tea towel in hand and nodded quietly as Iain's wife yelled on the doorstep.

Una's eyes sucked in Freda's ash blonde hair neatly tied back with a black ribbon, her unlined face and trim waist emphasised by a belted dress.

'Come in,' she said, stepping aside to let Una and the children into the softly lit hall.

'We're not staying. Could you tell Iain we're here to take him home?'

Una felt herself stiffen as she saw, through a glass panel in the door, her husband and Fergus seated at a table, their heads bent over some papers. He looked relaxed and at home. Una suspected he'd told them some sob story and Freda had taken pity on him.

Iain had arrived at the house in a bad state. He'd shivered in front of a roaring fire, unable to eat the hot beef sandwiches Freda had laid on the side table. His overriding feeling was that of having his side cut open and a hot poker shoved inside. He'd felt the shock for hours despite the brandy and a couple of prescription tablets. He'd pulled out the one photograph of the twins, scuffed around the edges from so much handling, and stared at it blindly. Now he imagined he heard their chattering.

Looking up he couldn't believe what he was seeing.

'Dad.' They wrapped themselves around him with such passion that he almost fell off the chair.

'Hang on a minute. Let me breathe! What are you doing here?' Iain beamed with pure joy.

'They were miserable in Spain so we came back. Are you ready? Iain?'

Fergus stole a look at his wife. He felt Iain was too fragile to return to Woodbourne House and if it meant a fight with Una, he was ready for it.

'We've brought you some presents. Open them.'

Iain gently pulled off the tape securing the gifts, pausing to exclaim his delight.

'Resin. Just what I needed. Oooh Johanna. French chocolates. Lovely.'

Paper slid to the floor in a heap as Iain piled up his treasures. A warm glow spread to his cheeks. Just having them at his side was the greatest gift. Fergus brought over a board game, partially played.

'You be red Johanna and you take up the blue James. Your Dad will show you how to play.'

Una's eyes narrowed. This wasn't the plan. She tugged at James' shoulder, feeling aggrieved as he pushed her off. She was aware that Fergus was watching her so she pulled a tight smile.

Freda proffered a platter of savoury tarts and mince pies.

'No thank you. We need to get home. The weather's getting worse. I can't match Freda's culinary skills but I'm sure we can pick up something on the way.'

Fergus got to his feet and pulled up his trousers. He'd abandoned his waistcoat for fear of bursting its seams. He rubbed his belly.

'We're going to church next door for a carol service. You're welcome to come with us. There's a community get together afterwards.'

Una straightened her back and inhaled slowly.

'No thanks. My children would like to spend time with their father in their own home.'

Freda lightly touched her arm.

'I'm sure they do. Let's go into the snug and let the men finish whatever they are doing first.'

She turned to her son who come back into the room, followed by Skips their aging border terrier.

'Tom, take the twins to have a play on your new drum kit.'

'Oh yes!' beamed James.

'Sure, can we raid the fridge first?'

'I don't know where you put it all. Help yourselves.'

Chocolate slice in hand, Una fired Johanna the 'Look' as she stood in the doorway considering her options. She could leave, demand that her family return to Woodbourne House where they belonged or spend some time in this lovely Arts and Crafts home. She couldn't help but envy anyone with such a house;

mullioned windows, sloping roofs, wisteria around the door no doubt. This should be hers she decided not that anaemic space they called home.

A fat ceiling-hugging Christmas tree with home-made decorations and gingerbread houses dominated the hall. She thought of a the poor imitation of tree she could offer the children and wondered if she was being unfair dragging them back.

'Come and sit here Una by the fire. This is women only territory. You can move those books and the cat onto the floor. Skips, down boy. '

Freda opened the antique drinks cabinet.

'What do you fancy? My friend brought me this Corbières from France. She lives down there. Shall we open it?'

Una's chest began to loosen as she settled back on the soft cushions. Her breathing slowed to allow her to savour the liquorice edge to the wine. She had to admit it was good.

'How was Spain? I heard the weather was unusually bad.'

Una stretched out her legs. She was finding it hard to keep her eyes open.

'You could say that. Miserable and wet. Rude staff. Disgusting hotel. The twins were moaning so we came back. I wanted to give Iain some space.'

Freda topped up their glasses and took a seat by the fire.

'I always fancied spending Christmas with my sister in Sydney.

She sends photos every year of them barbequing turkey around the pool of their house. Then she says she wants to come here for the snow. I guess we always want something different.'

Una felt her defences mobilise against what she heard as a criticism. She was annoyed with herself for dramatizing the situation at the airport as it now left her feeling vulnerable. She wanted to ask what Iain had told them but pride stopped her. She felt trapped in this small, overheated room with Freda saying little but no doubt thinking plenty yet the thought of going back home was not appealing either.

Snow was drifting down the side of the windows giving a picture post card feel to the village green. Timeless Bournville, legacy of the Cadbury family, was named after the Bourne brook which ran through the site of the factory. From the house, Una could see gingerbread like cottages, oozing a fairy tale charm, an eclectic mix of black and white buildings and the listed octagonal rest-house, now the visitor and craft centre.

The domed copper cupola above the tower of the famous carillion stood proud at the top of the main road next to the junior school. Una got to her feet and went to the window. Freda pointed out the edge of Selly Manor, a fifteenth century yeoman's house, moved and reconstructed by George Cadbury.

'Why not take a walk around the village. I've got some snow boots somewhere if you need them.'

The idea appealed to Una, if only to get out of the house. She accepted a wax jacket which hung on her like a tent. At the door she heard giggling coming from the garage which had been converted into a music room. Iain's deep baritone voice could be heard above the electronic piano making Una feel like an outsider. It was clear Iain was at home here. Una had little appreciation of music other than an occasional song which caught her attention. Iain's cello playing left her feeling depressed and excluded.

She tramped round the slushy streets, along the canal towpath, under the railway bridge and past the rows of Edwardian terraces which sold for a premium in this much sought after part of the city. Bournville had stood the test of time. Neighbourly, tranquil with a community spirit rarely found in a city.

She had to admit that if they did sell up and move here it would make life easier but then stamping off the snow outside the house reminded herself that she wasn't going to be told what to do by Iain or anyone else. As she rang the bell she felt a bit calmer and more willing to be sociable.

Tantalising smells wafted from the large kitchen diner where everyone was dipping home-made bread into soup. Stomach growling with hunger, she accepted a small bowl and perched on the stool by the breakfast bar. She heard them talking and laughing as if it was coming from another room.

Iain looked hopefully at Una, relieved that the tightness of her mouth had softened. He admired the way Freda had handled his wife's frosty demeanour. He didn't know why she had to be so abrasive. All he knew was how it made him feel. Apprehensive and fearful. Anything that didn't fit with Una's world view seem to bring out the worst in her. For a moment he nurtured the idea that the New Year would bring changes.

He hoped he could persuade her to think about moving home and starting afresh. It wasn't the house that was the problem but what it seemed to mean to her.

'Sit down everyone. I'll dish up. Una, I hope you will eat with us.'

Una watched Fergus carve the lamb which fell off the bone into the pomegranate and rhubarb sauce. Roast potatoes, perfectly crisp and colourful vegetables were spooned onto her plate until she raised her hand. One taste and despite herself she was hooked.

Freda sat back, eating little but with a delicious feeling of contentment. She loved feeding people and watching them enjoy it. It didn't matter if she had to get up at five am or go to bed at midnight after clearing up.

The twins groaned with pleasure as they dipped the last of the bread in the sauce.

'Thank you Mrs. O'Neal. That was wicked,' said James, hoping to be allowed to leave the table.

Fergus groaned.

'I don't know if I can sit still in church. I am so stuffed. Why don't you take the twins Iain? It's a children choir. They're very good.'

'Will you come with us Una?' he asked.

She realised that if she went home, Iain would be without transport. A frisson of annoyance crossed her face. She felt manipulated.

'Let's go home Iain. The children have had a long day.'

Iain didn't respond straight away. He wanted to say no. He wanted to demand to know what right she had to come back and dish out orders. Instead he made his apologies and collected his stuff. His need to be with his children overrode any desire to get even.

When they arrived back, Iain bent down to light the fire while the children went in search of the decorations which had been stored on the top floor.

Una entered the room and shut the door.

'What the hell did you think you were doing?'

'Sorry?' Iain struck a match and watched the flame lick the rolls of paper.

'Showing me up in front of those people. I came back because of you. The least you could have done was come home when I asked.'

'That would have been rude. I'm not a child Una so stop treating me like one. Fergus and Freda have been very kind to me. I was devastated when you walked away from me at the airport. Can't you imagine how I felt? '

'It's always about you and your feelings. It was no picnic for me either with those miserable kids. If you'd not been behaving so erratically over these past few months I wouldn't have needed to get away from you.'

Iain stood up, feeling the creak in his knees as a sharp pain. He felt old and weary.

'I don't know what you mean Una. Honestly I don't. I've just been my usual self. Playing music, trying to get work. Nothing out of the ordinary. Please, come and sit down. Don't let the children hear us argue.'

Una continued to lean against the door.

'Either you've got a serious memory deficit or you're becoming two people. Maybe that's it. You don't know when you slip into your alter ego.'

'Alter ego? Una, you've lost me.'

Una threw herself across the room and grabbed his jacket.

'Stop playing games with me Iain. Are you trying to drive me as crazy as you are? You talk to your imaginary friends. You go into some sort of trance then throw your fists at me then lo and behold you play the innocent, pretending nothing happened. You waste your days driving me insane with that bloody scraping…'

'Mum? Dad? Can you come and reach the tree lights?'

Una stood up and opened the door.

'In a minute.'

Iain leaned over his knees and looked into the fire. He felt so emotionally drained. Una's moods were becoming so unpredictable. She was a like a broken barometer. He wanted to escape into his den and lock out the world but his children were home so with forced jollity he went up the stairs to help.

'Don't you think it's late to be putting up decorations? Christmas is over.'

'No Mum. There's another ten days to go.'

James dragged down the bags and poured them over the floor.

'Where's Jo?'

'Fallen asleep on the bed.'

Iain got on the floor and helped his son assemble the tree. They worked in a companionable silence until every bauble and piece of tinsel covered the plastic branches. James yawned and went in search of some water. His mother was in the kitchen nursing a glass of wine.

'Bedtime James. You can open the rest of your presents tomorrow.'

James hugged his father before trudging up the stairs to his attic room. He'd sneaked a couple of presents under his dressing gown.

Iain went into his den and closed the door. What he wanted most in the world was for his wife to invite him back into their bed.

CHAPTER FIFTEEN

'Dad, Daddy,' wailed Johanna, carrying her new tablet into the den. She was crying as she scrolled down her Facebook page to show Iain a picture of some orangutans.

'Lovely sweetheart,' he said, turning his eyes back to his composition. He felt mildly irritated at the interruption. His new piece, 'Regret' for strings and horns needed his full concentration.

'Look what they've written about me. *Johanna Millar's long lost relatives.* It's cos I've got red hair. I hate it. I'm going to cut it all off.'

Iain wondered where his wife had got to. Worried he would say something to make it worse, he felt at a loss as to how to reassure her. James was spending the last of his holiday with his new hero, Tom, so Iain knew he had to do something. He put his arm around her waist and pulled her close. He felt her warm breath on his cheek, smelling slightly of cheese and onion crisps. His daughter was hurting which meant he was too.

'Tell me what's being going on. Are these girls at your school?'

She nodded, pushing her hair out of her eyes.

'They say horrible things about me when James isn't around then write things on the wall.'

'The wall? You mean at school? Don't the teachers tell them off?'

'No Dad. I mean on Facebook. Look, like this.'

Iain shook his head in horror as he scanned some of the nasty comments. He wanted to contact the school immediately about these bullies who were clearly making his daughter's life miserable.

'I don't want to go back to St. Mingers, Daddy. Can't I stay here now and go to school?'

Iain wanted to say yes, yes, yes but knew he couldn't make a unilateral decision. He rubbed his eyes with his thumb.

'Jo, I really do know how you feel but it's important not to run away and let these girls think they've won.'

'I don't care about that. I don't want to see them ever again. Please Daddy.'

'You are a strong girl and you know how much I love you. These girls are very insecure about themselves and they're probably jealous of your lovely hair and of you. If you ignore bullies they tend to go away.'

Johanna rested her head on Iain's shoulder and twiddled the ends of her hair around her finger as she thought about what'd he said.

'I suppose I could unfriend them,' she said.

'Well if you can do such things then that's a very good idea.'

Iain felt lost and confused in this new world of technology and wondered how he could contemplate going back into the world of proper work. He'd been feeling proud of himself for using Twitter and updating his simple website which, thanks to Tom, was drawing in adults keen on learning an instrument.

'Thanks Dad. You always listen to me.'

Iain's subconscious began surging out of the depths as he thought about Una's treatment of the twins. How many times had she batted away their questions as if they were annoying mosquitoes? Irritated by her lack of interest in her own children other than constantly checking their school reports, he vowed that when they did come home to go to school he would be there for them. Did she see them as some accessory to her successful life and not as people in their own right? Whenever she spoke to them it was in a voice that had started to grate on his nerves; abrasive, sharp, even with a hint of menace. It wasn't much different from the way she often spoke to him.

Iain turned back to his manuscript in an attempt to divert his daughter away from her troubles. She leaned against his desk, watching him teasing out some notes on his cello, frowning as he stopped to make some adjustments to the fret.

'Would you like to learn to play Three Blind Mice?'

Her face lit up. She tied her hair into a pony tail and followed Iain's instructions. It was a struggle for her to finger the strings and bow at the same time but after a few attempts she beamed with satisfaction.

'Well done. Maybe one day you could take over from me.'

Johanna had one foot out of the door then turned around.

'Dad, is it true you and Mum are getting a divorce? Alexa's

Mum's gone to Australia with her new boyfriend.'

Iain felt the bruising punch low down in his gut momentarily winding him. He saw in his daughter's troubled eyes a reflection of a failed father. Because of him her security had been threatened. It was his job to protect her and he'd not come up to scratch. He couldn't help but beat himself over it. He shook his head as he fought to speak.

'No sweetheart. Whoever has put this idea into your head is terribly wrong.'

'Miss Kennedy keeps asking if everything is alright at home and people keep saying weird things about you and Mum.'

Iain felt nauseous. Who had been talking about him? It had to be those people. The ones he couldn't see but knew were around him, watching, mocking, all the time. He cocked his ear to tune into their scratchy, rasping voices, competing to be heard over the cacophony of his screaming thoughts.

'Dad? What's the matter? You look as if you are going to be sick.'

Johanna panicked as she helped her father back into his chair and fetched him a glass of water.

'Shall I ring Mum to come home? I don't know where she's gone.'

'No. No. I felt a bit dizzy that's all. Didn't have any breakfast.'

'I'll make you some toast and coffee. Sit there.'

He looked into his daughter's face.

'That would be lovely. Shall we go out to Big Mama's for brunch? We could go to the cinema or bowling.'

She stamped her foot as something jolted her memory.

'I've got homework to do. I'd forgotten about it.'

Iain wanted to say she'd had all holiday to do her work but remained silent. She would hear the criticism and maybe turn against him. He couldn't bear the thought of that.

'Suppose you do your homework now then finish the rest of your packing for school then we can go out for the afternoon. Toffee popcorn at the cinema?'

She gave him a small smile and nodded.

'Jo. Just remember. Don't listen to other people. Some of them are out to cause trouble for the sake of it. I'm going to ring Martha to check the arrangements for tomorrow. It's very kind of her offering to drive you both back to Scotland.'

'Can't Mum take us? Martha talks all the time and drives too fast.' Groaning she trundled back upstairs.

Iain disappeared into his den to make his call. Much as he loved his daughter, he felt unable to deal with her moods.

'Martha? Happy New Year. Is everything alright for tomorrow?'

'Sure. I'll be round at your place around seven am. My meeting isn't till mid-afternoon so we can take our time with plenty of stops. My bladder has its own schedule.'

Iain winced. There was something unsavoury in his mind about discussing body parts. He was used to Fergus' crude humour but even sometimes he crossed the line.

'How are you now? Una said you've not been well.'

He bristled and without meaning to, snapped back a reply.

'I'm fine thanks. See you in the morning.'

In the kitchen he filled the kettle pulling it away from the tap as it spurted water over his front. What did Martha mean by that he kept asking himself as he hunted for a clean mug. Too many people were interfering in their family life he muttered, dunking a tea bag into the boiling water. Wasn't it against the Human Rights Act? He slopped in some milk not bothering to clean up the spillage.

He sniffed the carton carefully. It smelt off. He poured the tea down the sink. Someone had doctored it. Was Una trying to poison him? He paced the floor tapping the side of his head.

'That's it,' he cried in a eureka moment. 'I need to get it tested. Then we will know, won't we?'

'Who are you talking to Daddy? Is Mum back?'

Iain swivelled round, empty mug in hand, and stared at his daughter. She seemed and sounded different. He strode towards her and grabbed her shoulders.

'Who?'

'Mummy. Stop it, you're frightening me.

Iain's nerve endings were stinging. His eyes darted up, down, round, right and left as he strained to listen to the voice.

'Shut up Johanna and finish your tasks.'

She burst into tears.

'I need my suitcase. I can't reach it,' she said before running from the room.

Iain leapt up the stairs and crashed through the bedrooms, slamming doors and making the frame shudder. He caught sight of the piles of clothes piled on the bed. Sobs like hiccups came from behind the bathroom door. Suddenly his mind clicked back into place.

'I'm sorry Jo-Jo. My mind was elsewhere for a minute. I shouldn't have shouted like that. Please come out.'

'No. Go away. Mummy says you're mad.'

Iain felt the room sway as his knees began to shake. A mix of anger and humiliation grabbed his throat as he beat down a powerful urge to go and find his wife and drag her back home. She had to be accountable for feeding her own children lies.

A supercharged energy filling his body like gas in a helium balloon powered him to pull photographs of Una from the walls and smash them on the floor. For one manic moment he wanted to jump on the splintered glass but in the next he wanted to take a large shard and cut his arms. Anything to relieve the pressure building up over his eyes. He wanted to howl and bay and throw himself on the ground to kick and scream until exhaustion and shame took over. He stared at the damage and buried his face in his hands.

Johanna slowly opened the door and peered out. She saw her

father leaning against the window, his forehead pressed to the glass.

'I'm sorry too Daddy. Shall I clean up this mess?'

Iain turned round and pointed to the clothes.

'No. Leave it. When you've finished your packing, come down for some hot chocolate.'

His voice seemed to come from high up in the corner of the room, disembodied and reedy. Back in his den he dialled Una's mobile. He would order her to come home.

'Do you want to take that call?'

The poker-faced solicitor pointed to her phone then checked his Rolex. Una pressed decline and dropped it back in her bag.

'I want to know what I'm supposed to do. I've built my business Mr. Hall from scratch. I didn't have any bank of mummy and daddy to help me. I borrowed three thousand pounds fifteen years ago and worked my butt off. Do you have any idea what that's like? Not knowing where the next job is coming from or how you're going to pay your mortgage.'

Mr. Hall screwed the top back on his pen and sat back against his chair.

'No, I don't suppose you do.'

Una leaned towards him, her fingers drumming the black glass of the table.

'I am not going to let some teenage muppet from the tax office tell me how to run my business. Your job is to sort this out and not lecture me on my responsibilities as a company director. I know damn well what they are.'

'Miss Carrington. I understand how you feel.'

Una stood up so quickly, she knocked over her chair.

'You have no bloody idea. My livelihood is on the line. I've got two kids to support, a house, a husband who doesn't work. Is that your life? No, I thought not.'

She picked up her chair, sat down and folded her arms. He had no idea that her worst nightmare was to be made destitute or have to go on the dole. A horrible image of her and the twins sitting on sheets of cardboard in one of the underpasses, begging for money. She remembered shouting at one of the young able homeless about getting off his arse and onto his bike to find work. Now this could be her. A cold terror stole her sense of reasoning.

'Miss Carrington. I can't help you if you continue to be obstructive. I can't go outside the law to make something happen. I can however come to some agreement with your creditors but I need a true and honest picture of your finances. You don't seem to want to co-operate with that.'

'The company is limited by guarantee. I could go for voluntary liquidation as you say then work as a sole trader. They couldn't get a penny out of me then.'

Mr. Hall sighed. He'd heard this all before. Looking out across the churchyard where the alkies were swigging from cans he wondered what life would be life somewhere quiet and remote like Tahiti or Antarctica.

'You've been trading whilst insolvent. You've not taken proper precautions to prevent further loss to your creditors. Looking at these accounts you overtraded, spent wild amounts on air travel and entertaining. You are still running your high performance car which you should be selling or it will be taken by bailiffs. You could be made personally liable I'm afraid.'

Una absorbed this information with growing trepidation. Part of her brain registered that he was right but she wouldn't accept it. Couldn't accept it. Her whole being was built on being a successful businesswoman. What would happen to her if they took it all away?

'This is what I propose.' He handed her a file. 'Take some time to consider all options and what they might mean to you and your family then make another appointment. I can't keep going over old ground with you. A decision has to be made soon if there is no prospect of getting the required money to settle these debts.'

Una ignored his outstretched hand. The file felt like a bomb programmed to explode as soon as she opened it. On leaving the plush offices of cream sofas and fancy coffee machines, Una walked out, stunned, into the icy January air. Despite being wrapped in layers she felt her bones had turned to stalactites. Stepping on and off the pavement to avoid the lunch time crush, she hurried down Corporation Street, cursing when someone blocked her path.

Her white trench coat flapped around her legs as she searched deep in its pockets for her phone, narrowly missing the outstretched legs of a beggar and his dog. She tossed him a few coins thinking that one day that might be her. The children would be taken into care and as for Iain… well she couldn't go there. Iain was the reason they were in this mess she kept telling herself as she waited her for business adviser to pick up. After a few minutes the line went dead.

Grabbing a strong Americano in Coffee Fix, Una fired up her laptop and began calling up former clients.

'Sorry Una. We've signed up with Go Training. They've got us some funding.'

'Head Office has put a moratorium on training,' the HR manager of I Love Clothes told her before cutting her short.

'Not after the last fiasco. We should be asking for our money back,' said a dry voice from the city council.

Flushing with humiliation and cursing Anita for her incompetence, she packed up and crossed the road to the bank. Told she would have to wait, she became agitated and unable to concentrate on anything. She knew she would have to mortgage Woodbourne House again and it put the fear of Hades into her. She could see her father wagging his finger and saying, 'Whatever you do Una, you never, ever put your house on the line. It's your security.' A month later he'd disappeared and put their lives in financial crisis.

'Ms. Carrington? Come through please.'

Una was unaware that her face had frozen into a mask of disappointment. She knew that a woman was going to be more difficult to win over. They sat in silence at opposite side of the desk, an expression of incredulity passing across the face of the business adviser as she quickly perused the files.

'You can't draw any more money on this account,' she told her flatly. 'You will need to consider how you are going to settle this overdraft which is way over the limit set. If you have assets, then now is the time to liquidate them. '

She closed the folder and rested her hands on top. Una's eyes were drawn to the perfect French manicure.

'If you'd responded to us sooner we could have drawn up a plan. Six letters have been sent out to you including two recorded delivery. I suggest you come up with a plan and make another appointment. In the meantime, I am cancelling your credit cards.'

Una's hand flew to her throat where a blockage had formed. She gulped down some water from the dispenser in the corner of the office. This couldn't be happening she thought.

Back in the fresh air, she called Abdi in Dubai.

'Una.' She detected a note of irritation in his voice. 'I'm about to start a meeting. Can you be quick?'

'Are you coming to Birmingham any time soon? I need some help.'

'I'm afraid not. My wife's about to have another baby. Ma'Shallah.'

'Your wife?' Una's heard her voice rise half an octave.

'Surely you knew I was married. We had some fun times

Una but now I must take my responsibilities seriously. Ma'a as-Salamah. Goodbye.'

Una stared at her phone, shivering with shock as she realised she'd been used. 'Bastard,' she muttered, storming along New Street. All she really cared about at that moment was getting her hands on some money. There has to be a solution that won't involve selling anything she told herself as she stamped her way back to the Mailbox car park.

As she clicked the remote to release the locks on her car, her phone trilled James' personalised tune.

'Where are you Mum? We've made dinner for you. It's special as we're back at school tomorrow. You promised to come home early.'

'Ok, Ok I'm on my way.' She felt bad for forgetting her promise.

Una sat in her car without turning on the engine. She didn't want to go back to a house that soon might be taken away from her. Turning on the radio, she was surprised to hear a recording of Iain's string quartet. She didn't remember him saying anything about it. Typical of him, she thought. So bloody secretive about everything. The cello solo touched something in her but she would never admit that to Iain. That would feel like giving in to him.

An idea struck her. His cello was an inherited antique. It must be worth something. As soon as the twins were out of the way she would do some investigating. She grinned into the rear view mirror as she smoothed on her favourite lipstick.

CHAPTER SIXTEEN

As an icy blast shot through the hallway of Woodbourne House, it rattled the letter box making Martha jump. She stood, resplendent in her white faux fur coat over lime green trousers and shiny ankle boots. Iain chatted to her as he piled up the bags, pausing to give Johanna a big squeeze as she sat dolefully watching them from the stairs.

'That's some coat,' said Una, appearing suddenly from the back of the house. 'Did you skin a polar bear?'

'Thanks a lot. I'll know where to go next time I need an ego boost.'

'You look cuddly,' said James, heaving his bag onto his shoulder. 'I'll put this stuff in the car.'

Martha went to ruffle his hair, laughing throatily as he dodged her hand.

'Put your coat on Jo. Martha needs to get off. Come on, come on.'

'You just want to get rid of us.'

Una stole a look at her husband who was rubbing an eye behind his glasses. She noticed a blob of superglue on one of the arms. It irritated her. Why did he have to patch stuff up all the time and show her up?

'James?'

He stood limply while his mother hugged him and made a fuss about him looking after himself and his sister. Jo grabbed her rucksack and settled herself on the back seat of Martha's spacious car, headphones plugged in, blanket pulled up. She closed her eyes.

'Take plenty of breaks and go easy on the gas, Martha. Jo gets car sick.'

Martha squeezed behind the steering wheel and started the engine. She leaned out of the window.

'I drive 40,000 miles plus a year Una. I think I know what I'm doing. Stop fretting. Belt up kiddiewinks and let's hit the road.'

James turned to give a small wave to his father. His stomach was squirming at the thought of leaving him. His mother's constant shouting and hitting the wine bottle had ruined their holiday.

Iain watched the car merge into the traffic, wishing he could put his arm around Una's shoulders in solidarity but she'd gone back in the house. He couldn't work out if she didn't care about her children or if she couldn't show it.

Una was hunched over her laptop at the kitchen table, a large mug of steaming coffee in her hand.

'Those kids are so ungrateful,' she said, not moving her eyes from the screen. 'I made sure they had a good breakfast and packed them up some snacks but they couldn't wait to get away from us.'

Iain stood at the sink, his back to her. A robin sat cheekily on the windowsill. He studied its plump orange-red breast thinking he might compose a piece about different birds. A few bars danced about in his head.

'Are you listening to me?'

'I heard what you said but I don't agree. Johanna is very unhappy in Scotland. I wasn't happy about her going back.'

Iain leaned against the dishwasher, a glass of water in his hand. His stomach had been feeling sour so he'd decided to make cutting back on the whisky his new year's resolution. James had slipped him a letter from school requesting a deposit for a German trip to Berlin. Iain needed to raise it with Una but judging by the look on her face was wary about saying anything. He made a note to talk to the investment people who managed the school trust.

'What's up with you? What are you hiding?'

Una stood up and arched her back.

'James needs money for a school trip.' Iain waited for her reaction. His trepidation reminded him of the few times he was called before the headmaster to be disciplined.

'Well he can't have it. I don't have it. Do you?'

'I'll find the balance if you can send him the £100 to secure the place.'

Una strode up to him, hands on hips, and stared into his face.

'And how will you find the balance? Sell your cello?'

'Don't be ridiculous. That's my livelihood.'

Una fixed her gaze on him for a moment then stepped away. She picked up a cloth to wipe down the table.

'It's an antique isn't it?'

Iain looked at her warily with a feeling of unease.

'It was Uncle Frazer's. He played it in the Scottish Chamber Orchestra.'

Una applied unnecessary force to a coffee stain.

'Must be worth something then.'

She moved on to change the bin bags and clean up the spilled cat food. Beethoven yawned as he watched her from his bed.

'It's priceless, Una. It's an heirloom and the best cello anyone could have. I am very lucky. What about this trip?'

'If you want him to go, then you fund it. I've got bigger things to worry about.'

Iain disappeared to his study and shut the door to search for the trust fund papers. Maybe there was a way of releasing some money for his son's trip. If not, he would get a job cleaning lavatories if necessary.

Opening his cello case, he sighed with the pleasure reserved for meeting an old friend or slipping into a dressing gown on a rainy night. His new bow, a present from Fergus, rested in his hand as he tightened the screw for the perfect tension. His hands seemed steady for once but playing pizzicato was still a problem. Fergus had commented on the mistakes he'd made in the last rehearsal for the Bartok.

'Bloody hell Iain. That sounded like a cat having its guts plaited.'

'My fingers are stiff.'

Iain had rubbed them on the rough sleeve of his jacket to kick-start the circulation. He recalled how miserable he'd felt at letting them all down.

Outside the metal sky cast a gloom into his den matching his mood. He struggled to shake off a feeling of hopelessness. Was this to be his life from now on? A man needs work for self-esteem but Iain needed his wife to understand how he felt and above all he wanted her support.

A crack of his shoulder bones reminded him of the passing of time. Holding his cello close, he picked up a cloth and he ran it gently over the polished rosewood, down the sides, over the scroll, marvelling at its beauty. It was one of Tweedale's finest English cellos. Iain had treasured it, protected it and watched over it for the past ten years. It was the only thing in his life that felt real to him.

Una had shown no interest until now which made Iain anxious. Closing his eyes he eased the bow over the strings, revelling in its suppleness as it became an extension of his hand. Why was Una asking so many questions about it? What did she want? Who'd put her up to it? He laid down his cello and cocked his ear towards the door. Sensing her outside, he flung it open, brandishing the bow.

The shock of seeing his face, grey and scowling, made Una jump, a tray jerking out of her hands. Tea dripped onto the beige carpet but Iain made no attempt to help clear it up. He vanished back into his room and drew the curtains.

An hour later, Una gently opened his door and placed a mug on the side table. The hostility that seemed to emanate from him felt unnerving. Seeing him sitting in the dark, hunched and silent triggered a flicker of guilt.

'What's the matter?'

She cleared some papers off a chair to sit down. This silent cave was his territory and it was clear he didn't want her there. Looking around at the oak bookcases and the dark heavy furniture he'd inherited from his family gave her a feeling that the room held dark secrets. Unwashed glasses and plates were stacked up in a corner. His sofa bed was pulled out, the bedding spilling onto the floor.

Una's chest heaved. Blood pounded in her temple as she surveyed the mess. She shouldn't have to live in this chaos. It was disgusting. He was disgusting.

'What do you want Una? To have another go at me? To tell me to get a job?'

Lifting his head to look at her, he felt a dull pain in the back of his head. As he tried to stand, a dragging sensation in his calves pulled him back down. Una felt contempt for this stranger in his shapeless grey cardigan with the missing buttons.

She studied her new gel nails, red lips tightly pursed.

'We're going to have to sell this house Iain.'

The words hung heavily between them. Iain frowned thinking

back to when she'd refused to consider it when he'd raised the matter. His brain was bubbling with confusion. Was this some sort of game she was playing he asked himself.

'Why?'

'The business is in debt,' she said simply.

'But I thought things were going well since you were always out working and flying off to see clients. I don't understand.'

'No, you wouldn't. As long as you're cosied up here with that bloody thing,' Una kicked the cello case, 'you can forget the real world exists. The world where men are out working, providing for their families, you know, the normal stuff of life.'

She paced the floor, punching a fist into the palm of her hand. Suddenly she stopped and pushed her face into his. Iain could smell his own fear as her hot breath burned into his cheeks. He started to hyperventilate.

'How do you propose I find 50K in the next month? A few stints off the Hagley Road?' Iain winced at her strident tone. 'Who's going to kerb crawl a 40-year old? Eh? Look at me, Iain, goddamn you. Face reality. We could end up homeless.'

Una felt a growing agitation pump through her veins. She picked up a family photograph which lay on his desk and stared at younger self. Hopeful eyes, under a fringe of long dark hair, met hers. She didn't recognise this Una with wriggling babies in her arms, a soft smile on her face.

An ominous silence descended over the room as if waiting for two gigantic demons to square up to each other. Iain cocked his ear as the voice became clearer, mocking him from behind the curtain.

'See what you've done,' it said. 'Useless you are.'

He clamped his hands to his ears and looked at his wife. He saw a distorted red mouth with tombstone teeth and bulbous black eyes.

'I'm sorry for what I've done. I need to be punished.'

He got on his knees and handed her the cello bow.

'Get up you fool. What are you playing at? Get a grip for fuck's sake.'

'They kept telling me to do it. I didn't want to hurt you but they told me I would be dead if I didn't follow their instructions.'

Iain crumpled into a pile on the floor, his hands pressing into his ashen face. Tears burst through his fingers, trickling down into his beard. Every part of his body crackled with a pain that felt as if it was burning through his skin, creating strange purple patterns on his arms.

Something in Una was pushing her to get down on the floor beside him and take his shaking hands in hers in a promise of reassurance but her emotions stuck in neutral. The sinister shadow of her husband which seemed to burst unbridled from his unconscious mind, awakened in her a primitive fear.

She sat on the edge of the chair wishing she smoked.

'Iain, I don't understand anything you are saying. Who told you to do what? You need to explain and get up off the bloody floor.'

He stumbled to his feet, and grabbed a paper weight as his eyes darted around the room. A demon sound came from his throat.

'Don't play games with me. You're trying to destroy me and my family. I did what you said but no more.'

He fell backwards against the desk, knocking over the lamp against Una's leg. Wrenching open the drawer of his desk, he pulled out a hammer wrapped in a dishcloth.

'Stay back,' he ordered.

Una stumbled backwards, cursing as she rubbed her leg. Fumbling with the camera on her phone, she clicked the red button to record him.

'You've gone mad. Put it down Iain. For God's sake.'

As Iain ranted, Una reached over and grabbed the hammer by its head. Her finger began to ooze blood. Iain swore and picked up anything he could find to throw in her direction.

'I'm calling the emergency doctor or the police.'

In a fleeting moment her hand slapped his face. Her body began to shake as his eyes rolled to the back of his head in some sort of fit.

'Iain, Iain, wake up,' she said grabbing his arm to drag him into the kitchen. She folded his hands around a mug of strong coffee while he struggled back to awareness. A swarm of thoughts passed through Una's mind as she called the doctor. Thank goodness the twins were away at school was the most pressing one.

The doorbell brought Iain back to his senses. He looked around him, bemused.

'What happened?'

Una kept the locum doctor in the hallway while she told him what had happened. She scrolled down to the photograph on her phone.

'He does things then seems go blank. I don't feel safe with him at the moment.'

The doctor followed her into the kitchen where Iain was sitting calmly at the table stroking Beethoven.

'Hello. I didn't know we were expecting company. Please take a seat.'

'I'm Dr. Weston. Your wife called the surgery earlier saying you've not been feeling too well.'

He asked Una to leave the room.

She hung about in the hallway, trying to catch snippets of the conversation but felt on edge as if the door was about to burst open and she would be caught eavesdropping. An hour later he came out of the kitchen, a tight expression on his face.

'How is he?' Una angled her chin towards him.

'I'm sorry but I can't discuss this with you other than to say I'm making an appointment for your husband to see a specialist.'

'What sort of specialist.'

'You will need to ask him. Goodbye.'

The following day

'You look like the risen dead. What's up?'

Martha tugged her freshly styled hair as she eased herself onto a stool in the busy café. The tyre around her middle felt uncomfortable so she shook her head at Una's offer of the almond twist.

'Look at this.' Una showed her the photograph.

Martha looked at it hard. It was a man with a hammer in his hand.

'Well? Now do you believe me?'

'Are you telling me this is Iain about to whack you with a hammer? I find it really hard to believe that about him and how did you manage to snap it on your phone?'

'Thanks very much.' Una briefly told the story but Martha was finding it difficult to fit the pieces together.

They stirred their drinks and stared out at the people sheltering in shop doorways out of the rain. One or two bent over their unlit cigarettes, flicking lighters, impatient for their nicotine fix.

Una was used to her friends agreeing with her. She felt betrayed by Martha challenging her truth.

'I sometimes wonder whose side you are on. I'm in debt – shit, the business is going down the pan – and now I've got a crazy husband. I'm the one in the pressure cooker but you don't see me attacking people, especially my family. Why do I get the feeling you are blaming me?'

Una's raised voice was attracting attention.

'Shhh. Calm down. I'm not taking sides. I don't know enough about it. I like Iain and find it hard to believe the things you say about him. Get a divorce if it's so bad.'

'You just don't get it do you? '

'Oh I do. You want me to agree with everything you say and I'm not going to. To me, Iain is a gentle soul who's had a rough deal. He's doing his best but you undermine him at every turn. You're not meek and mild like you try to make out. I'm sorry Una but I find some of this hard to believe. Besides if he is as ill as you say then you should be supporting him.'

Una was about to spit back when a short, middle aged woman with a grey bobbed hair hovered next to them.

'Sorry to interrupt but I need to say something to Mrs. Millar. I'm Emily Hartman's mother. Your husband was her music teacher at St. Hilda's'.

Una shook her head, irritated by the woman's fluty voice.

'I've nothing to say to you. Go away.'

'I want to apologise for what Emily did. Dr. Millar didn't do any of those things.' There was a rush of blood to her cheeks. 'We did punish her you know.'

'You'd better leave now or I shall do something I regret. You've no idea what damage your slutty daughter has done to my family.'

'Una,' Martha cautioned. 'The manager's watching.'

'The manager can go fuck himself,' she said in a voice loud enough for him to hear. 'And so can you,' she said to the woman who seemed to quiver in her brown, shabby coat.

CHAPTER SEVENTEEN

Iain felt nauseous, partly from the dull ache in his jaw and partly from the painkillers he'd taken to relieve it. He explored the tenderness in his neck, fearful that he needed a much overdue dental appointment. Iain dabbed some whisky on a blob of cotton wool and wincing pressed it onto the gum. Once the workshop was over he would go to the dental hospital if he couldn't get an NHS appointment.

He doubly checked that all the music and lesson plans he needed were arranged in order in the folders before packing them into his brown briefcase that now curled at the edges. He paused as he tried to recall its age. Must be over forty years now he mused, remembering his father awkwardly handing it over to him as a reward for doing so well in his exams. Iain ran his finger over the leather as he thought about his childhood. His parents had lived comfortably together but in parallel universes, unlike the drama that infiltrated his marital home. Money was a taboo subject even though he remembered times when his mother had to go to work in a department store on Princes Street.

A heavy sadness settled on his shoulders as he thought about his little sister Mairi. A tragic swimming accident had left her unable to breathe unaided, forcing his parents to agree to the termination of life support. She was just nine years old. Closing his eyes, he remembered how the grief had dug into his mother's face never to let go. Iain brought Mairi's face to life with ease. Long red hair, like Johanna's, chunky freckles across her upper cheeks, a front tooth chipped from falling off her bike, brought fresh moisture to his eyes. Would she have married and had a family? What would she be saying to him right now? As he tried to hold her face in focus, she tripped away, giggling, swinging her hair and giving him a big wave. For a transient moment, he wanted to run after her.

'Bloody hell Iain. I've been ringing that bell for hours,' Fergus was blowing on his hands as he entered the hallway. 'It's chilly in here.'

'Come through. Have you time for a drink?'

'If you mean whisky then may I remind you it's not even 10 am but if you mean coffee then no. We'd better get on the road. There's been an accident on the M5 so we'll go down the A38 through Bromsgrove.'

Fergus stepped back out into the hall.

'Where's Una?'

'I've no idea. I didn't hear her come in last night.'

Fergus didn't let on that he was relieved. He felt a sinister chill run through Woodbourne House whenever Iain's wife was at home. She barely uttered a word so obvious was her contempt for him. It didn't bother Fergus. In fact it amused him but he was growing more concerned for Iain who seemed to shrivel in her shadow.

Iain bent down to lock the cello in its case, wincing as a pain shot through his back teeth. Please not today, he muttered.

Once in the car, they talked about the young musicians' workshop Fergus had arranged for a substantial fee.

'Music and money,' he grinned. 'Followed by whisky and women.'

'I assume that's for alliteration purposes only. Watch out. You nearly took the side of that car off.'

Iain breathed out as Fergus pulled back into his lane, humming and cursing alternately.

'It should be a good session. Lots have signed up for your composition class.'

'I thought I might stay over at a B and B and do a bit of walking afterwards. See if I can get rid of this pain in my neck.'

'Charming, and I thought we were friends.'

'I'd stay as well but Freda's got one on her today. Says we don't spend enough time together.'

Iain let his mind drift as Fergus exercised his gift of the blarney stone. He wanted to spend more time with Una the way they used to before the twins but she was always out of reach as if an invisible electric fence had been rigged up between them. She was tense and on edge whenever he was around but his new awakening made him realise it was his fault. No wonder she was scared of him after what he'd done. Somehow he had to make amends.

As they headed towards Malvern, Iain turned his attention to his classes. He'd chosen to teach the adults who hadn't picked up an instrument since they'd been forced to learn at school.

Even if the day was full of screeching violin strings he was determined to have some fun.

'I will lift mine eyes up to the hills,' sang Fergus in his wobbly tenor voice, which to Iain's ears sounded more like one of the Gibb brothers. 'Look at that magnificent wintry sight.'

As they approached the small town of Great Malvern, Iain noticed how much more relaxed he felt than in Birmingham. He wound down the window to take in deep breaths of the crisp air, peering to get a better view of the Grade 1 listed Priory, once a Benedictine monastery. Out of breath shoppers paused against the wall to chat or complain about the racing cyclists who mounted the pavement to pass the roadworks.

'I love this place,' said Iain with a sigh of contentment. 'If only I could persuade Una to move here.'

'Not ideal for a business woman. If you're considering moving, why not Moseley? It's got an arty farty crowd and is still close to town. Freda wouldn't consider moving out of Bournville. I shall be buried along with the rest of the Cadbury misshapes.'

Fergus swung the car into the drive of the academy, scraping the boot as he manoeuvred into a space. As Iain reached into the boot, people milled around carrying music stands interspersed with the clarinettists screwing their instruments together, a small guitar group strumming away, a spaced out look on their faces and Fergus running around the car park trying to grab loose sheets of music before they blew into the brackish pond water.

The halls of the old school reminded Iain of St. Mungo's in

Edinburgh. The names of former head boys and sports trophy winners were etched into the oak plaques, reminding Iain that no matter how great you were in life it was no guarantee of happiness or success in the future. St. Mungo's had given him the best opportunities but what had he done with them?

'Come on dreamer. I know you wish you were still back at school but we've got work to do. The class list is over there.'

Iain put down his cello as he made a note of his schedule which didn't seem too onerous. Trundling down to his room which overlooked a bare patch of garden, he fumbled with the equipment Fergus had requested. Iain looked around for someone to help him find the on button.

A fellow cellist came into the room and seeing Iain's confused expression helped him set up.

'John Tatum, Cheltenham Cellos. I've heard a lot about you Dr. Millar.'

Iain felt his heart banging. What had he heard?

'All good of course. You're in the right place for an Elgar enthusiast. I love it here. It's as if the old man is watching over us. Sounds a bit daft but ...'

'Not at all. Some places absorb great genius.'

Iain paced the room waiting for the onslaught of students. He kept checking the list of fifteen wannabe song writers, hoping he would be able to entertain them as well as teach them some rudiments of constructing music. As they filtered in, looking as apprehensive as he felt, he welcomed them with a warm handshake, an offer of tea and biscuits and ice-breaking conversation. He was amazed that so many had travelled from Oxford and even South Wales just for his workshop. As his confidence took hold, he launched into the session.

'Will you join us for lunch John? We're going to amble up to the Foley Arms. Ah, Fergus. Meet John Tatum. Cheltenham Cellos.'

The three trudged up the hill, Fergus lagging behind as he pulled up his shapeless trousers.

'Where's the fecking oxygen?' he panted as they reached the door.

'Ignore him. He's always like this,' Iain said, leading the way into the warm but empty bar.

'So John. How's business? Many cellos changing hands?'

John sipped his orange juice before replying.

'Some interesting stuff passes my way. Antique stuff mainly. A bit like your Old English.' He nodded at Iain. 'What a beautiful instrument. Worth a fortune in today's market. Some of the old dears that bring them in have no idea of their value.'

'You do tell them I hope,' said Iain, leaning back as the waitress placed their hot plates on the table.

'Oh yes. We don't get involved in anything underhand like some dealers I could mention.'

John went on to tell them some stories of dodgy transactions which made Iain's skin prickle.

'It's amazing how many of these strings are in demand by the overseas market. I hope yours is well insured.'

Iain's appetite deserted him. Una had been making the payments but he'd not checked the policy for some time. Pushing his plate away, Fergus dived on the left over chips.

'We should be getting back,' said Iain, tucking his scarf into his coat. 'Round two.'

Fergus and John were so deep in conversation that they didn't spot Iain lag behind to make a phone call. Agitated at having to leave a voicemail, he flipped his mobile shut and turned it off. Consumed by the fear of his cello being stolen or damaged left him unable to concentrate fully on the afternoon session he'd dedicated to Elgar. Some of his students were accomplished players and soon became bored.

'Why don't you play something for us then explain your technique,' suggested a middle aged woman with purple spikey hair.

Trying to appear nonplussed, Iain handed out some pieces from the Enigma variations and asked for volunteers to play with him. The purple woman hastily declined but John and a few other students were keen to share their talents.

By the time they'd unpicked the music, discussed techniques, and the motivation behind the pieces, someone poked their head round the door to indicate the end of the workshop.

'Thanks very much Iain. That was a superb day. Come down to Cheltenham with Fergus and we can do our own jamming session.'

John closed his cello case with a click and headed off, almost crashing into Fergus in the corridor.

'Nice bloke,' said Fergus, flinging himself down on a chair, shirt hanging over his trousers. 'We should meet up with him again.'

'He did suggest that. What do you think he meant about dodgy dealers?'

'Stolen goods I suppose. What you getting your G string in a twist now about?'

Iain held onto the seatbelt without slotting it into the clasp. Something was nagging at the back of his mind but he couldn't give it shape. Hadn't Una been asking strange questions about the cello recently despite never showing any interest previously? He wished his memory wasn't so cloudy. Picking out snippets from different conversations over the weeks made no sense. She wanted to know about the trust fund as well or was he getting the two things mixed up?

'Are we going to sit here all night and turn into stalagmites or shall I drop you off at this B and B? I assume you've booked it?'

'Booked what?'

'Your bed for tonight. You wanted to go walking tomorrow. Have you forgotten already?'

'Seems like it. I meant to do it at lunchtime but then…'

'So what to do my friend? It's tar black and I'm not going over those hills tonight with you but we could walk round the edges or over the common maybe. I could do with the exercise.'

'What about Freda?'

'Oh well. Yes, there's a conundrum. We'll only be an hour or so. We can get some fish and chips to replace the lost calories.'

They drove to a place Fergus was familiar with from previous trips. Iain felt foolish for taking up his friend's time but he needed the company from someone he trusted. His very private thoughts tumbled around in his head most of the day, tormenting, exhausting and confusing him to the point he could no longer pinpoint reality with any confidence.

'Let's have a wander. There's a torch on the back seat.'

A few dog walkers picked their way over the clumps of tough grass, pausing to light a cigarette or check their phones. The two men tramped the common with Fergus complaining about it being a bloody daft idea every two minutes but realising it was something Iain needed. They talked a bit about the workshop and plans for organising some more in Birmingham.

'It was good to be able to teach again,' said Iain. 'I've missed it.'

'You're good at it. You've got a lot of patience especially with beginners and adults can be much more motivated than kids who are forced into learning an instrument because Mummy thinks carrying a flugel will elevate her status. '

'You're becoming cynical in your old age Fergus.'

'World weary more like. Nothing is ever as it seems. Take Freda. Everyone sees her as a meek and mild docile wife who's given everything up for a life of domesticity. But… but…' Fergus waved his hand in conductor mode, 'Freda is fluent in Russian and worked for the intelligence service in her heyday. Recruited straight out of Cambridge.' His voice was puffed up with pride. 'See, you can never tell.'

Now that he'd given Iain an opening, Fergus walked ahead in silence. Iain formulated some words in his head but they sounded ridiculous. He didn't know if they belonged to him or those who came to plague him.

'I'm worried about my hands,' he said after much agonising.

Fergus slowed his pace, waiting for Iain to say more.

'What I might do with them.'

Biting down a witty one-liner, Fergus said,

'Not sure I'm with you.'

'They shake sometimes and I think they've got a life of their own that has nothing to do with me.'

Fergus puffed his cheeks and exhaled.

'Best if you see a doctor about those tremors. I had noticed.'

'He will tell me I'm crazy.'

For a moment, Fergus shared the same idea.

'Come on. It's freezing out here. Let's get a fish supper then head off home for a rest.'

Picking the batter off his fish, Iain examined his greasy fingers. Were they really capable of hurting Una? Horrified by the realisation that he did things that he later forgot about, he wrapped up the uneaten food and stuffed it into a carrier bag.

'The cat will have that,' said Fergus, tossing it on the back seat. 'You sure you're alright? You've got a very strange look in your eye.'

'I don't feel too well.'

'Make that appointment. Let them give you a once over and put your mind at rest.'

Iain felt his mind could never be at rest. He didn't say that he could hear a rasping noise in his ear which told him to murder his wife.

CHAPTER EIGHTEEN

February 2015

Una had left the tax office, her ears ringing with accusations of misappropriation of funds belonging to the Crown, and was striding angrily up New Street, past the Iron Man statue in front of the Council Offices and into the nearest bar. She gingerly fingered the deep cut on her hand which should have been stitched but that would have led to difficult questions.

Her brandy glass sat untouched as Una pulled out the A4 sheet of dense computations, unable to tear her eyes away from the final figure. The numbers swarmed on the page like drunken flies causing Una to grasp the arm of the chair. This is a mistake she told herself, adding water to the brandy as she attempted to reclaim some control. She felt it strip the back of her throat as she took a long swallow. She would appeal. Martha knew a good insolvency lawyer who would get this thrown out of court. Una picked up the paper and studied it again, convincing herself that she had a strong case. She called Martha out of a meeting.

'It is urgent. I need to see you asap. I'm in Rococo.'

Una heard a sigh of irritation.

'I'm really busy. I've got two minutes so tell me now. Make it quick.'

'I can't on the phone. It's complicated.'

'It always is with you isn't it? Stay where you are and I'll meet you in an hour but I can't stay long. I'm in the middle of planning a big launch.'

Una got the feeling that she was being brushed off. Her relationship with Martha had cooled since Christmas but she couldn't see how that was her fault. Martha could blow hot and cold depending on whether there was a man in her life. Cradling the brandy glass in her cool hands, she sat back to observe the other late afternoon drinkers and to think more carefully about her plan.

Iain was becoming more closed down and secretive. Their yes-no communication, now punctuated by chasms of hostile emptiness, was making Una feel uneasy. She was finding it harder to engage with him on any level and any attempt to discuss their financial situation pushed him back into his den or out of the door. If she was to successfully execute this plan she needed to bring him back into the fold.

Martha announced her arrival in a red trouser suit and cream shirt. She'd lost weight Una observed but in her perverseness decided not to comment. Martha hadn't even taken off her coat before Una launched in.

'Look at this.' She waved the papers at her.

'Hang on a minute. Let me get a coffee.'

Martha perched on the edge of the seat quickly scanning the source of Una's angst.

'Oh dear.'

'Oh dear? Is that all you've got to say? They're going to make me bankrupt. You've got an accountant type lawyer friend. That one you brought to the Custard Factory. Would he take this case on?'

'I don't know. He has a long client list. You would have to ask him.'

'Would you do it for me? He probably owes you a few favours?'

Martha bristled and gave Una a cold stare.

'I hope you don't mean what I think you mean. If so, you're on your own girlie.'

She stood up to go.

'Don't be so dramatic. I didn't mean anything. Figure of speech that's all.'

Martha went quiet, letting her coffee go cold as she inwardly seethed. Una's obsession with money was turning her into one of those unpleasant women who could never let go of a grudge and grabbed every opportunity to bore people with it. She fumbled in her bag for her phone, scrolled down the contacts list and scribbled a couple of numbers down on a serviette.

'No guarantees,' she said, handing it to Una. 'If it were me then I would be going for voluntary insolvency. Take your lawyer's advice. Do a deal then start again. Sometimes Una you enlarge things more than you need to.'

'If Iain…'

'Stop blaming Iain. You're responsible for this not him. I know things aren't easy between you but you can sort this out if you really want to. Sometimes I wonder. Now I've got to go. Let me know how you get on.'

Una stood up to exchange the usual air kisses but Martha was at the door. She turned and raised her hand.

The canal side where she often walked was deserted. A plastic bag flew in front of Una's feet as she side stepped some dog muck. A shopping trolley was upended in the dirty water giving a neglected look to the area. Una felt neglected as she walked slowly away from the cafes and bars of Brindley Place and down towards an impoverished part of the city. Terror took hold in her blood as she imagined them all living in some vile social housing block overlooking a filthy space which passed for a play area but littered with needles and condoms. She had to get herself out of this mess even if it meant leaving Iain and the children behind. Work was plentiful in the Gulf. She could have a good life without the responsibility.

The possibilities churned round in her head as she battled suffocating feelings of entrapment. One thing Una was sure of was that she had to have a solid plan. She could simply walk away tomorrow and never look back but deep in her core she knew the guilt would destroy her. She paused on the ornate cast-iron foot bridge to catch her breath. The faces of the twins were burnt onto her retina as she imagined their stricken faces. To them she would be as good as dead.

Exhausted from so much rumination, she flagged down a black cab to take her home. Work, what little there was of it, would have to wait another day.

A week later

Iain shuffled into the O'Neal's living room, his arm in a sling, his face badly bruised down the left side. A sterile pad was stuck to his temple. Freda laid down a mug of hot chocolate and some freshly baked biscuits. He looked up and smiled his appreciation. His mind was confused as another flashback took hold.

He remembered falling as something solid hit his collar bone. Surely it wasn't a frozen chicken. That was his mind playing tricks. He reran the fight Una had started. She'd screamed a lot of nonsense about him having an affair with one of those schoolgirls. He'd turned away, determined not to give her more ammunition. Was that when she attacked him? He touched his temple, screwing up his eyes as he forced himself to remember. Or had he attacked her in self-defence? That's what she told the police.

Iain's grey pallor concerned Fergus as he joined him by the fire. Freda had suggested that Iain should stay with them for a while. She had prepared the loft room as a cosy bedsitting room in the hope that Iain would agree. She liked his gentle manner and realising he wasn't well wanted to help without interfering.

Iain was touched but torn. Afraid of what Una might do, he said he needed to go home first to collect his cello and some documents. After a comforting lunch of pasta with a rich meaty sauce dotted with plump mushrooms, Fergus insisted on driving Iain back to Woodbourne House then on to the Barber Institute to listen to the UK's leading viol ensemble playing

Tudor music. Iain had long wanted to try out the vertically held six string instrument which looked like a cello but offered a more gutsy sound.

Iain's injury mean that he was unable to play for a while and that had thrown him into a deeper state of depression. The doctor in A&E had said he needed to rest as much as possible. He'd noticed some old bruises on his arms and upper body but Iain had batted away his questions with explanations of clumsiness and aging.

Woodbourne House appeared like a house staged for a documentary about haunting. Iain felt eyes were peering out of every window. He turned the key in the lock to find it stuck. He tried again. Fergus put down his pipe and tried.

'You sure this is the right key?'

'Of course. Maybe it's stuck because of the damp. We've not had much heating on lately.'

Fergus put his shoulder to the door, causing a shower of flaking paintwork, and pushed several times as Iain manoeuvred the key. Iain walked round to the back door to peer in through the kitchen window. He called Una's number but there was no answer. Frustrated and angry he picked up a brick and aimed it at the window.

'Don't do it Iain. It'll cause more problems. We'll come back after the concert and try again. I know a bloke who's a 24-hour locksmith. Let's go or we'll miss the start.'

Throughout the performance Iain shuffled in his seat, unable to find peace in the music. His mind was on his vulnerable cello which lay out of its case on the floor of his den. Where was Una and what was she doing? She'd said something about going away for an interview but he couldn't remember if that was before or after the chicken throwing. Getting up from his seat he hurried to the exit where a student with a disapproving mouth opened the door. Breathless, Iain doubled up a handkerchief over his mouth. His harsh, dry cough rattled in his chest and it was a full two minutes before he could say anything to Fergus who stood beside him.

'I need my cello. I must get my cello,' he coughed, as he allowed Fergus to guide him back to the car.

They drove back to Woodbourne House in silence. Iain pressed his hands to his knees then to his face, his shallow breathing being the only sound.

'You sit here. Give me the key.'

With some effort and juggling, Fergus managed to open the door against which he propped the brick he'd taken from Iain's hand.

'Anyone in?' he called.

As his voice bounced back off the high ceilings, he pushed open the doors to the downstairs rooms. An open newspaper, a discarded cup, a vase of wilting flowers told him nothing but the kitchen spoke of danger.

A chair had been overturned and a large knife stuck out from under some papers on the table. Cupboard doors were open from which it appeared crockery had been wrenched from the shelves and hurled around the room. The waste bin lay on its side having spewed its contents over Beethoven's basket. Fergus put a sleeve over his nose as a rotting smell assailed his nostrils. A crazy idea hit him. Hell's teeth, he muttered as an image of Una chopped into pieces and stuffed behind the dishwasher loomed large.

'Have you got the cello?'

Iain stood in the hallway, rubbing his hands.

Fergus closed the kitchen door, and followed Iain into the den.

'Oh frigging hell,' he said.

They both stared in horror at the mess before them. Contents of drawers and book cases had been vomited over the carpet. Music scores torn into shreds and scattered like confetti spoke of a vicious act of vengeance by someone who wanted to cause maximum pain. An oak box which stored music paraphernalia had been overturned and seemingly kicked around the room. As Iain bent down to pick up a broken bow, he felt a blockage in his throat like a large lump of meat.

'The cello,' he rasped, staring at the empty space on the floor.

'Where did you leave it?'

He watched Iain shrivel like a sparrow's broken wing.

'It was there. Right there.'

Iain stood on the spot, his eyes lasering the pattern off the carpet as if trying to reproduce his cello through the power of his mind.

'Someone's taken it,' he said finally, looking around in the hope it might be hiding from him.

Fergus stumbled up the stairs and tore through the bedrooms, opening the children's old toy boxes, flinging open wardrobe doors as he went. He felt he was in the middle of a comedy drama like the old Brian Rix farces except this wasn't funny. It was gathering nightmarish proportions.

'Calm down and think,' he told himself. 'There's no evidence of a break in so there must be a logical explanation.'

'What the hell are you doing in my house?'

Fergus stared down the staircase at Una's flaming cheeks. Her hair looked like rusty spikes.

'Thank God you're here,' he gushed. 'I mean you're not dead.'

Iain was pacing the floor, muttering to himself.

'What are you talking about? I've been at a meeting. Why are you here?' 'She looked at Iain. 'Is somebody going to tell me what's going on and what the hell is all this mess in the kitchen?'

Iain went to have a look. Maybe the cello was there somewhere. He looked in the chest freezer, baffled by its emptiness.

'Where's my cello?'

Iain blocked her exit as she tried to push past him.

'I asked you a question. I came to get my cello and it's not here. Where is it?'

'I've no idea. It looks as if someone has broken into the house looking for something. Maybe they've taken it.'

'Don't you care?'

Una folded her arms and walked into his study.

'Not really,' she said, turning her back on the mess. 'But I do care that we might have been burgled.'

Fergus bristled.

'I'm going to call the police. That cello is worth a lot of money.'

Iain got back in the car where he sat shivering under a blanket. His shoulder was throbbing despite the painkillers. He tried some finger exercises to distract him from the waves of hot pain down his arm but his mind was glued to his missing instrument. A severed arm would be less gut wrenching.

Fergus refused to leave the house despite Una's abusive tirade. He was beginning to understand something about this woman with the crazed look in her eye. She couldn't intimidate him but it was obvious she was trying to break Iain but then he'd practically confessed to hurting her despite the growing evidence of his injuries. Nothing made sense to him and he wished the police would show up so he could go home.

It took a patrol car over an hour to arrive at the house. A female officer went inside whilst her male colleague spoke firstly to Fergus then got inside the car with Iain.

WPC Barnes cautioned Una twice for her foul language.

'Just give me your side of the story Mrs. Millar and stick to the facts please.'

Una said how she could give them any facts when she didn't have any.

'I came in. The house was turned upside down. My husband's cello is missing. End of story.'

'Are you having any financial difficulties at the moment?'

'My finances are nothing to do with you. If you are suggesting I've got anything to do with a theft, then you are out of order.'

WPC Barnes sighed lightly. She was tired and a stroppy witness was the last thing she wanted.

'I am not suggesting anything but I do have to ask the questions.'

DI Clifford knocked on the door and entered the house.

'I've talked to your husband but he's in shock. I'll call in forensics so please don't touch anything. In fact, if you've got somewhere else to go tonight that would be helpful.'

Una pursed her red lips into the shape of a cat's bottom.

'Is he saying that I've been violent towards him?'

'We're here to deal with a possible robbery. If you'd like to get your stuff together we will secure the house and let you know when you can return. There's a cheap hotel off New Street if you need it. WPC Barnes will take your mobile number.'

Una didn't like his tone but knew she needed to co-operate for her own sake.

CHAPTER NINETEEN

Una sat on the edge of the hotel bed watching a spider stretch its legs up the pedestal of the grimy washbasin. The cell-like room smelt dank with a dull orange glow from the street light pushing its way in through a threadbare curtain. She kept her coat and boots on shuddering at the idea of getting into the single bed without protection against the billions of germs she imagined lurking in the sagging mattress. Somewhere outside a mechanical voice warned people against crossing a barrier. Its repetitiveness was driving Una to distraction.

The receptionist had made out that she was lucky to find a room at a bargain price considering that every hotel was full because of the International Spring Fair at the National Exhibition Centre.

Una pulled out some disinfectant wipes and ran them over everywhere her skin might make contact. As she reached over the bath to clean the mould on the rubbery seal, she had an urge to vomit. Leaning back on her haunches she paused to wonder what Iain had told the police once she was out of earshot, especially if encouraged by Fergus O'Neal. Surely they would realise that his incoherent mutterings were the sign of someone unstable and maybe that was the reason they suggested she vacated the house for the night.

Wiping down the remote control, Una flicked through the TV channels as she toyed with the idea of calling her husband. She pondered her feelings for him as she stared at a loop of cobwebs in the far corner of the ceiling. When he was in her presence she felt sick to her stomach at what he had done to them. He'd tried to dress up his dismissal as a suspension, reassuring her that it was girls being stupid and they would eventually withdraw their allegations. Una had seen something hidden behind the blankness of his eyes and even though she had wanted to believe him, something had whittled away at her reasoning until she was left with a pile of shavings. Doubt heralded its arrival. Iain's only real interest in life was his cello. That had hurt and angered her in the early years but that didn't mean he wasn't capable of casting his eye elsewhere. Despite the allegations evaporating into smoke, Una couldn't let it go. She knew she was punishing him and it was only when Iain seemed to gather some inner strength that she pulled back in case she lost him. Without her target, Una was well aware that she would be forced to look in the mirror.

Intellectually Una realised she should be feeling some sort of real emotion and not the dumbed down pretence of guilt but she felt as if her mind had split from her heart. For Una feelings were best left in the freezer. She didn't understand what it meant to be passionate about anything other than work and that was only because of the financial reward it brought. Detachment kept her safe and in control.

Una awoke as dawn shivered in through the curtains. She was exhausted from a disturbed sleep. She checked her phone half hoping to see a message of apology from Iain. Her coat was crumpled as she got up to put on her boots with an urgency to escape. She planned to go back home and tell the police to screw themselves.

Pouring boiling water onto a coffee sachet she yanked open the mini bar and took a miniature brandy. She held it to her lips then screwed back on the lid. Martha's voice danced on her shoulder. 'Well done girl. Drink never served any good.'

***

The sight of Iain's dishevelled clothes into which his body appeared to be shrivelling shocked Fergus to the point of him bringing in a substitute violinist for a concert at Coventry Cathedral so that he could stay with Iain. The news of his missing cello had torn him apart. He sat motionless in the chair staring into the fire, his supper untouched on the tray beside him. The tremor in his hands was more noticeable and on a couple of occasions a cup of hot liquid had slipped onto his lap. Iain hadn't leapt up in pain tugging the fabric of his trousers away from his skin like most people would have done. Instead he'd allowed his legs to be scalded as if to punish himself, refusing Freda's insistence on treatment.

Fergus was aware of his inadequacy in trying to help Iain out of his depression. He waited for Freda to go shopping before tapping out the numbers for Dr. Gordon's surgery. He was in no mood to humour the gatekeepers.

'No, he's not in danger to others but he might be to himself. How the feck do I know? I'm not a doctor but he needs to see one. Now.'

There was some resistance from the receptionist until Fergus lost his temper.

'If you don't get somebody round here then I shall take him

to A&E. Last time I was there it was jammed to the gills with people who only needed to see their GP,' he yelled, mopping his forehead with the back of his hand.

Fergus stared down the length of the garden at the patches of late snowdrops. A few shoots from spring bulbs dotted the dark earth and disturbed pieces of bark lay in clumps on the wet path. It was probably the fox, thought Fergus, pushing some more tobacco into his unlit pipe. His mind turned to Iain's overturned study and the obvious theft of his cello. Nobody could convince him that someone had broken into Woodbourne House, chosen not to take the various gadgets Una had left lying around, but instead focused on a musical instrument which to any regular burglar would have no value whatsoever.

Fergus pressed on his breastbone as a wave of acid surged into his throat. He tossed the pipe aside and went in search of some of the horrible pink liquid Freda kept for him in the medicine cupboard. He took two deep swigs from the bottle before making some decaffeinated coffee for himself and a full strength Americano for Iain.

He sat back in his winged chair as the silence between the two men hung like a heavy blanket over them.

'There's a new recording of Saint Saens string quartet I was thinking of getting. It's time to add some more stuff to the repertoire,' Fergus said, lifting the spoon from his mug.

Iain barely moved a muscle. His face was taut with the pain of the loss he felt so profoundly that it could not be expressed.

'We'll get the cello back Iain.' Fergus wanted to add,' I promise,' but didn't dare raise his hopes. Until the police had completed their investigations what had happened to the cello was nothing but speculation.

'Until then, it's no problem to get a replacement on hire. Steve's got a couple going spare.'

Iain wasn't interested in cellos or concerts at that moment. He wanted to get access to a computer to search for information on the best way to end his life. The dense fog was lifting to show a faint outline of a path he could take. Una would get his life policy and the bit of pension he'd accrued. She wouldn't have to worry about money or debt anymore. He was so convinced that it was the best way for everyone including his children that his mind became fixated on the plan. Leaning back in his chair, he half smiled as the flames warmed his ankles. The hectoring voices had won but he was fine with that. He agreed that he needed to be punished for what he'd done. He closed his eyes and thought about his funeral music. It would have to be the Elgar Cello Concerto he concluded.

'I can arrange that Iain. I've plenty of good contacts in Malvern.'

Iain's eyes flew open.

'What?'

'You were talking about Elgar.'

Iain struggled to sit upright in his chair, a nerve twitching violently in his cheek.

'I must have dropped off. Sorry, I've let the coffee go cold.'

Fergus poured him a small measure of whisky and topped it up with soda water.

'Have you heard from Stuart lately? What's he up to?'

'Stuart? No. Not recently. He's got a teaching job in Muscat. Sultan Qaboos University I think. He wants to keep his Arabic fluent.'

Fergus pondered on his next words.

'I think Tom would like to travel in that part of the world before he goes down to the LSE. Would it be alright if he got in touch? Email maybe?'

'I'm sure he'd like that.'

'Ok. Tom's come up with a plan. For the cello.'

Iain's sudden mood lift dissipated as he swilled the golden liquid round in the tumbler.

'He's going to launch a social media campaign to get it back. The more public it is the more likely some thieving toe-rag will want to dump it or do a deal.'

The doorbell chimed snapping the tension between them.

Fergus went to open the door and in a low voice told Dr. Gordon what he could.

'Hello Iain. Now don't get mad. Fergus is concerned about this tremor in your hand. You can't be a cellist if we don't get this sorted out. I think an appointment with a neurologist is due.'

'It's not necessary,' Iain said levelly. 'I won't be playing for much longer. I've got other plans.'

'Take your jacket off and roll up your sleeve.'

The doctor pushed a cuff onto Iain's arm.

'And what might they be?'

Iain bit down on the inside of his lip to prevent him from saying anymore.

'Your blood pressure's a bit on the high side. How are you feeling in yourself?'

Iain shrugged. He felt irritated as he was unable to express any feelings other than a deadness which acted like weights on his legs and arms. His chest felt as if a lorry had dumped a load of bricks onto it.

'How are things at home? Fergus tells me you're staying here for a while. It's a good plan Iain. You need rest in a calm environment. You're better here than in a hospital.'

'Why should I need to be in hospital? I'm not ill.'

Dr. Gordon closed his bag and sat on the chair Fergus had vacated.

'Iain, you're showing all the signs of clinical depression. You're losing yourself. I'm going to prescribe a course of medication to help you get your foot on the first rung of the ladder out of the well. When you feel a bit better we can talk about counselling or therapy. I'm no specialist but I want to get you the best help available.'

Iain stood up and put his jacket back on almost in an act of defiance.

'There's nothing wrong with me. I've not lost my marbles. I feel very calm.'

Dr. Gordon found Fergus in the kitchen tidying up some papers.

'I want you to get this prescription made up today. Iain needs to start this medication immediately and you're just the man to help me to help him.'

Fergus folded the green paper and slipped it into his pocket.

'I'll try but he can be a stubborn old mule sometimes.'

***

A phone call from the police requested Una's presence at the house within the hour. Several calls to Iain's phone had diverted to voicemail. The urge to vent her frustration became so overwhelming she could barely contain it. She believed he was playing games, egged on by Fergus, in order to drive her crazy. If he'd not got involved with that man maybe he would have been a proper husband and got a job. She was not in favour of house husbands seeing them as lazy spongers wanting to write books or fiddle with their paintbrushes. Where were the real men? The ones who came home with dirty fingernails not bloody manicures and talked loudly on the phone about the Nikkei?

As her taxi pulled up outside the house she saw two patrol cars parked nose to tail on the drive. A small team of officers followed her up to the front door.

'SOCO, West Midlands Police,' said a tall, thin man as he led the officers into the house.

'What exactly are you looking for?' asked Una, fumbling for a lipstick.

'Fingerprints, traces of hair, fibre, footprints. Can I ask you to wait in the conservatory please Mrs. Millar? We won't be too long.'

Wishing she had kept the coffee maker in the Victorian domed addition to the back of house, Una paced the floor, breathing into her wrap and rubbing her gloved hands. It was obvious that they would find trace evidence of her and Iain and even the cat in the study but her anxiety levels were shooting off the graph. She needed the proof that someone else had been in the house. Una kept an anxious eye on her watch, wishing they would leave. She tried Iain again but the reception on her phone was poor. Damn him, damn, damn, damn.

'We're finished, thank you.'

Una rushed to the door.

'Did you find anything?' Her eyes flashed as she lifted the latch.

'You'll get a call when the evidence has been examined. Sorry to inconvenience you.'

Una watched them go, trepidation creeping into her lungs. She needed a drink. Pulling an open bottle of wine from the fridge, she knocked off the top and swallowed hard. A rancid taste hit her mouth and she spat out the liquid into the sink where she filled a glass with cold water in the hope it would calm her down. She felt the house was sending down vibrations of disgust as she walked through its empty, neglected rooms. Her laptop winked its blue eye at her from the kitchen table. Una couldn't face dealing with the emails that would have piled up from disgruntled clients, angry creditors and offers of Viagra. All she wanted to do was curl up in a darkened room, under a thick duvet and not wake up again.

When Martha called round the following day, she assumed Una was out. Noticing her car parked at the side of the house, Martha banged the knocker and rang the bell simultaneously. The folds of her fluorescent pink skirt flapped in the wind.

'Come on you drunken skunk. Open up.'

Martha went round to the back of the house where Una usually worked but it was dead apart from a rat which shot over the lawn.

'Bloody hell, Mrs. Open up before I get nobbled by some giant furry thing.'

The commotion and Martha's loud voice which could push a cruise liner across the Atlantic with no help, forced Una out of her room.

'Oh my life. Look at your face. Black, blue, pink, purple.'

'Give it a rest Martha. I've got a banging headache and a tongue that's been in a chemistry lab.'

'You been drinking again?'

'No lectures please. We've been burgled. I had to stay a night in a stinking hotel… oh never mind… The fingerprint men have been. It makes me feel dirty.'

'Good god Una. You didn't?

'Shut up Martha. Not everything's a joke. Iain's left home and I've got one shit of a mess to sort out. Now if you've nothing useful to tell me, please go.'

'Fine. I will. It's the last time I show any concern for you Una Carrington. You're turning into a prize narcissist.'

CHAPTER TWENTY

March 2015

Fergus sat in his backroom study drumming his fingers on the keyboard of his laptop. He flexed his fingers as he made another stab at writing to Stuart without sounding dramatic. He wasn't sure what he wanted to achieve by making contact with Iain's elder son other than to let him know his father wasn't well. Fergus didn't want to guilt trip him into coming home, knowing that he was about to start a new job at a prestigious university but he felt strongly that he should have a heads up in case the situation became more serious. With Iain in hospital he felt it was his duty.

A knock on the door made him jump and he hastily blanked out the screen.

'Come in,' he called.

Freda, looking tired and flushed, brought him some coffee and a couple of his favourite homemade orange biscuits.

'You've got that guilty look on your face?'

'Moi? Surely not.'

'Fergus,' her tone held a warning note.

'Ok, ok. I'm letting Stuart Millar know about his father. He might want to come over so I've hinted he can stay with us.'

Freda lifted a wobbling pile of books from a chair, cringing as they crashed to the floor. She'd given up offering to tidy this room years ago.

'Have you rung the hospital this morning? '

'I've got a meeting at St. Chad's later so I'll pay a visit. I don't think he'll want to do much talking but at least I can be there. Apparently Una's in Dubai.'

Freda smoothed down her skirt to distract her tongue.

'Do they know if it was a stroke?'

'No idea yet. Probably one of those TIA thingy bobs. Mini strokes. It's affected his left eye and arm but they said it will pass. He's on a glucose drip but that's all I know.'

'Poor Iain.'

Freda stood up and put her arms around her husband's neck.

'Ahhhh. You're strangling me.'

'Stop exaggerating. I want to show you how much I love you.'

She plonked fat kisses on his plump cheeks then disappeared back into the kitchen to attend to the next process of the soda bread she was making.

Fergus re-read his email and pressed send. He hoped Stuart would contact him on Skype so they could talk camera to camera. Nibbling the edge of a biscuit, he scrolled through the concert plan for the next few months. He would have to find a stand in cellist and someone to take over Iain's tutorials. Una had been indifferent to the news of Iain's collapse, a reaction he couldn't comprehend. Freda would have been like an unexploded firework until the doctor arrived but Una had simply said, 'I'm about to board a flight.' What was it that made her so indifferent, so aloof to her own husband's suffering? Maybe she was one of those people who had never developed empathy.

Tired of trying to figure it out, Fergus picked up his violin and played bits of his new composition, *Meditation for Strings*. He wandered through the ground floor of the house and out in to the backyard where the dense pink blossom of the cherry had burst into life. Fergus loved its simple beauty, so short lasting it reminded him of the fragility of life. Its ephemeral nature was a stark reminder of the need to be mindful of the present moment. He thought about composing an ode to it in the way that Housman had done. 'Loveliest of trees, the cherry now, is hung with bloom along the bough,' he murmured. He would write a particularly lovely cello part he decided, dabbing the corner of his eye as he thought of his best friend immobile in a hospital bed.

Fergus hurriedly wound up the meeting of the Birmingham Guild of string players and went in search of his car. Narrowly avoiding a collision on the Pershore Road by Cannon Hill Park in his haste to get to the hospital by the university. At least he had some positive news to share with Iain.

'Just make sure he stays in hospital as long as possible,' Freda had urged. 'They're too quick to tip you out of bed if there's any sign of breathing.'

By the time Fergus had pushed open several sets of swing doors and made false turns down dog-leg corridors, he spotted Iain in the corner of a four bedded ward. Iain was lying back against the pillows, face tight, eyes closed. He was drumming his fingers on the cover.

Fergus used the heel of his hand to dispense the antiseptic gel before pulling a chair up to the bed.

'How are you doing?'

Iain's eyes flickered open and pulled Fergus' face into focus.

'Not bad. The headache's gone.'

Fergus looked around at the other visitors. Some were talking in whispers, others laughing loudly as they shared out the chocolates, most appeared awkward.

'That's progress then. What have the doctors said?'

Iain shuffled against his pillows as he tried to get traction on the mattress.

'Not much. The neurology chap said I didn't have Parkinson's which is a relief. They're doing some more tests.'

'Right. Good.'

Fergus pointed to a carrier bag he'd placed by the bedside cabinet.

'Something to keep you amused,' he muttered. 'When are they going to let you out. You can tell them you are coming back to stay with us.'

Iain nodded, conscious of the pain in his shoulder and neck.

'Una didn't mean it you know. It was an accident. I'm the one to blame really. I shouldn't have lost my temper.'

Fergus unfastened his pink satin waistcoat and leaned forward.

'I'm not with you. What accident? What's Una got to do with this?'

Iain closed his eyes and travelled back to the afternoon he went back to the house. He wanted to confront Una about the cello but instead he threw a chair across the room in frustration. She'd picked it up and smashed it against his arm. That's all he remembered and the bruising proved it.

'Nothing. It doesn't matter.'

Emotional pain was etched like deep tram lines in the hollow of his cheeks. Like a tongue exploring the gaping hole after a pulled tooth, Iain kept going over the terrible words she'd fired at him, each one of them tearing off a piece of his skin to expose the nerves underneath. His dignity and fight had been punched out of him by those words.

'I've got some good news. The Guild of Strings is going to use its contacts to chase up your cello. Billy was furious and promised to ring round his mates tonight. You know what he's like when he gets wired up.'

Iain smiled weakly.

'Thanks but don't put yourself out. I won't be playing anymore.'

'Whaaaat?'

'Sir, would you keep your voice down please. There are some very sick people trying to rest.'

A middle aged woman with wisps of grey hair glowered at Fergus over her black glasses.

'You can't say that,' Fergus hissed. 'As soon as you're better you're going to play. Steve's sorted out a cello. Get back on your horse and stop being a wimp. I need you.'

Something the size of a bulb had lodged in Iain's throat. He reached for the glass of water and tried to swallow. The liquid wouldn't go down and Iain began to panic.

Fergus helped him into a better sitting position and taking his arm encouraging him to breathe slowly.

'It's alright my old mucker. Nothing is going to happen to you.'

'I can't go on like this. It's over. I'm sorry.' Iain rambled on as if talking to a disembodied voice, asking questions and providing answers. His bad eye twitched as he stared over Fergus' shoulder towards a spot near the door.

'Don't go anywhere.' Fergus got up and made for the nurses' station.

'I think my friend needs a doctor. He's hyperventilated and is hallucinating.'

A tiny young woman with olive skin and straight black hair echoed his words as if trying them out for size.

'The specialist is due to see him tomorrow. I suggest you leave him to rest now. Mr. Millar gets overexcited.'

'Dr. Millar. Show some respect.'

'Can you leave now please? You're upsetting the other patients and visitors.'

Flushed with anger, Fergus strode back to where Iain had fallen asleep and whispered, 'Everything's going to be alright. Have a listen to that CD that's in the bag. There's an old disk player in there with new batteries. If you need anything let me know.'

***

Freda was sitting at the dining table doing some craft work. She was so tightly focused on cutting some felt into star shapes that she didn't hear the front door open.

'You ok?' Fergus hung his coat on the peg in the hall.

'You've had a call from Stuart Millar. He wants you go call him on Skype later.'

Their old cat stirred from his basket and weaved his thin body through Fergus' legs getting the brush off for his efforts at being friendly.

'How's Iain?'

'Hard to say. His mental state is weak. He talks like a man who's given up.'

'Well at least he's talking. Not many men do that. They keep it all inside then one day they explode. Male suicide rate in the 40-50 age group is on the rise. I listened to a programme about it. You ready for some dinner? It's salad.'

Freda laid down her scissors and jabbed his overhanging belly with her finger.

'Maybe it's because their wives give them salad,' he mumbled, following her to the table. A pink, moist salmon fillet on a bed of green salad stared at him from the plate as if to say, what's your problem mate?

***

An unexpected visit from the police had left Una on edge. She'd arrived back from a fruitless trip to the Emirates, her confidence in shreds. They'd questioned her again about the alleged break-in making it clear that the only trace evidence they'd found belonged to her and Iain. Her statement had been picked apart in such a way Una knew they were looking for anomalies.

The female DC wanted to search the upstairs of the house but Una refused, telling her she would make a formal complaint if she so much as stepped onto the bottom step.

'Get a warrant,' she snapped.

'We will do that Ms. Carrington if we think it's necessary.'

'Where's your husband?'

The officer looked around the kitchen as if expecting Iain to pop out of the fridge and say boo.

Una was caught off guard.

'He's in hospital. Queen Elizabeth. He collapsed.'

'Theft is a stressful business,' said the Inspector who Una disliked intensely. It was the way he studied her without seeming to blink. 'You don't seem too bothered if you don't mind me saying.'

'I do mind actually.' Una dragged out the syllables of the last word. She was aware of how like a pouty teenager she sounded but couldn't help herself. 'I mind you being here. I mind you insinuating that I am involved with this cello business and I damn well do mind you telling me how I feel.'

Una opened the door and folded her arms.

'Now if you don't mind,' she said with sarcasm, 'I've got work to do.'

Una watched them into the car before slamming the door. In the hallway she pressed her hands to her ears and screamed. She leant against the wall and allowed her body to slide down to the floor as her legs folded beneath her. An avalanche of envelopes fell in a pile beside her. She kicked them aside then reaching over to pick them up, tore each one into four pieces. Her mind chewed on and regurgitated the trauma of being told she did not have the right technology skills for the jobs she'd applied for in Dubai, the implication being she was too old. How dare they, how bloody dare they she shouted, pulling herself up to answer the phone.

It was the nursing home calling to say her mother had died.

'I'm so sorry Una. She passed away early this morning. I was with her last night. She had a moment of lucidity which is not unusual. She said, tell Una I love her.'

Una felt she should cry but her face was too stiff with shock. Words like funeral, sorry and gloves appeared before her eyes like the coloured specs in a kaleidoscope. She picked up on the mention of her mother's glove collection.

'Please pack them all carefully and I will collect them. My husband's in hospital so it will be in a day or two.'

Una paused, running her tongue over her lips.

'Did my mother leave a will?'

'I'll give you the details when you come up. Again, I'm really sorry for your loss.'

As Una poured some wine she felt nothing at all. Her mother's death had been expected for a long time and Una's way of dealing with it had been to detach and that feeling was even stronger as she turned over the idea that she was now without parents. In one way she felt liberated. If her mother had any money left from the nursing home fees it would come to her. The glove collection had some value although she remembered the feel of the tan calf skin ones which she would keep as a memento. It could go with her many lipsticks she thought wryly.

Una felt an urge to talk to someone, to speak the words out loud, my mother is dead. She called Martha.

'I'm so sorry. What can I do?'

'Nothing. I just need to tell someone.'

'How are you feeling?'

The memory of that moment she'd received a call from St. Kitts to say Momma had died was as sharp and poignant as if she was hearing it for the first time. She rubbed her eyes dragging flecks of mascara onto her cheeks. Nothing made up for the loss of your mother. Her heart went out to Una.

'I'm fine. I was expecting it but it's still a shock. Iain's in hospital and before you ask no, I didn't get offered any of the jobs. The police are still hounding me over the cello so all in all things are shit.'

'I'll call round later and bring some food. You can't be on your own. I'll come with you to Yorkshire if you want. Drive you up there. Just let me know.'

Una had no energy to argue. All she wanted to do was shut the curtains and lock herself away in the bathroom with a bottle. A hissing in her ear told her to visit her husband. She told it to fuck off.

CHAPTER TWENTY-ONE

Iain was allowed out of hospital a few days later. The consultant advised him to note any changes to his movements and contact his doctor without delay.

'The mind can play havoc with the body,' she said kindly. 'Prolonged stress, even when we don't recognise it, will interfere with normal functioning. I've recommended that you get some counselling or some relaxation therapy. I've heard colouring books are all the rage.'

Iain half smiled but shook off any idea of seeing some therapist. As he packed his stuff into a battered rucksack he wished he could flick a switch to turn off the thoughts which did circuits round his head all day stopping only to tune into the voice that demanded his ear every so often. He was sure the grating noise was external even thought he'd read that it was possible the sounds he heard were from his own mind. When it was telling him he would do everyone a favour if he killed himself, it didn't feel like a product of his imagination.

He sat on the bed and opened his manuscript notebook. The squiggles and dots executed in a shaking hand looked both alien and familiar. He felt the skin around his throat turn damp as he tried to hear the music in his head.

'Yo'm look washed aht ar kid,' said a fellow patient as he hobbled past Iain's bed. 'Mrs been getting at yer? I dumped mine years ago.'

Iain eased himself onto his feet and into his shoes, politely ignoring the large red faced man with his tumbling wall of blackened teeth. Iain felt agitated as the man continued his monologue. He felt the urgent need to get outside and take in gulps of fresh air to get rid of the overpowering smell of sickness.

'Dr. Millar, you've not been discharged yet,' called a nurse as he walked down the ward towards the double swing doors.

Iain ignored her as he saw Fergus turning the corner towards the café.

'Whisky for me,' he called, trying to catch his breath as he hurried towards him.

'You're out of luck. It's not even lunchtime. You can have coffee and be grateful I've come to rescue you.'

Fergus bit into his bacon sandwich, oozing with fried tomatoes. A dollop of brown sauce landed on his lime green waistcoat, bringing a smile to Iain's pale face.

'Bugger, 'he said, trying to wipe it off with a serviette.

Iain stirred his coffee but made no attempt to drink it.

'I've got a confession,' Fergus said, through a final mouthful of bread. 'I've been talking to Stuart.'

'Stuart? Why?'

Fergus ripped open a sachet of sugar as he thought about what to say.

'To tell him that you've not been feeling too well.'

He waited for Iain's response.

'I'm fine and he's busy. I hope you didn't suggest that he came over here.'

Iain felt a frisson of annoyance.

'No. He said he wanted to and he arrived last night. He's staying with us. He's an adult Iain. His choice.'

'You mean he felt obligated.'

'Nonsense. He's on a long weekend from his college. Some sort of religious holiday so he's pleased to be back. Freda's doing her usual of feeding the poor lad till he bursts.'

'Does Una know he's in Birmingham?'

'Doubtful. We've not told her. Stuart doesn't seem particularly interested in seeing her. Now, you're coming back to us for an extended stay. Just till things get a bit more on an even keel. Freda won't take no for an answer. She's got your room all ready. I've got Steve to sort you out a cello. Nothing as grand as your own but at least you can still teach and play. Tom's put a message out of Facebook to say lessons will be at Bournville and created a bookings page. You've got two rearranged and two new students.'

Fergus grinned.

'We just need to get you formally released from this prison.'

Iain sat back nursing his cold coffee, seeing his surroundings as if behind a glass screen. People appeared out of focus as if floating around in a fog. He saw Fergus's lips moving but the sound was turned off. There was a safety in the disconnection with the world as if it pushed him into a cocoon that nobody could penetrate. He remembered Johanna telling him that when she wanted to pretend she was the only person in the world she would pull the duvet over her head.

'Here. Look at this.'

Fergus swiped his tablet to display Tom's campaign to recover the cello.

'There's this website, Stolen Strings, which specialises in this sort of thing. See, violin stolen at Putney station, reward for finder. Another one here in Italian so it must be a world-wide site for marrying strings up with distraught owners. Bloody brilliant idea. Wish I'd thought of it.'

Iain pulled his attention back to take a closer look.

'There's no mention of the mark on the back. It looks like a bird. Something unusual in the wood. Look.'

Iain showed him the picture he carried in his pocket.

'Well I'm blowed. I've never noticed that before.'

'Dr. Millar. I've been looking everywhere for you. Come back to the ward now.'

A large framed nurse with cauliflower grey hair stood over him, her square face taut with frustration.

'I'll wait here,' said Fergus, giving the nurse a wink as he opened up a broadsheet.

Two hours later Iain was allowed to leave. Fergus was apoplectic.

'I'm playing at the Town Hall at 4pm. It's almost 2. Come on.'

The Bristol Road past the university and through the usual bottle neck of Selly Oak was clear. As they turned left towards Bournville they were welcomed into the arms of the village by the delightful sound of the carillon.

Iain was ushered into his room by Freda carrying freshly laundered towels. A couple of framed photographs of Iain receiving an award from the Mayor of Birmingham and one from the Conservatoire hung on the wall above the fireplace.

'Thank you,' he said quietly, succumbing to exhaustion.

'I'll bring you some tea then leave you to rest. Stuart will be back later.'

Kicking off his shoes, he sank into the armchair and tried to get his thoughts into order. His head felt like mashed potato. Dr. Gordon had explained that the fuzzy head, dry mouth and constant churning in his stomach were symptoms of anxiety. The tablets were supposed to take them away but they made Iain feel nauseous. Dark thoughts of walking into the North Sea fought with the desire to return to Scotland and live on an island where nobody could reach him. He would play his cello and live off cabbages.

'Oh God. The cello,' he groaned, dropping his face into his hands.

He thought about the twins. He had to pull things together for their sake. He'd heard little from them since they went back to Edinburgh.

Iain declined the offer of going to hear the afternoon concert with Fergus. He should have been playing not sitting in the audience. The need to sit alone in silence was greater at that moment than his love of music. The borrowed cello sat in a dark corner of his room like a wallflower at a school dance. Iain felt nothing but a crushing despair as he listened to the sounds of the O'Neal family down below. He'd had to leave his home and rely on the kindness of friends. He had no job, no money of his own and now no means of earning any. Freda brought him a plate of quiche and chips but he said he wasn't hungry.

'Stuart's here,' she said gently.

He tore his eyes away from the fire and looked at her sadly.

'Shall I send him up with some whisky?'

Iain nodded slowly, pulling a rug tighter round his legs. Despite the warmth of the room he felt as if he'd been lying on a slab of ice. His knee joints felt stiff as he stood up to clear a space for his son to sit down.

'Dad.'

Stuart Millar, six foot four, pushed back his thick sandy hair as he eased his rugby player frame into the chair. Iain noticed how he'd grown out of the awkwardness of the teenage years and into what his own father would have called a 'fine young man.'

'This is a surprise but good… good to see you.'

Iain patted him on the shoulder as he picked up his glass.

'How are you Dad?'

'Och I'm fine. Nothing the good doctors can't sort out. Fergus fusses too much.'

'He's worried about you.'

Stuart picked up a handful of crisps and laid them on his palm. He could see how much his father had shrunk into himself. His eyes were so empty of life it upset him to witness it.

'I heard about the cello. Any more news?'

Iain shook his head, staring into his glass.

'The police have been again but I couldn't tell them anymore. The insurance documents are missing and I can't remember the name of the company. Una dealt with that sort of thing.'

'What has she told them?'

Iain sighed heavily, not wanting to recall their last fight. It had turned ugly with both of them to blame. All he could remember was lifting a hammer to defend himself. The rest was blank.

'That we were broken into but the police say there's no evidence for that. My cello is missing and I want it back.'

'Tom's doing a good job with the campaign. Lots of people offering to help locate it.'

Stuart noticed the tears in his father's eyes as he leant over to give a reassurance squeeze of his arm. He could kill whoever had done this to him. His thoughts turned to his stepmother.

'I know. He's a good lad. If it's been traded on the international market then there is no chance. It was to be your inheritance.'

Stuart swallowed hard. He didn't know what to say. His father's grief was etched all over his face and in his hollow voice. They talked for a while about Muscat and the new job but Iain's eyes closed and within minutes he was asleep. Stuart saw a man whose bones seem to be folding in on him and his heart in lockdown. He covered him with the blanket before slipping out of the room.

A week later

Una sat in the freezing carriage of the Birmingham to Euston train, arms folded, and face hidden behind the woollen scarf. She'd been told there would be no buffet owing to staffing shortages and it added to her darkening mood. She'd picked up a small training contract in South London, all her overseas options having come to nothing. It meant she had to take the train every day as the client refused to pay for her gas gobbler. The company specialised in green issues and insisted that all their suppliers used public transport. Una dismissed them as a load of lefties in sandals who knew nothing about business but research showed they turned a significant profit every year.

Her job was to go out to companies and carry out 'green consultations.' She knew she was out of her depth but desperately needed the fees. Every time she was asked about alternatives to bleach or what's wrong with palm oil she wanted to scream,' I don't bloody well know.' She was tired and had been up most of the night with a sore gut. Iain's sneaking away to stay with the O'Neal's had made her feel powerless especially as his phone kept switching to voicemail.

As the train waited outside Euston, Una sent him a text. She'd tried different ways to engage with him, exasperated with his refusal to talk.

'Damn you, damn, damn,' she muttered through gritted teeth, as she stepped onto the platform and headed for the tube. The hub and rub of people swarming down the stairs left Una feeling breathless to the point where she had to step aside and catch her breath. The overwhelming feeling of needing to get away from everything made her turn round and head for the next train back to Birmingham.

A searing pain in her gut made her grab the first seat where she drank deeply from a bottle of water. A fumble in her bag brought out a new lipstick, cherry delight, which she applied quickly and thickly over her tingling lips. As the train pulled out she pressed her face to the window. Feelings of calm spread through her body and she began to feel foolish for panicking. She emailed the company to explain but didn't expect to hear from them again.

By the time she got back into Birmingham her stomach felt so acidic, Una wondered if she'd developed an ulcer or if it was the searing hunger she felt. She spent the last couple of pounds on a drink and had nothing left to buy even the simplest sandwich. Her stomach growled in protest but all it received was a couple of chalky tasting tablets.

In tears she rang Martha who curtly said she couldn't keep running out of meetings because Una wagged her pinky.

'I'm near M&S. Go in the café and I'll see you in ten minutes,' she finally conceded when she realised Una's distress was real.

She saw Una slumped at a corner table, the contents of her bag spilled over the bench.

'You don't half get yourself into some messes. I'll get you some hot food. You look done in.'

Una plunged her fork into the lasagne and didn't speak until she'd finished.

'I've broke. We are broke,' she said, pouring tea into a china mug. I baled on a client today so they won't be having me back. Work's dried up. I've tried getting a job in the Middle East but my age seems to be against me.'

Una stopped talking.

'Why are you looking at me like that?'

'Because you've brought all this on yourself. I don't have much sympathy for people who insist on blaming others. Most of us have had to suck up bad luck and get on with it. You just wallow in it and play the woe is me card.'

'That's unfair. I'm trying to get out of the mess but...'

'But Iain shouldn't have lost his job blah blah blah. I've heard it all before Una. Change the record.'

'I've got an offer on the house,' she said quietly.

'So Iain agreed to the sale? That's a step forward at least.'

'He doesn't know about it.'

'What? Are you crazy girl? Don't tell me you've been forging his signature.'

Una blew on her tea but said nothing.

'He's not around.'

'That's not the point. It's fraud. What were you planning on doing? Telling him it's sold and putting his stuff out on the drive? You are seriously demented. What about the twins? Where do you plan on living?'

Una slammed her hands to her head.

'Stop it. Stop the questions. I don't know. I don't bloody well know anything right now except I have to protect what assets we have before the bailiffs turn up. You don't understand. I've lived under the shadow of being homeless most of my life. My mother was vague about money. She'd take stuff to Uncle Tom's the pawn shop to pay the gas bill after it had been cut off or get stuff on tick from the corner shop. She fell apart after my Dad died. I had to go to work in a shoe shop to help us stay afloat. I couldn't forgive her for that.'

'I'm sorry. I didn't know that.'

'Why should you? Now I've got her funeral next week and according to her solicitor she left no money to speak of. Just enough for a headstone.'

Martha pulled out her wallet and counted out some notes.

'It's not much but it will help you out until after the funeral. We can talk then. The offer to drive you up there still stands but Una, you have to get your shit together for the sake of your kids if not for you.'

CHAPTER TWENTY-TWO

Back at the house Una sat with her coat on in the kitchen, the only warm room in the house. The silence hummed around her as she pottered around cutting the mould off the heel of a granary loaf and slicing pieces of hardened cheddar. She found herself missing Iain's mumblings and the deep, richness of his cello. Beethoven strolled warily around her feet, daring her to break her habit of not feeding him from the table.

Una poured some wine into an unwashed glass, twisting in her chair as a sharp pain tried to dismantle her ribcage. A spurt of acid soured her mouth forcing her to spit into the basin in the cloakroom. She shuddered and screwed her face as she tried to dispel the horrific taste. Swilling around mint mouthwash, she leant over the bowl as a wave of nausea hit her throat.

Una hated being ill, especially when she was alone. What if she choked? There was no one to take charge. In the twelve years of living at Woodbourne House she'd made no attempt to befriend the neighbours and she was sure the nosy couple across the road would relish every moment of her distress.

Only Martha was there for her but even that friendship seemed to be tottering on a precipice. They'd argued on the way back from Isla's funeral because Martha had accused her of not organising a wake for the few people who did turn up at the crematorium.

'I don't know those people. Why should I spend money I don't have on feeding their faces?' she yelled as they walked down the promenade under a sprinkling of rain.

'Because it's what you do. It's about expectations. My Mum…'

'OK, OK. We can go to the pub if you want but the others were just nursing staff and some woman from Age UK.'

'You didn't even seem that upset. I don't get you sometimes. Most of the time.'

They'd spat and hissed at each other until the damn of emotion had burst in Una for the first time that day. Martha had held her until every last sob had shaken itself out. They'd walked arm in arm on the beach, pausing to throw pebbles into the water because Una had said that was one of her positive memories of time spent with her mother.

Back on the motorway, Una had been silent, brushing off Martha's questions about Iain. Una's head was full of him. She wondered what he'd been saying to Fergus about her. The man's disdain shone through every time he caught her eye. Iain's thought process was distorted and his memory non-existent. Iain could make up anything and Fergus O'Neal would believe him and back him up.

Martha suggested she stayed at Woodbourne House but Una was firm in her rejection. She'd made up her mind to drive over to Bournville. It was the only way she was going to get to communicate with her husband. He didn't know about Isla's death so it was a good enough excuse. She'd persuade him to come home.

She sat in his study with a glass of water and looked around at the untidy display of books and the muddle of papers on the desk. The people who'd offered on the house hadn't even seen it. They were coming home from Melbourne and had cash. She'd found them obnoxious and demanding. At that moment she decided to tell them there was no deal.

Getting up quickly, she picked her car keys and headed for the door. In ten minutes she was standing outside the cottage where she could see Iain sitting in a corner of the living room, a blanket over his knees. She was annoyed that he could allow himself to disintegrate into a pathetic old man.

Fergus came to the door. Seeing Una's tight red lips, he folded his arms and waited for her to speak.

'Can I see my husband?'

'What do you want him for? He needs peace and quiet not more hassle. Doctor's orders.'

Una put her foot in the doorway as she attempted to push her way in.

Fergus squared up to her and for once was grateful for his bulk being the right size for the doorway.

'He needs to come home to be looked after.'

'Oh yes? Since when were you around to look after anybody Una? You didn't even visit him in hospital.'

'That's none of your business. My mother has just been laid to rest so I've had other things on my mind.'

'Sorry to hear that. Come in for a few minutes but if you cause any trouble…'

Una followed him into the room where Iain sat listening to music through headphones. Feeling someone was standing next to him he looked up but said nothing.

'Iain? Can we talk? My mother's died. I've just come back from Scarborough.'

Iain continued to study the score on his lap.

Una stared helplessly at Fergus who shrugged.

Pulling off his headphones, Iain turned his dead eyes towards her.

'Where's my cello?'

'I don't know Iain. They're trying to find out and get it back for you.'

'Did you steal it?'

Una opened her mouth to reply.

'Tell me the truth for once in your life. Look at me and tell me the damn truth.'

Fergus laid a hand on his shoulder and whispered something.

'I… No.'

'Who did you give it to? How much did you get?'

Una sat down quickly as the stuffiness in the room got to her head.

'I don't know what you mean. We were burgled. You know

that. I'm trying to claim on the insurance for us. For you.'

The lies slid easily off her tongue. She pretended she was in a play where she was reciting the lines written for her character.

Iain turned his head away, his body stiffening with every word she spoke. He waited for the voices to give him an instruction but they were strangely quiet.

'I don't believe you,' he said.

'Let's talk about this when you are better.' Una moved towards him but as she slipped her arms around his neck, his hand jerked up and struck her across the face.

'Iain. No.'

Fergus helped Iain to his feet and out of the room.

'You'd better go,' he called to Una over his shoulder. 'You've upset him.'

Gingerly fingering her reddened cheek, Una hit back.

'You saw what he did. This isn't the first time. He has a selective memory.'

'Just go,' he yelled, 'before I throw you out myself.

'I want my cello,' cried Iain as Freda scurried out of the kitchen to help him upstairs.

Fergus followed on Una's heels to the front door. He grabbed the belt of her coat.

'Get off me.'

'Do you have any idea how heartbroken Iain is over his cello?

You have no clue how important these instruments are to musicians have you? It would be like someone cutting off your arms so you couldn't drive that fancy car of yours. Imagine that.'

'Don't be so dramatic. I'm leaving.'

'I've not finished yet.'

Fergus closed the door behind him.

'You know that cello is worth a fortune don't you? You've got debts. Iain told me everything. I forced it out of him so don't go blaming him. Put the two things together and who am I looking at?'

'You're as mad as he is. I'm not listening to this crap.'

'The police will though when Iain makes his statement about the violence you've inflicted on him.'

'Ha ha ha. Now I know you're crazy. I'm the one with the bruised arms and eyes and the broken fingers after he'd slammed a hammer on them. Believe what you like Fergus but you are so very out of order.'

Una zapped the car lock with her gadget. She narrowed her eyes and held his for a several seconds.

'This is none of your business. Remember that.'

Two weeks later

Fergus had called a meeting of a select group of string players and urged Iain to go along. As they shuffled along the benches of the Selly Oak community club house, Iain had to field questions about his cello.

'Shocking business,' said Joe, holding tightly onto his viola case. The others muttered their agreement. 'Any more news on it?'

Iain shook his head.

'Tom, that's Fergus' son, says there's been a lead from his campaign and he's following it up.'

'Message for you from the Stolen Strings website as well. There's a number to call for information,' Fergus added.

Iain pocketed the scrap of paper until he could turn his attention to it properly.

'Attention everyone please.' Fergus waved his bow in the air.

'Now that you are suitably watered, let us turn our hearts to the new ensemble and our minds to helping Iain.'

Fergus outlined his plans for the new strings group which would play an eclectic mix from baroque to jazz, pop to highbrow classical.

'We need to be in touch with everyone's taste these days,' he explained. 'Versatility is the key to success. If anyone has an idea for a name, let's have it by the end of the meeting.'

'How are we going to get the gigs?' asked Moira who played the viola.

'Good question. My son Tom has come up with a marketing plan. It will be done mainly through social media and the usual posters and flyers.'

A groan rippled through the group.

'Yes, yes, I felt the same until I realised how cheap and effective it can be. Everyone seems to be linked to everyone else these days. It's how we've managed to get over 3,000 hits on Facebook for Iain's cello.'

The Coffee Shack was filling up with people escaping the downpour. Iain felt claustrophobic, sandwiched between Moira who had a habit of banging his ankle with her case and Kerry who was a recent graduate from the University. She played cello but did a good line in giggling.

'So are we all in?' Fergus rubbed his hands and looked around.

Murmurs of agreement were punctuated by a clink of mugs.

'We can rehearse at that place on Hampton Street. We've used it before. How about Sunday afternoon for a warm up, say 2 till 4? Good. Good. Now onto this cello business. We need all of you to contact everyone you know that plays an instrument, sells them, especially strings, has children who use all the different social media outlets to get on the case. Anything to get the word out there. The details are already circulating on the net so take what you need.'

'You kept that very quiet. I didn't think you were serious about starting a new group. Won't we be competing with ourselves?'

'No. These days we have to be entrepreneurial or we will be end up as has-beens. It's good to see you looking a bit brighter.'

'Must be the tablets,' said Iain a bit of a sparkle back in his eyes.

Now that he had more energy he could think about executing

his plan. He'd discovered a number of websites which helped people to end their lives but all suggestions were met with horror. Iain couldn't imagine him hanging himself from the garage door nor getting hold of a rifle and shooting himself behind the shed. He tried to picture himself in different scenarios before coming to terms with the fact he would get so far then not be able to follow through. He supposed he could drink himself to death but then who would find him.

'What are you so wrapped up in?'

'Nothing much. Just thinking about a text message James sent me this morning.'

'Nothing wrong I hope.'

Iain shrugged his arms into his coat.

'I don't know yet. He says Johanna cries every day and wants to come home. I need to give the school a ring.'

'Oh dear. Something else to worry about. Don't forget to call that London number.'

'Eh?'

'Your cello?'

'Mmmm. Ok. I'll do it when we get back to your place if that's ok. My phone's run out of credit.'

Iain spent the afternoon in his new den. He knew he would have to go home eventually if only to sort things out with Una. Knowing it would lead to an acrimonious dispute and he would end up with nothing other than unpredictable access to the twins made Iain feel exhausted. He had no energy to do battle. After all he wasn't the one at war.

He thought about the conversation he'd had with Miss Kennedy. Johanna was distressed but wouldn't talk about why. Her grades were dropping and she'd been found in the games cupboard sobbing instead of being on the hockey field. Iain felt so helpless. All he could do was wait for his daughter to call him after school.

The number he'd called about his cello was unobtainable so he assumed Fergus had written it down incorrectly. He couldn't be bothered to follow it through at that moment.

Stuart popped his head round the door.

'Tom said there's been a lead. Any news?

Iain shook his head.

'You try the number Stuart. I can't get through. It's a dead line.'

'Ok give me a few minutes to check it out. Dad, I've got to go back to Muscat in a couple of days. Do you fancy coming into town for an early dinner?'

Iain was on the verge of declining but had second thoughts. He'd spent very little time with his elder son since he went to Exeter so it would be good to get to know him again now he was a fully grown man.

'I'd like that.'

'In an hour? I've got some emailing to do first and I'll make this call.'

**

Una took another call from the insurance company.

'I've told you everything I know. It's been weeks since the burglary so why haven't you processed the claim?'

She drew on a cigarette, angry with herself for taking smoking up again. As she pulled it away from her mouth, the paper stuck to her lips.

'Look my husband is a professional cello player. That instrument is irreplaceable so don't tell me it's only worth £5,000. It's insured for £30,000 for God's sake. Don't you read your own paperwork? Lost, stolen, zapped up to Uranus makes no difference to the claim and don't tell me to calm down.'

Una threw her phone across the room where it skidded against the skirting board. The feeling of being out of control was making her gut growl in pain. She stubbed out the cigarette and quickly brushed her teeth to get rid of the sour taste. The two messages from the school asking her to call them as a matter of urgency were ignored as she knew there was some more trouble she would have to sort out. Una felt as if she was in an airless house made of thick stones and no windows. There was no exit. Every time she tried to remove a stone to reach out someone ran round and sealed it up again. Lipstick and alcohol had kept her panics at bay but she became ill from drinking and her blood red tubes had lost their power since the death of her mother. She was beyond making sense of it.

She wandered around the house with a packet of antibacterial wipes and for the next few hours she waged war on germs. Scrubbing away marks on the kitchen surfaces she convinced herself that it was the first step to enlightenment.

'Mum, tell me what to do,' she said, digging fiercely into the grease on the hob. 'I just don't know what to do.' Her tears fell in fat blobs onto the shiny black surface.

CHAPTER TWENTY-THREE

All Iain could remember was that he heard a clock downstairs chiming quarter past three in the morning. His tortured cry brought Fergus bounding up the stairs, gasping for breath as he flung open the door to the attic rooms.

'What the hell…'

Clutching his chest he took one look at Iain's ashen face and terrified eyes staring into the middle distance and called Freda to bring some brandy. Iain sat transfixed in his bed, sweat soaking his face and dripping from his beard as he shouted at his invisible tormenter.

'I want a divorce,' he demanded.

The sound seemed to come from the bowels of the earth. Fergus felt as if his skin was crawling with a million ants. He'd never witnessed anyone in this state before. It was surreal like something from a Vincent Price horror film. Rooted in helplessness, he watched Freda perch on the edge of the bed and talk quietly to Iain who flung the glass of brandy towards the fireplace as he struggled to his feet.

Iain and Freda exchanged glances.

'It's me, Freda. You're safe. There's no one in the room except Fergus. Iain, can you hear me?'

Iain waved an agitated hand towards the window, his body shook with terror. He tried to make them understand that he was being watched and in his frustration he grabbed Fergus by his dressing gown collar and pulled him to the window.

'She's out there. Una and those girls. Laughing, pointing at me, waiting...'

'Calm down Iain. There's nobody there. Just the trees and the old fox who strolls across the green most nights. You've had a bad dream that's all.'

Iain clutched the windowsill as he peered into the gloom. Shapes were shifting and distorting as he tried hard to focus on Una's face which has been so clear with its grinning red mouth. Now it was gone. He craned his neck to listen to the voice that had been taunting him but there was nothing but a faint hooting of an owl in the distance. Somewhere in the depths of consciousness, Iain knew he was losing his mind.

Fergus dragged himself out of his shocked state and helped Iain into a chair, indicated with his head for Freda to leave.

'I'll bring up some tea,' she said.

As Fergus bent down to turn on the electric fire he noticed the spilt contents of a plastic folder. Shuffling them into a pile his eye caught sight of a newspaper cutting showing Iain outside the Law Courts with a man he presumed was his barrister. Another picture showed three girls in the green and black uniform of St. Hilda's. Something in their faces showed a mix of triumph and shame. Fergus felt disturbed as he scanned the report.

The two men had never discussed the case in detail as Iain had pushed it down into the archives of his memory and slammed the door.

'I know what you're thinking,' said Iain after a while.

'I'm not thinking anything other than how to get you the right sort of help. I know nothing about trauma except from bits I've read but it seems to me you've buried this for so long that it's decided to explode.'

'I didn't do anything to those girls. It was a conspiracy. They set me up to lose my job but then I keep thinking I must have done something that I don't remember.'

'You're not the first male teacher this has happened to. Remember the case of that Maths teacher in Coventry? He had to resign and leave the country in the end. His wife didn't support him because she said there's no smoke without fire or some trashy cliché. He was a mess.'

Iain's hands tapped relentless on the wooden arms of the chair. He began to make rocking movements which he felt unable to control.

'I was teaching music to year 9, girls aged between thirteen and fourteen. I'd been warned by other teachers about some of the girls but they seemed so pleasant and hardworking. Isabelle Marchand wasn't a good violinist. She had no feel for the instrument or music. Her bowing action was very lax. One day I got frustrated and stood behind her so I could guide her arm into the right position.'

Freda pushed open the door and laid down a tray. Iain paused to take a sip of tea.

'I had another lesson with her and two other girls. They came to the composition class whenever they felt like it. Emily

Hartman and Amanda Jessop-Hall. She's the daughter of that well known doctor who treats soldiers for post-traumatic stress.'

'Yeah. I've heard of him.'

'The Hartman girl dropped her manuscript paper on the floor. I bent down to pick it up for her and she started screaming I'd been looking up her skirt.'

Iain's felt his face burn. He couldn't believe he was saying these words out loud.

Fergus looked up from his cup.

'And were you?'

For a long time Iain didn't reply.

'I can't remember,' he said finally.

'Oh God.'

'The other girl, Isabelle told the deputy head I'd touched her … her … chest. She called me a dirty old man. A perv. I didn't even know what the word meant.'

'Have a biscuit,' was all Fergus could find to say.

'I didn't. Wouldn't. It's not my nature but my brain is so fuddled I keep thinking that maybe I did by accident. I was told not to apologise as it would be seen as an admission of guilt but I ignored that advice. It all got out of hand. The head said she was sure it would all blow over but I would have to be suspended pending investigations. The Marchand girl's mother decided to take legal action. I was cleared but blacklisted across the city as being a risk.'

Fergus rubbed his face and stood up. His back was aching and he was longing for his bed.

'Is this the first time you've talked about this?'

Iain shook his head.

'I was offered some counselling but it was a waste of time. Una refused to come.'

Fergus sat down again, frowning.

'What has she to do with it?'

'It was affecting our marriage. She paid the legal bills and hasn't let me forget it but I know she doesn't think I am completely blameless. I really thought I would go to prison. Young girls, older male teacher, witnesses… it's press fodder.'

'Witnesses? Good heavens man. They made it all up. They even admitted it in the end. You should have countersued for defamation and ruining your career.'

Fergus's cheeks were flaming.

'No point. Una said we'd run out of money and I didn't want any more to do with it. I thought I'd be able to put it behind me. She's never forgiven me you know.'

'But it's made you very ill, Iain. I've seen the changes in you this past year. You're exhausted with the stress and you're not yourself. You've got to get some proper help.'

Iain leant forward to refill his cup.

'It's better for everyone that I'm not here.'

'What? Freda would be furious if you left.'

'I don't mean that. I mean not here, around …'

Fergus looked at him hard.

'No, no NO. You've got the twins to think about. This isn't the answer.'

Fergus paced the floor as he enumerated all the reasons Iain needed to stop thinking like a daft idiot. An idea came to him. He grabbed the phone and pressed it into Iain's hand.

'Call the Samaritans. Talk to them. They'll talk you out of these mad ideas.'

Iain laid the phone carefully on the table. The clock struck 6 as dawn stretched and yawned her arrival.

'I don't want to talk to anybody. I've told you the story because you're one of the few people I can trust.'

'But these girls. You can't let them get away with this?'

'Fergus leave it. Please. I'm so tired I can hardly get through an hour without wanting to block it all out.'

Fergus sighed heavily.

'Look, go back to bed and get some shut eye. We can talk tomorrow. Maybe if we get this cello back you'll feel better.'

'It no longer matters,' said Iain as he turned over and closed his eyes.

***

Una dialled the number of the insurance company, still pursuing the cello claim.

'I've already been through this a hundred times with you,' she said to the pedantic claims officer. 'You've got the paperwork so what's the delay?'

'There's a time delay of a month to see if the cello turns up.'

'Turns up? TURNS UP? We're not talking about some wayward teenager. This is my husband's livelihood. It's not going to catch the bus and walk back in the house is it?'

'Ms Carrington, we've had some information we need to look into. I can't say more than this. Dr. Millar did take out a more recent insurance policy so we need to talk to him personally. Perhaps you would ask him to call.'

'Yes I know that but I play the bloody premiums. Get me your manager.'

'I'm sorry but if you continue to be abusive I shall end this call.'

The line buzzed in Una's ear. She strode into the kitchen and picking up a pile of plates from the draining board, she threw them against the wall. The pressure to pay down her debt was building but whichever way she turned she faced a brick wall. The daily fear had attacked her stomach causing it to throw up a vile tasting acid into her throat.

She sucked on her finger where a fragment of crockery had caught the skin. Pacing the house, she picked up things, put them down, shuffled through paper work ignoring the post that had piled up on the hall floor and the flashing light on the answering machine. Wearily she sat on the staircase, leaning her head against the wall. Her mother's face swam before her. Una had once boasted that grief was for the weak but as pulled her jumper down over her knees she felt her body burst in an explosion of feelings. To Una it felt like a sudden storm that the weather forecast had failed to mention. She held onto the bannister as she rocked against its force. The face of a young boy came into view. Una screamed.

'I didn't do any of those things Daddy. He slipped in the paddling pool. Oh God, please go away. '

In the earthquake of her mounting grief, Una slid down the stairs and curled into a ball on the cold, unforgiving floor.

'You believed those boys over your own daughter. I didn't try to drown him. Mum knew that yet you walked out on us because you said I was a dangerous kid to be around.' Una sobbed out the words and she wrapped her arms around her heaving chest.

It was dark by the time she opened her eyes. Dreams of her childhood left her shivering as she moved slowly into the kitchen. She took a bottle of wine from the fridge then returned it to the rack. She had no stomach for it. Anxiety constricted her throat as she bent over the sink to catch her breath as the feeling of being smothered became overwhelming. Una breathed in deeply through her nose and closing her eyes breathed out slowly through her mouth. She felt her head slowly clearing. Splashing water over her face, she set about cleaning the kitchen and making coffee. As the sense of control returned, Una felt calmer and switched on the radio for company.

***

Iain had woken from the longest sleep he'd ever had. The feeling of renewal was a shock to him as he half expected the new buoyancy to evaporate.

'Is the Wolverhampton concert still on tomorrow?

Fergus replied through a mouthful of crumpet.

'Are you up for playing?'

'Yes, I think so. I'm very hungry,' he added with a sheepish look in Freda's direction.

Iain's eyes glistened as he threw himself into the practice session for the Bach Concertos despite the ache in his fingers.

'Damn fine performance, said Fergus on the way home. That pizzicato was perfection.'

Iain shuffled uncomfortably in his seat. He didn't think he's played well at all but he had to admit it had restored some sense of normality to his life.

'Tom said there was a message on the Stolen Strings website. I don't know what exactly but we can check it out.'

'Plonker,' he yelled as someone cut in front of him. 'Shall we grab something at that new place on the Hagley Road? Tom said he'd meet us there.'

Fergus spun into an illegal U turn triggering the rage of drivers behind him. Iain sank into his seat. He could feel his mood plummeting. He tried to block the volley of swearing by putting his hands over his ears. His nerves jangled as if being hit by an electric current. Pulling his shirt collar open, Iain dabbed the moisture from his throat.

The moment they entered the heaving restaurant, Iain turned back to the door. Fergus grabbed his sleeve.

'You sit over there in that alcove and I'll get the drinks.'

He plonked two pints of beer on the table spilling some down his trousers.

'Funny place this. What's with the Hobbit theme?'

'I think Tolkien used to come here when it was something else.' Iain looked round at the painted characters and snippets from the book.

'There's some funny folk around. I heard you can go to these Middle Earth events at Sarehole Mill and dress up as one of the characters.'

Fergus took a long sip of his drink as he scanned the menu.

'I really fancy the fish and chips but Freda's on to me about losing weight.' He sighed as he patted his protruding stomach. 'I could rip a cow in half I'm so famished.'

Iain's appetite had left him so he chose soup and a sandwich. He shrugged out of his jacket and pushed himself further into the corner out of sight.

The student waitress who brought their food smiled and asked Iain if he needed anything.

Iain jumped.

'No, no thank you,' he said quickly.

'Enjoy your meal.'

Iain was about to ask for some brown sauce but the words

stuck to the roof of his mouth. He felt the room sway. His hand reached for the edge of the table as the faces of the people around him turned into snarling caricatures with exaggerated features.

'Iain? Are you alright?'

'I told you I was being watched.'

Fergus turned round to see a young woman with long black hair and a stud in her eyebrow. She was staring at Iain. Amanda Jessop-Hall put her hand to her mouth as the colour drained from her face.

'Dr. Millar. Oh my God!'

In her panic to escape she knocked over a chair, sending a tray of drinks on a table behind hurtling to the floor. A flustered twenty something, blonde streaks through his hair and a Manager badge slapped to his chest, hurried over.

'Mand, clean this mess up.' He pasted on a smile and turned to Fergus.

'Everything alright with your meal?'

He turned to Iain.

'If this gentleman isn't well maybe you should leave. There's nothing to pay.'

He looked round anxiously at customers waiting to be seated.

'There's nothing wrong with him. He's had a shock.' Fergus eyed his chips wistfully. 'If you want to be useful a glass of water would help.'

Iain swayed as he stood up, holding on the table for support. He glanced at the people watching the scene and saw disgust in their eyes. His skin felt as if it was covered in a thin coating of slime which he was desperate to scrub away.

'I'm going,' he mumbled as he pushed past the anxious looking manager.

'Don't let her drive you out. I don't know who she is but I've a good idea.'

Fergus followed him out in the half light and grabbed his arm as Iain felt his knee joints suddenly fold. Once in the car, Iain closed his eyes as the scenario played out yet again. He tore at his hair as he fought to recall the truth about that day. He knew it was naïve to even touch her hand as he adjusted her bowing action yet the voice, now insistent in his ear, told him he'd wanted to touch her, that he'd got a thrill from being so close to her breasts.

'No NO, I didn't, I didn't', he cried convinced that he was going mad.

Fergus was at a loss. He put the car into gear and drove carefully towards home. Half a mile before Woodbourne House, Iain told him to stop.

'I'm going home tonight. I want to see my wife.'

'You're in no fit state.'

'YES. Just stop here.'

Fergus sighed and pulled to the kerb.

'Well I'm waiting here.'

'No, go home Fergus. Please.'

'Fine but I will be back in two hours to pick you up. No argument.'

Iain shuffled up to the front door and rang the bell. Una appeared, a sour expression on her thin face. Fergus watched them go inside and with a heavy heart headed for home.

CHAPTER TWENTY-FOUR

Iain and Una stood awkwardly in the kitchen as if waiting for the understudy's prompt. He searched her face for something to tell him she'd missed him but her eyes told him nothing.

'How've you been?' Iain asked, picking up a couple of unopened circulars from music groups.

Una bent down to open the dishwasher and pulled out two clean mugs.

'Fine,' she said.

'I was sorry about your mother. Even when you know it's imminent it's still hard to take in. You remember when…'

'Look Iain. Forget the small talk. What do you want? When are you going to come back and face your responsibilities? That's all I want to know.'

Una arched her back to release the tension in her spine.

Iain eased himself into a chair, ignoring the jibe. The cat flap rattled announcing the arrival of Beethoven who with a loud meow jumped onto Iain's lap.

'I wanted to see you.'

'If you're after money, you're out of luck,' Una scoffed, putting his mug of coffee on the table.

'I don't want money. I want us to resolve these problems together. Like couples do. Through talking and planning.' He looked at Una, desperation filling his tired eyes.

'I need you to tell me the truth about my cello. It's the only way I can make money.'

'Pennies aren't going to solve this mess. I know as much as you do. Is this why you've come here? To harass and bully me? That's what the police have been doing and the insurance people. Talk about being guilty on demand.'

'I've no energy to bully anybody,' he said, his hand pressing onto his throbbing left cheek. He needed an urgent dental appointment but that cost money. Freda's clove remedy hadn't helped. As soon as he mentioned it he watched her face darken.

She leaned over him, hands on the arms of his chair as her eyes bored into his. A nerve at the corner of her unmade up lips twitched. Iain could feel her stale breath on his cheeks. He pushed back deeper into his chair.

'I don't have any money. Which bit of that don't you get? Maybe it's you that stole your own cello. Maybe that's why the insurance company won't pay out. Poverty stricken musician and all that. It's been done before no doubt.'

Iain leapt to his feet.

'Don't be so bloody ridiculous. That's a wicked thing to say. You're the one with the morals of a pimp. What worries me most is that Johanna has started to act like you.'

As soon as the words were out he wanted to push them back in his mouth. An acrid taste surged into the back of his throat as he struggled to swallow. His stomach was contracting with fear as he waited in anxious expectation for the blow he was sure would come. He'd excused her behaviour all through their marriage putting it down to a fiery temper and a model of behaviour set by her own parents, but despite his fragile mental state he wasn't going to be bullied any more.

Una hesitated before moving away from him to pour the last few drops of wine into a glass. She walked around the kitchen rhythmically punching a fist into a palm. The house waited with baited breath.

'If you want to put things right then you help me dig us out of the enormous debt we're in. Get some happy pills then sign on at the job centre. Cleaning, driving, delivery, whatever you can get. Being unemployed is not an option Iain. It's embarrassing having you lounging around feeling sorry for yourself. I've not been able to focus on my own work which is why the business has all but collapsed.'

Bemused at her lack of reaction he felt some confidence returning.

'You can't blame me for that,' Iain said quietly running his hand over the cat's tail. 'You have to take responsibility for your own actions Una if I am to come back here at all.'

She swung round and before Iain realised what was about to happen, felt the sting of her knuckles against his cheek. He fell back into his chair banging his knee against the table edge.

'Who do you think you're talking to?' Her face pressed into his. She grabbed his wrist and twisted it until he cried out.

'All I'm saying is that we have to start from the beginning and work as a team. I won't be your scapegoat anymore. We've both got to be honest with each other.'

'Oh well that's rich coming from you. You lied about what happened at St. Hilda's and I chose to believe you. I know you lied because I've heard other versions of events since.'

Despite the pain in his legs, Iain jumped out of his chair. He felt his fingers tingling with the urge to fix them around her neck. The voices urged him on.

As she tried to step past him, he pulled back his shoulders and blocked her path, pushing her back with hands that seemed to find a new strength.

Una growled as she fell against a rack of coat hooks. A pain shot through her shoulder.

'You're a bloody idiot Iain. I'm not frightened of you. I could crush you if I wanted. Just stop provoking me. You force me to slap you to bring you to your senses.'

Iain grabbed her arms and pinned them against the door.

'*Kill her*,' said the voice.

'I'm sick of your broken record. Sick of you undermining and threatening me when you feel like it. You've controlled everything in our lives and I've gone along with it but not anymore Una. Not anymore.'

Iain clamped his lips. He was becoming afraid of his own power surges. He felt them as burning coals behind his breastbone which gathered heat and whooshed up into face and hands causing his mind to explode.

'Oh the little man has spoken, urged on by fatty Fergus no doubt.'

She felt her chest collapse inwards as his pupils widened with a glazed look. For a moment he appeared as someone she didn't know so sinister was the grimace on his face.

Iain pushed closer to her, resting his hands on her neck.

'Go on, go on, we dare you. It's what she deserves.'

'Shut up,' he said, slowly articulating each word. She watched, petrified, as his face took on different expressions but it was the dark empty void in his eyes which frightened her the most. It was as if Iain had been abducted and an alien was staring at her through the sockets.

When he began to engage in an incoherent dialogue with some invisible person, she smelt the stench of real fear in her nostrils. Taking advantage of his distraction, Una bent double and pushed through his barricade. Iain stopped talking, pulled his focus back onto his wife and grabbed her hair.

'Where do you think you're going? You're going to listen to me for once.'

He shoved her into his den and onto the sofa. She'd never experienced Iain as anything other than meek and mild.

'If I was a real man I would force myself on you right now. You've not been a proper wife for years and I've put up with it. You're a pathetic excuse for a mother. My children are frightened of you and James even said he hated you last time he was here. Are you proud of yourself Una?'

She attempted to pull herself up into a sitting position, noticing that the sleeve of her top had been torn. Her arms felt as if they'd been put through a mangle. She stopped fighting in the hope that he would let go. Didn't they tell you to do that in a rape situation? That it's the struggle that gets men excited? Or was that a myth? Maybe not fighting him off was giving him the message she condoned his violence. Her head swarmed with long archived bits of information.

'You're just a self-hating piece of crap Iain, projecting your inadequacies onto me. You've obviously lost your mind with all this insane raving. You'd better go.'

Iain felt an electric shock through the arms which were pinning her down. He shot backwards and looked around him. His hair was like damp thatch. Una watched the wild look in his eyes fade.

'You have no idea how upset and miserable I am. How deeply hurt and humiliated by what's happened to me these past few years yet I've tried to keep it to myself. Poison which goes in will explode at some point. If you'd helped me…'

Una's jaw physically dropped. She pulled herself to her feet, nursing her right arm.

'Helped you? What do you think I've been doing? If I'd divorced you where would you have ended up? I stayed with you to make sure you were alright.'

'Not because you had any love for me? Just because you didn't want to see me on the streets?'

Una opened her mouth then closed it again. He'd taken the

words out of her head.

'I can't sleep at night for worrying about money, the twins, your madness, the responsibility I have to shoulder alone. You bury your head in music so you don't have to face reality. Of course I'm angry with you Iain. Who wouldn't be? It's me who's the victim here.'

'You, you, all about you!' Iain lurched towards her again as a new wave of unbridled anger gripped him. 'We've got two children who are distressed but you don't care about them. You don't listen to what they want. Did you know that Johanna went missing a few weeks ago? No, I thought not. I didn't tell you because I knew how you'd react. Morag went down to Edinburgh to help sort it out. She's going to take the children to Inverness for a while. She is at least a proper mother.'

Una squealed like a wounded cat and grabbing clumps of his hair, head butted him in the face. Blood spurted from his nose and onto his shirt.

'And you're a fucking pervert,' she yelled in his face. 'You're disgusting.'

Iain limped in agony to the front door. Slowly he eased his arms into the sleeves on his coat. His shaking hands carefully positioned his hat. His black scarf was arranged around his face. With a shaking hand and a look in his eyes which reflected back the broken man he felt he'd become, he said, calmly and without emotion, 'True colours always come out. Eventually. Now I know how you really think and feel. I'm going to leave. I should have realised before now the sort of person you really are. You just want to control me, the children, everything and I don't want it anymore. You're not a wife. Not for me anyway.'

***

The threat of rain reflected Iain's mood as he tramped into the city centre, pausing occasionally to reconfigure the cotton handkerchief that was pressed to his nose. The bleeding had stopped but his face continued to throb. He hoped that when he arrived at the dental hospital they would treat him as an emergency and not charge him. When he discovered that he had to make an appointment through some agency he went ballistic. He called Fergus, his whole body trembling.

'Iain I can't understand what you're saying. Calm down a bit or you'll end up in the cop shop and not the dentist's. I will sort it out for you. Where are you?'

'I don't know,' Iain sobbed into his phone. 'I don't know what's happening to me.'

Fergus ran his hand through what was left of his wild red hair.

'Find a café, get a strong coffee then call me back. OK?'

Iain stared blindly ahead of him, trying to recall a landmark but the buildings, the cars and people all merged into a blob of nothing.

'Iain? OK? Coffee then ring me?'

'OK.'

Iain ambled around in a circle, afraid to cross any roads. He clung to clusters of people crossing from Moor Street Station to go under the underpass to the refurbished New Street. Seized with an idea of getting on a train and going up to Scotland, he realised he had no money. Rustling in his pocket he found a few coins which he dropped into a busker's paper cup.

'Thanks mate,' said the man as he began to strum his battered guitar and sing along to some tunes from the sixties. Iain listened to him, appreciating the music and the deep timbre of his voice.

'How did you get here?' asked Iain, when the busker paused.

'You mean on the streets? Like everyone. A mistake then I lost it all. Except this beauty.' He broke into some wild flamenco which had Iain tapping his feet.

'That was fantastic. You should be playing professionally.'

'Me and all the other buskers,' he laughed.

Iain stood back as people rushing past almost knocked over his cup.

'Do many people give you money? Sorry, that was a rude thing to ask someone.'

'More like coffee and food. They probably think I am going to buy drugs or something if they give money. I do ok.'

'Are you er… homeless?'

'No fixed abode. Yeah mate. That's why I can't get benefits. Why are you so interested? You a social worker or something?'

Iain shook his head, realising his toothache had eased.

'I'm a musician like you. Cello.'

'Cool. Sorry mate but…'

'Sure. See you again.'

'If you're bringing sarnies, please no chicken. I'm a veggie.'

Iain raised his hand as he left.

'I'm Simon by the way,' the man called. 'I used to be an accountant.'

Iain's thoughts were interrupted by the chirruping of his phone.

'You were going to call me. Have you discovered where you are?'

'New Street station. Fergus, I met this really interesting man.'

'Never mind that. I've got you an appointment with the dental hospital for tomorrow morning. Now I am coming into town to pick you up. Tom's insisting we call this number he keeps picking up from the Facebook campaign.'

'But I've had an idea.'

The line buzzed in his ear. Iain went into the first café he found in the Bull Ring and taking his hot chocolate to a corner table he felt his mood lift. He decided against telling Fergus his plan after all. He wouldn't understand. Iain wanted to go back to speak to Simon again and take him a veggie box from the café but he didn't have the money. Maybe a cake he thought. He wanted to know more about his life on the streets. No hassle, free to move where he wanted, play his guitar to suit his mood. It sounded ideal. He imagined himself picking up a cheap cello and playing jazz. People would gather to listen and toss coins into his hat. He'd smile benignly as they tapped their feet. Simon had suddenly become his hero.

Fergus called. 'I'm in town. Where the feck are you? You're like will o the wisp.'

'Park down the side of Debenhams and I'll meet you there. I was going to get the train back to Bournville.'

Fergus swung the car on the pavement to get off the yellow lines. A snogging couple gave him a mouthful.

'You could have killed us, you tosser.'

Iain had barely shut the door before Fergus pulled out into the traffic, not bothering to indicate.

'You've had us worried. You've got quite a shiner. Have you seen your face?'

Iain pulled down the sun visor to look in the mirror. He knew that it was pointless to lie anymore.

'Bit of a mess,' he muttered.

'A bit is an understatement.'

'I probably deserved it,' was all he was prepared to say.

CHAPTER TWENTY-FIVE

By the time they arrived back in Bournville, Iain had lost his nerve to make the phone call. Maybe it was a trick; a scam to lure him into a trap. Maybe it was a set up by those girls. Part of his brain was telling him he was being foolish but the other, more insistent part where the voices lived told him something different.

Fergus handed him the crumpled piece of paper on which Tom had scribbled the number.

'Well? Are you going to do it or shall I?'

Iain carefully pressed the numbers and his magnified heartbeat echoed in his ears. His sore gum began to pulsate with the climb of his blood pressure.

'Record the conversation,' Fergus hissed. 'Press that button. That red one. There.'

After listening to it ring out for what seemed to be several minutes, Iain was about to hang up when a gritty voice said, 'Yes?'

'Er, My name's Iain Millar. Dr. Millar. I'm a cellist.'

The voice waited.

'My cello has gone missing and I believe you might know something about it. Tom O'Neal gave me your number.'

'Never heard of him.'

'It's an Old English.' Iain went on to describe it.

'Gotya. A dealer rang me about this a couple of weeks ago as he knows I buy for the overseas market. Mainly China. Are you saying this is your cello? I don't handle stolen goods if that's what you're implying.'

'No, no I'm not but I want it back. You see it's got sentimental value.'

The man laughed throatily.

'It's got more than that. Look, you need to speak to Curtis. He might have sold it by now though.'

'Where can I find him?'

'Now wait a minute. Are the police involved?'

Fergus, whose ear had almost attached itself to the phone, shook his head and mouthed No.

'No,' Iain replied dutifully.

'You sure because if they are I know nothing about this. Ok?'

'OK.'

'I did tell him at the time that something smelled nasty about this and I wouldn't touch it. He said he was contacted by some vicious tongued female who said it was hers.'

The man gave him a contact number then hung up.

'I doubt that's his real name,' said Fergus, wandering into the kitchen in search of food. Since Freda had gone away on some drama course his stomach was losing the will to live.

'I think I'll do a bit of practice on that cello you hired for me.'

'Good. It's about time. What about Curtis?'

'I'll do it afterwards when I feel a bit calmer.'

'Elgar?'

'Hmm. Maybe a bit of jazz for a change. Oh that thing I was going to tell you.' Iain turned to look out over the village green.

'Earth to Iain.'

'I need a solicitor. I'm divorcing Una.'

Fergus didn't know whether to cheer or commiserate.

***

Fergus strained his ears to hear the snappy rhythm coming from an instrument that prided itself on its solemnity. Something seemed wrong about it and about the weird noises Iain was making. Was he actually slapping the body of it like an overenthusiastic double bass player? He stirred sugar into his coffee losing count of the number of spoonfuls as he stood at the foot of the stairs.

Iain was enjoying himself. He swung the cello round on its spike, plucked the strings to a tune that danced around in his head and laughed crazily as it all seemed to make sense. To him at least. Exhausted he flopped on to the bed and spread eagled his arms, laughing at whatever popped into his head.

Two days later

'Hey mate. What you up to?'

Simon was sitting on his new fold up chair, a gift from one of his fans, rolling a cigarette.

'I've come to join you.'

'Whaaaat? Cool. What can you play?'

'Jazz. Listen.'

Iain unlocked the case and pulled out the cello which he'd covered with homemade stickers.

'Right. Cool cello.'

Iain's performance attracted a few people who clapped and threw some coppers in Simon's hat.

'That's some gig. Let's blend the guitar.'

Iain's euphoria rocketed as coins were tossed into the hat. He plucked and bowed and swung like his life depended on it.

'Hey, you look a bit flushed. Sit down and take a break. I'll go solo.'

'No. I'm fine.' Iain was becoming agitated at being told to stop.

'Coffee break then. Let's spend the takings. You pluck away till I get back. Something soothing eh? What about one of your Elgar pieces?'

Iain agreed and mopping his brow flopped onto the chair. He spent a long time preparing his bow. Elgar seemed to be from a different lifetime. Unable to remember anything he scraped out a few notes and got told, 'Go home Grandad,' by some teenagers. With his coffee he took his dose of antibiotics and suddenly felt tired.

'Where do you sleep at night?' he asked Simon.

'Depends. Sometimes a shelter if I get enough money. Mostly around the Alex Theatre. There's quite a few rough sleepers so it feels safer. More like a community.'

Iain was beaming.

'Mate, it's not funny.'

'Sorry, sorry, no. I wasn't laughing. I've had an idea.'

'What's that then?' Simon tentatively sipped his coffee through the hole in the plastic lid. Who had lips shaped like a pillar box he wondered?

'Can I sleep with you tonight?'

Simon moved back so quickly he fell over his open guitar case sending coins and shopping trolley tokens spinning on their felt bed. His face changed shape and colour as he put his hands up to keep Iain at a distance.

'Whoaaa mate. I thought there was something a bit off with you. I'm not… don't do… you know…'

Iain felt the sweat form a necklace across his temple. He pulled out a bunch of crumpled tissues and carefully folded them into a neat square.

'No. Neither am I,' he said in measured tones. 'What I meant was I would like to spend the night with you… in a shop door way or the hostel. To see, well, um,' Iain turned his face away to cough, 'what it's like.'

'Mate. You go home now. You need some proper grub inside you and a good rest. Get those cuts and bruises looked at and that tooth. Your cheek looks swollen.'

Iain's humiliation was complete. Not even a homeless busker wanted to spend any time with him.

'I didn't mean to be offensive. It's just that…'

'You'd be surprised how many men come up to me and say they dream of a life on the streets away from the world. Fantasy or delusion but after one night they soon scuttle back home. I wouldn't have left if… well… it doesn't matter. It's been a long time and anyway,' Simon packed away his guitar and snapped the locks, 'it's time for me to move on. I've got enough to go up to Manchester. Here, take your share.'

The green canvas chair was folded into his carrying case which Simon slung over his shoulder.

'Come on, you've earned it. You're good. Very good.'

Iain shook his head without making eye contact. He'd made himself look a fool and grossly misunderstood yet again. He watched Simon walk away the length of the underpass, tossing his grubby scarf over his shoulder, his long fingers offering a semblance of a wave before he turned the corner out of sight.

He shuffled his way through knots of people in New Street looking out for a spot where he could sit and play some soft classical. It didn't matter about the money. He just needed to be amongst normal people. He found himself in Centenary Square by the 'Real Birmingham Family' statue that had caused so much controversy.

Sitting on a low wall, he closed his eyes and began to play some bits of Bach he remembered. Quiet applause made him open them again. Some silver coins lay at his feet. With mixed feelings and an uncertain smile of appreciation, he picked them up and put them in his pocket. The dark shadows which followed him seemed to slip out of sight as Iain thought about where he could pitch up and chat to others like him. He was sure they were out there. Men like him who needed some peace of mind and needed to talk and be heard.

He played until the commuters poured out of offices and shops, his fingertips raw, his muscles taut and painful. He'd heard his phone vibrate several times in his pocket so he pulled it out, flipped it open and turned it off. Biting the wrapping off a packet of biscuits he winced as a sharp pain shot through his jaw. He swallowed the last two painkillers with a swig from his bottle of flavoured water and hoped the pain would subside at least enough to get him through the night.

It was late when he found some people in Pigeon Park swigging from cider bottles and trying to get comfortable on broken benches. The women dragged heavily on cigarettes, bearing their blackened and broken teeth in greeting.

'You got any pop?'

'No. Just water.' Iain patted his pocket from which a bottle of Highland Spring poked its neck.

'So wachyo a doin 'ere?'

Iain smiled and sat down next to her. The stench was overpowering. He stood up, ostensibly to ease the crick in his back.

'Sorry to trouble you. I'll just get some shut eye over there.' He pointed to empty bench.

'Ere. You can get some cardboard from the back of the Arcade.'

The woman's yellowed eyes fixed on him.

'Yo ay done this afore an ya?'

'Er. No'

'Thought not. Well,' she lit a cigarette from the end of the one she'd just finished, 'you'll be ok here. The dead won't bother ya.'

She threw back her head and swallowed hard from a can.

'Is that your coffin you're carrying?' Growls of laughter rumbled from the men who paused in their drinking to watch him. Iain clung to the cello as he went in search of some covering for the night. People wandered through the park from their nights out in the wine bars or a late night at one of the Colmore Row firms, taking care to skirt the area for fear of being contaminated.

Homelessness is catching, thought Iain as he tossed and turned to find some comfortable position for sleep. Lying on his back he closed his eyes and thought of the twins. For once he was glad they were not at home to witness the shame he'd brought on the family. He deserved punishment he thought and waited for the voices to agree but they were silent.

'Come on. Speak out. You usually have an opinion,' he shouted into the still night air.

'Shut yer cake-hole,' a man's voice called back.

Iain sat up to search his pockets for the last bit of a sandwich somebody had given him. Hunger bore into his stomach like a pneumatic drill but Iain knew no amount of food would fill it. He'd planned this night with a sense of heady release but the images of his family, his failure to support them and his desire to release himself and them from the ongoing torture had taken on psychedelic proportions. Rubbing his hand over his unshaven chin, he felt dirty outside and in. The shirt he'd worn for two days had stiff patches of dried sweat under the arms. The pocket in his corduroy trousers was torn from constantly pulling out and pushing back his phone. He tried to picture himself in his concert clothes but he couldn't grasp the image for long enough to make it real. As the cathedral clock chimed three, Iain lay down his head and wept.

It was the woman who found him in the morning with half his face set in a stiff mask. Giving him a rough shake, she shouted to wake him up. He opened his eyes and looked at her blankly. As he tried to sit up, his right arm felt numb. Rubbing it, he allowed her to help him to his feet before collapsing again.

'You've been on the pop,' she said with a hint of accusation.

Iain's words tumbled out in a jumble of sounds.

A passer-by on his way to work, stopped to look at Iain. He bent over him, checking his pulse and looking into his eyes. He made a quick, authoritative call.

'This man's had a stroke. Do you know him?'

He turned to the street sleepers who had huddled around Iain's pitch.

'Never seen him before. Looks a posh bloke. Not one of us.'

'I've ordered an ambulance and I shall wait here till it arrives.' He turned to people who stopped to gawp and told them to get on with their business. Once the paramedics pulled up, he had a quiet word with them then hurried away.

***

'Bloody hell, Freda. I've just had a call from Una. It seems Iain's been sleeping rough with the winos and has had a stroke. He's in Heartlands.'

'You mean he didn't come home last night?'

'Not here. And clearly not there either.'

Freda slapped down her tea towel and untied her apron.

'You are not making any sense. I go away for a weekend and look what happens.'

'Don't blame me over this. I'm not his keeper.'

Fergus flopped into his chair and sighed heavily.

'Let's not fight about this. I'm going to the hospital to see what's what.'

His wife put her arms around his neck and kissed him lightly on the top of his head.

'I'm sorry,' she said. 'Shall I come with you?'

'No. He won't talk if you're there. I really don't know what's going to happen this time. He was supposed to ring this Curtis bloke about the cello but... Oh I don't know. It's a bloody mess. Can you call Steve and ask him to conduct the practice tonight and to sort out substitutes for Iain and me. I'll be back as soon as I can.'

As he pushed the key into the ignition, his phone galloped into the William Tell overture. It was Una. She left yet another message. Fergus couldn't help but hear desperation in her voice. For a fleeting second he felt sorry for her.

CHAPTER TWENTY-SIX

The first thought Una had when she woke up, fully clothed on the kitchen floor, was that she would never drink alcohol again. She heaved as she noticed streaks of vomit down her black cashmere top, barely making it to the bathroom before she disgorged the rest of the sour bile. Flinching and squirming as the acid burned her tongue and gums, she scrubbed her teeth to get rid of the vile taste but it stuck with her. She bent her head over the basin and closed her eyes as the cooling water washed over her face, mingling with the tears that pooled in her eyes.

The first stirrings of dawn brought a realisation that she was finished. The pile of papers that had arrived by personal service were strewn over the floor but she didn't need to read them to know that their home was being repossessed and she was being sued for bankruptcy. Yet as she read and reread the letter from some one-man band solicitor in Selly Oak, it was the fact that Iain had filed for divorce that had upset her the most. She was sure that Fergus had been behind it.

Waiting for the coffee to trickle through the machine, she could feel the anger building up from her gut, swishing more acid into her throat. The coffee tasted so vile she threw it down the sink before reaching for the phone. Iain's mobile went to voicemail yet again. She screamed and was about smash the cup against the wall before realising that she needed to change tack. She hoped Freda would be home.

'Hello Freda. It's Una.'

Unnerved by the lack of response she bumbled along.

'Is Iain there please?'

'No he's not.'

'Ok. Do you know when he'll be back? The twins are wanting to talk to him.'

'Well you have our number. They are very welcome to call here.'

Una stared at the clock for inspiration. It was not even 8am.

'Sorry for calling you so early. I didn't realise the time.'

'Is that all? Would you like to hear that your husband is back in hospital? He's had a stroke?'

Una prickled at the unmistakable criticism.

'Am I the last to know what's happening to my family?' she snapped, all pretence at being friendly dissipating.

The line snapped shut.

She called back.

'I don't like being cut off like that Freda. I want to know where Iain is. Why haven't they rung me?'

'I've no idea. Try Heartlands.'

Una showered quickly, threw her dirty clothes in the washing machine, picked out the papers that Iain needed to sign and set the satnav for Bordesley Green. It was an area she knew only by repute so decided to take a taxi instead. As she got out, she caught sight of Fergus having a smoke in the designated shelter.

Marching up to him she said in acid tones, 'What the hell are you playing it? Why did nobody tell me about Iain?'

'Not my responsibility Una.' He ground the butt of the cigarette against the wall before tossing it in the bin.

'You're his friend aren't you? You're the one that took him away from his family? Damn right you have a responsibility.'

Una felt her cheeks blazing as she chiselled her eyes into his. Unable to articulate her anger she stormed through the entrance and demanded to see her husband.

'I'm sorry Mrs. Millar but your husband can't see anyone today.'

'Don't be bloody ridiculous. I'm his wife.'

'Please keep your voice down. Let me check on him. Wait here please.'

Una circled the floor to keep the nausea at bay. The smell of sickness reminded her of Isla and how she'd failed her in her last few years. Had she failed Iain too? The idea was nonsense she told herself. It was Iain who had failed himself yet a pin prick of reality was making itself felt. The thinnest of cracks was beginning to appear in her delusion. She pushed it away and straightening her back followed the nurse through to where Iain lay perfectly still in a side room overlooking the garden. Una was horrified at how shrunken he seemed. His face was grey with a knot of burst blood vessels down one cheek. Una stretched her fingers towards them but held back waiting for him to acknowledge her presence.

Pulling up the one visitor chair she leaned forward and said,

'Iain. Iain it's Una. I've come to see how you are.'

As soon as the words were out she felt gauche and foolish. Is this what their marriage had become? A vacuous exchange of pleasantries? Una pressed her hand to her bare lips. She hadn't been all that pleasant to him. As she transferred her gaze to the drip in his arm and the various monitors by the bed, it was becoming clearer that in fact she'd been anything but a wife.

Iain moved slightly and opened his eyes. One eye seemed permanently dilated and it fixed on her. Una bent to pull out the papers from her bag but stopped. He wouldn't understand what she was talking about.

'What happened?' she asked.

Iain tried to shake his head but winced with the effort.

'The nurse said you'd been sleeping rough. I don't understand. I thought you were with Fergus.'

Still Iain said nothing but watched her hands move around her face, into her bag and finally settle on her lap.

'There was no need for any of this. We could have moved away, taken the twins out of school, started again in a new county, maybe gone back to Scotland so you could have taught again.'

She thought she spotted a mere flicker of acknowledgement. Her thoughts were scrambling as she tried to form them into sentences. Leaning forward she touched his hand and was shocked when he slid his away.

'Sello,' he said.

'Sell up you mean? That's what I want to talk to you about.'

The bed cover twitched as Iain moved his legs.

'Sello.'

'I don't know what you mean.' Una struggled to keep her voice calm.

'Time to leave Mrs. Millar. Your husband is getting tired.'

'But I've only just arrived.'

'And you were lucky I allowed you five minutes with him. You might want to take this back home with you.'

The nurse clattered down the corridor in her sensible navy shoes and brought back an old cello with two of the strings missing and a broken fret.

'That's not my husband's. His cello …' Una felt her heart stop. Acid shot into the back of her throat. The nurse deftly passed her a sick bowl.

'Follow me. I can see it's been a shock. Dr. Millar was lucky. A consultant from the dental hospital found him laid out in the churchyard with all the winos. He's had a mild stroke but he'll recover physically.'

She accepted a plastic cup of water but it did nothing to ease the hot and cold shivers which flashed through her body. For a moment she felt she was about to faint. Flinging off her coat, she ran down the corridors and through the automatic doors marked exit. Fergus had gone.

Tom was waiting by the car which was parked carelessly across two spaces in the hospital visitor parking. He'd been on the phone to Curtis Longton threatening to get the police involved then promising not to if he was prepared to see them that day.

'Dad, you look wrecked.'

'Thanks son. So where are we going exactly?'

'We're to meet him at an address in Putney at 4pm.'

'But I'm starving.'

'I'll drive as far as Northampton services. Mum packed some bits for us.'

Tom tossed a plastic container onto the Fergus' lap and started the engine.

'I hope he's not going to go flaky on us and disappear. He sounded weird on the phone. What are you going to say to him?'

With a mouth full of cheese and chutney, Fergus mumbled that he'd make it up as he went along. At the services they stopped for coffee but neither felt like food. Fergus was still suffering from indigestion from the hospital bacon baguette. Tom was eager to get the business over with. Something was bothering him about his conversation with Mr. Longford although he did feel a bit excited at the idea his social media campaign had given them such a strong lead.

'I'll drive this bit into London. I know it I think. Forget the satnav. We don't want to end up in the Thames do we?'

'Supposing he wants a shed load of money to get it back? We don't have it.'

Fergus set his mouth in concentration as he navigated lane changing into fast flowing traffic. In Birmingham he was used to crawling and gear grinding, shouting his impatience when the mood took him but as they approached London he felt less brazen. A bit scared if he was honest.

Flustered and sweating he barked at Tom to find a parking space.

'Bloody unbelievable these charges.'

Eventually he got lucky and many manoeuvres later sandwiched them in between a Porsche and a white van.

Fergus beamed.

'Well I got us in but I can't promise to get us out,' he chuckled, dragging a piece of old rag down the front of his jacket. The stain was adamant it wasn't going anywhere.

Balancing on the broken top step of three, Tom pressed the bell marked Longton. They waited. He pushed again. Nothing. Fergus got the feeling they were being scrutinised from a top floor window. He stepped back, almost falling, and was proved right.

When the door buzzed open, they edged their way up a narrow flight of wooden steps which seemed to extend into the ether.

'ID.'

'Dad?'

'What. Oh. Driving Licence.'

Fergus went through all his pockets until he found his wallet.

They followed the tall, lugubrious character into a high ceilinged room bursting with string instruments. All top names, all extremely valuable. Fergus' eye locked onto the violins; Stradivari, Luthiers, Guarneri and Amarti cellos. His eye travelled to the darkest corner where Iain's beloved cello lay. Forlorn, unloved and afraid it seemed to reach out to him.

'That's it. That's the one,' he shrieked through his fit of coughing. He couldn't remember when he'd taken so many stairs in one go.

'You're not the owner so I can't do business with you. You said you wanted proof. Now you have it.'

Curtis smoothed down his clipped moustache with the side of his thumb.

'Here's the proof of ownership and a letter from Dr. Millar authorising me to deal with it,' said Fergus.

The outstretched papers were ignored.

'This puts us all in a difficult position Mr. O'Neal.'

'Fergus.' He stretched out his hand but there was no attempt at cordiality. 'This is my son Tom.'

'I agreed to pay £13,000 for this instrument for a client in China.'

'£13,000? That's outrageous.'

Tom cut in quickly.

'What my father means is that's far too much money. We don't have it. And this cello was stolen from Dr. Millar's home.'

'Then the police must be involved.'

Fergus and Tom denied it in the same breath.

'Has money changed hands?'

Curtis unfolded his long, lean body and took a pace towards the window.

'It's not the way I do business.'

He sat on the low window ledge and steepled his fingers in thought. Traffic rumbled towards the complexity of lights and signs at the junction.

'So where do we go from here?

Fergus began pacing the long narrow room, pausing to sigh at the array of violins for which he would donate all his remaining teeth. He caught Tom's gaze.

'I can't let you walk away with this instrument today. You could be anybody. You could even be part of the fraud.'

'What the feck are you talking about?' Fergus' voice rose half an octave. 'You're handling stolen goods so you're part of it too. Give me strength.'

Tom stepped between them.

'Dad's right. You need to tell us what you want us to do. We've come a long way and now you're telling us you want money for taking back something that belongs to us. To Dr. Millar that is.'

Curtis gave Tom a poisonous stare and the tension between them became steamy. Pulling out a red handkerchief he dabbed his upper lip as he slowly paced the length of the room. Fergus demanded to examine the cello. He needed to check the markings that made it unique. Satisfied he decided to change tack.

'Mr. Longford. None of us want to be involved in something criminal. If I give you £500 cash within the next fifteen minutes…'

The response was a long throaty guffaw of laughter.

'Come on Dad. Let's go to the police.'

'Now you wait.' Curtis grabbed Tom's shirt collar. 'We agreed no police. I will contact the vendor…'

'Don't bother. We know who she is. We'll be visiting her as soon as we get back to Birmingham.'

'Ok damn you. Five thousand pound handling fee and I will bring the cello to Birmingham next week.'

'5k? Are you insane?'

'Probably for allowing you to come here. Take it or leave it.'

Fergus was about to explode into a rant when Tom grabbed his sleeve.

'Deal,' he said, holding out his hand. 'Dad?'

Curtis Longford handed him a card.

'This is the address you will come to. Don't bring anyone with you or tell anyone about this. I will call you.'

'It's blackmail,' Fergus spluttered.

'It's business,' Longford replied flatly.

CHAPTER TWENTY-SEVEN

Una visited Iain each day in the hope that he would be well enough to sign the papers she needed to return to the new solicitors. Marvin Braithwaite had proved to be on the ball but had made no promises about Una's position. Fortunately for him, he'd made no reference to his client's irresponsibility. 'It happens,' was all he would say.

She talked softly to Iain in a voice that didn't quite belong to her about things she hoped would trigger some memories of happier times; camping in Skye when the tent blew away into the sea and Johanna starting nursery and giving her lunch away every day to a girl who told her a tale about living in a cardboard box. Pausing every so often to wait for his response, she dabbed his forehead with a damp tissue shocked when he jerked away from her, his empty vacant eye watching as she moved back to her chair. Una concluded that the stroke must have been more serious than the ward manager was prepared to say. She tried holding his fingers which felt rigid in her hand but she got the feeling that if he had the energy he would slap her with them. She planned to speak to his consultant.

'Iain. I don't even know if you can hear me but there are things I want to say.'

She put her bag on the floor and edged closer to his bed.

'I don't know what has happened to you other than the bit that nurse told me. She asked me if you self-harmed. I didn't know what to say to that. She mentioned some old bruises he found when he did the examination. What have you been telling her? I know you get confused sometimes.'

Iain turned his head with great effort to look out of the window. He smiled to himself as he saw a blackbird perched on branch so close he could see some unusual white markings on its feathers. He thought about how fortunate birds were to be born with the ability to be able to fly up and off whenever they wanted. Did they think about it he asked himself or was it instinct?

'Iain?'

Una gave his arm a gentle shake.

'Why are you smiling like that?'

Iain sighed inwardly. He wanted her to leave. In fact, he'd never wanted her to visit him in the first place but was unable to tell the nurse. They'd told him his speech would return and it was his closely held secret that it had. He felt a bit like the Chief in One Flew Over the Cuckoo's Nest. The only way he could communicate with her was to remain silent. It was a trick he'd learned from her after all. All those years of using the silent treatment to control him. He quelled the knowing smile that threatened to burst onto his lips.

'Iain, if you drop the divorce then we will sell the house and start again. That's fair isn't it?' Hmm? I know you want the twins to come home and well, we can work something out. I'm going to start a new business providing the bankruptcy proceedings don't come to anything. I've been advised to go for an IVA …'

'Shut up. Shut. The. Fuck. Up.'

Una stood up quickly and backed away. She could feel the burning hate pouring from his eyes. Dashing into the corridor she looked frantically around for a nurse.

'Come quickly. I think there's a problem. My husband's having another stroke.'

The middle aged woman reluctantly stopped her conversation and wobbled towards Iain's room, the ladder in her black tights stretching with every move. Iain grinned at her and held up a glass to be filled with water. He wanted to show off the renewed steadiness of his hand.

'He's not been speaking at all then he comes out with this foul language.'

'Well at least he's speaking one we all understand. There's some odd cases about people recovering from a stroke speaking a foreign language or even with a foreign accent. Mind you, there's not much English spoken in here anyway.'

Una opened and closed her mouth. All instincts told her to challenge the woman's racist attitudes but she let it go. It was no longer her battle to fight.

'So what is the matter with my husband?

Una bent over to fasten the jacket of Iain's borrowed pyjamas before the nurse did her tests.

'You can go now Mrs. Millar. Doctor will need to see him.'

'I need to know now. There's some urgent business to conclude that needs…'

Staff nurse Jamieson had seen it all before. Sick husband, bullying wife, inconclusive evidence of assault, blame pushed onto both sides one minute then fiercely protective the next.

'Go home. You look exhausted. When Dr. Millar is feeling up to visitors we will let you know.'

Una was about to stand her ground when she realised that the hospital really did employ security officers and CCTV. Gathering up her coat and bag, she bent down to kiss Iain's cheek.

'Bye darling. I'll be back soon.'

Una pulled out the mirror she kept in the glove compartment and spiralled up the tube of peony red lipstick. She dabbed a spot in the centre of her top lip and slid it over the stretch of her mouth. After a final satisfying blot she ran a comb through her hair and wondered what to do next. A call demanded her attention. It was about the insurance claim for the stolen cello.

Una's stomach twisted itself in a pretzel as she listened to some senior manager advising her that that the claim was not going to be processed and they had reason to believe that the theft of the cello was not genuine. She began to shout, half realising that she was probably protesting too much but on hearing that there would be proceedings and possibly police involvement was terrifying.

'We also have evidence that you insured this cello with two different companies and you've made two separate claims. Dr. Millar's signature does not match what we have on record. I am sure you realise the severity of this situation.'

'Don't be ridiculous! Why on earth would we do what you're suggesting? We're respectable professional people.'

The claims manager let her rant, noting her language and behaviour.

'We will be writing to you to explain everything and to tell you the next step in the proceedings. Mrs. Millar I have to warn you that we do get anonymous tip offs about such matters. You might want to get legal advice.'

Una threw the phone onto the passenger seat and collapsed onto the steering wheel. Banging her fists and her forehead she yelled out all her frustrations in between bone rattling sobs. Reaching for the phone she called Martha and between nauseous heaving and waves of terror she told her what had happened.

Martha stretched out her fingers to admire the new manicure. She'd suspected Una wasn't as innocent as she made out. An old saying of her grandmother's came to her. *Di higher monkey climb di more him expose.* She gave Una the translation.

'Girl, the higher you climb the more you will be exposed. You've gone too far this time. Pride has come before your fall and what follows Hubris? Nemesis. I wish I could feel sorry for you Una but truth is, I don't.'

'Is that all you can offer? Stupid quotes?'

Martha thought for a moment.

'That's all I can offer. Bye Una. Good luck.'

A few days later

'Mum, I need the car. I'm picking Stuart up from the airport.'

'What? You didn't say anything before. I'm off to rehearsal and the room is a tip. Your Dad put all those boxes in there.'

'Stop fussing. I can do it when we get back. Just put the bedding out. Does this mean you need the car?'

Tom grabbed a freshly made scone and crammed half of it into his mouth.

Freda put her hands on her hips and made a moue of disapproval.

'No. I'm being picked up. I don't even know where your Dad has got to. When did you arrange this with Stuart? Explain please.'

'Facebook,' was all Tom would say as if that explained everything. 'Keys? Please. Mummy?'

'How long is he staying? Does he know about Iain?'

'Byeee.'

Stuart was in the first group to enter the arrival lounge. He was carrying a small holdall and an Arabic newspaper.

'Tom. Thanks mate. Nightmare flight. Some kid was screeching all the way from Dubai.'

Tom made a sympathetic noise and led the way out to the short stay carpark.

'I've only just told Mum you're coming so she's still in shock. Nice shock though. You know what she's like.'

'Even my mother doesn't know I'm here. I'm glad you told me about Dad. It sounds awful. Poor Dad.'

'It will cheer him up to see you I'm sure. Do you want to go back via the hospital? It's just about visiting time I think. Dad was there earlier. He said there's some improvement.'

'He will only feel better when he's got rid of the witch,' muttered Stuart as he fiddled with the window winder.

Tom didn't comment.

'I've been offered a job in Edinburgh. Interviewed on Skype a couple of weeks ago. I wasn't going to take it but I think I'd better. It's a lectureship in Arabic and Middle Eastern Studies. It means Dad could come and live with me and the twins.'

'Wow. You have thought things out.'

'Don't say anything. I need to see how he feels about it. Is this the hospital?'

Stuart was allowed ten minutes to see his father only because he made a grand statement about having flown in from Muscat specially. He found Iain dozing in front of a repeat of Time Team from Salisbury Plain. He crept in slowly so as not to alarm him, whispering, 'Dad, it's Stuart several times until Iain opened his eyes. Stuart gave his frail body a long hug not realising how much he'd missed him until that moment. Iain struggled to find some words but sensed they were superfluous.

He let Stuart help him ease him up into the pillows and handed him the remote control. Turning off the TV Stuart told him about the uncomfortable flight back, some of the goings on at the college and finally about the job. Iain's face lit up. Pleasure and pride was etched over his gaunt face.

'When you're better we can talk about it. I'm going back with Tom now but I'll come in tomorrow. The nurse said you might be released in a few days.'

Iain nodded and reached for his son's hand. He felt very fortunate he thought to have a son who travelled thousands of miles to see him. Not many twenty somethings would do that. Sinking back into the pillows he raised his hand as Stuart left the room. He felt some of his strength returning and later that night was found shuffling slowly through the ward to make a phone call.

'Could I speak to James and Johanna Millar please? I know it's late but I really would like a few quick words. I would appreciate it.'

'Dad, what's wrong?' James' voice trembled slightly.

'Daddy!' squealed Johanna. 'You are naughty. You're not supposed to ring at bedtime.'

'Nothing's wrong James. Don't sound so worried. Johanna, sometimes it's good to be a little bit naughty.' Iain felt a gentle laugh swell up from his stomach. 'I just wanted to tell you and your sister how very much I love you. Very much indeed.'

CHAPTER TWENTY-EIGHT

Iain's night was restless. As he began to recover his balance and his speech he wanted to go home – but realising that the place he'd called home for ten years was no longer a place of refuge but a battle ground. He was ready for whatever fate was about to throw at him. Having his son home somehow made him feel things would work out. He stepped out of bed and drew back the curtains. Dawn was breaking over the city and he indulged a fantasy of being back in Edinburgh and going for a morning walk through the quiet streets before going to teach a few hours of music. The twins would stay at St. Mungo's as day pupils and they would spend time exploring Scotland as a family.

'Dr. Millar. What are you doing out of bed?'

He noticed the twinkle in the eye of the nurse as she handed him his stick.

'I think they call it living in the moment. It feels good.'

'Well don't go falling or they won't let you out today.'

Iain's face lit up.

'Indeed I won't. I shall be very, very good.'

***

Stuart had been unable to sleep at all. He sat in the window seat of his room sipping coffee and listening to six resonating chimes from the village clock tower. Seeing his father in such a bad way angered and upset him. Remorseful over not keeping in touch very much since he left he was determined to try and make amends. When he'd spoken to his friend Jed in Muscat about the situation he'd been dismissive. 'You're a grown up Stu. Let the parents wallow in their own messes. Not your problem.'

He drained his cup and pulled on some jogging kit hoping to slip out without disturbing anyone. He could hear Fergus snoring loudly from the next room. Walking briskly around the green helped to clear the brain fog. He nodded to a couple of early dog walkers on Oak Tree Lane as he trotted towards Rowheath park. He needed plenty of energy for what he was about to do. He paused to untwist the knots in his shoulders before breaking into a run through the lanes of Cadbury houses, around the boating lake, past what used to be the local college and back towards the house, pausing only to take sips of water from his flask.

Freda was up and about in the kitchen rolling out pastry. She waved a mug at Stuart as he bent down to untie his trainers.

'I wish you could get Fergus to go out with you. Maybe for a short walk. He really needs the exercise,' she sighed as she watched the coffee filter into the jug.

Stuart laughed and pulled out a stool at the breakfast bar, gratefully accepting a piece of toast and home-made jam.

'How was Iain?' she asked, joining him for a coffee.

'Better than I thought he would be. It's a good hospital.'

'It will be good to have him back. I think Fergus wants to have a chat with you about the arrangements.'

'Sorry Freda. I think that's my phone.'

He retrieved it from his jacket pocket and read the text.

'It's Dad. You must be a fortune teller. It seems that he can come home later today.'

'What's all the noise? My head is thumping.'

Fergus appeared in the kitchen, rubbing his temples.

'That's because you downed too much whisky last night Fergus. You really have to take your health more seriously.'

'It's too early for nagging. Is there any coffee left?'

Fergus perched on a stool but found his belly wouldn't allow him to balance.

'Feck.'

'Dad can come out after two this afternoon,' Stuart told him. 'I can bring him back in a taxi.'

'No need for that. Stuart.' Fergus paused to butter his toast, scraping half of it again under his wife's watchful eye. 'There are some things I need to say. I am probably out of order as it's not my place but your father and I have been friends for years.'

He crunched for a very long time before continuing.

'It's my view that your Dad has been under a lot of strain which led to the stroke. You know about the dirty business with the school.'

Stuart nodded and laid down his mug.

'Well, Una never really believed him and has been punishing

him ever since. Iain has been here and at rehearsals covered in bruises and with various injuries he's tried to explain away. I believed him at first but then I started to piece things together. Hell's teeth Freda. Is the heating on full? It's hot in here.'

Stuart didn't move despite the desperate need to scratch his calf.

'Una is a difficult woman to say the least. She can't stand the sight of me. The way she gives me the evil eye is a giveaway. Problem is, I've seen bruises and cuts on her as well. She's making out that Iain has been violent towards her because of some mental health issue he's got. Your father is very depressed but who wouldn't be with what he's had to deal with? The problem is I know your Dad and am sure he isn't the one that's being abusive to her. It's as twisted as a corkscrew.'

Fergus closed his mouth. He felt he'd said too much. Watching anxiously for Stuart's reaction he tapped a tea spoon on each of his knuckles.

'I've known for ages but not been able to do anything about it.'

'You've known? So I'm not being a daft old fool?'

The relief on Fergus' face was almost palpable.

'I lived with them for a few years don't forget. Dad was always frightened of her moods and would do anything to keep the peace. Money is her god, or at least the love of it. I wouldn't be surprised if she'd stolen Dad's cello.'

'Ah. Well. We think she is behind it and has been dealing with somebody in London to get it sold overseas. And… and she's attempted an insurance scam.'

Stuart's hand moved to stroke the scar on his forehead.

'So what are we going to do?'

'We're going to get the cello back. You've come over at just the right time. Your stepmother could well be facing a prison sentence for assault, theft and fraud but much will depend on what your father wants to do. All we can do is support him in his choice.'

'I want to go to Woodbourne House. I am going to confront her. This is my Dad we're talking about.'

'Stuart, Una can be dangerous. I know you're an adult but it's better if we both go. She could call the police and make up some story. Without a witness you are too vulnerable.'

He chewed on his lip as he processed the information before agreeing. He felt he should call Morag but to tell her what? That his father was at the mercy of a psycho?'

Fergus was about to pull up outside the house when he noticed police officers walking down the drive to their car. He glanced at Stuart to judge his reaction and for the first time recognised the similarity between him and his father. A slightly too long nose, high broad forehead and the way Stuart held his head slightly to the left side as if listening to something.

They sat in the car waiting for the police to leave. They were taking their time and just as Fergus was about to open his door, he found himself head to head with a female officer.

'Are you visiting this house sir?'

'Yes, as a matter of fact we are. Is there a problem?'

'Are you a relative of Mrs. Millar?'

'I'm her stepson. What's happened?'

'For feck's sake will somebody tell us what's going on?' Fergus got out of the car and stamped the cramp out of his foot.

'Can you tell us your business here sir?'

'I've come to collect some papers belonging to my father who's in hospital. He needs them.'

At that point both men turned to see where the commotion was coming from. Una, protesting and resisting what appeared to be an arrest by two more officers, appeared on the doorstep. Her face was poppy red with anger.

'Tell them Stuart that they've made a mistake. I've done nothing wrong.'

Stuart looked at her through narrowed eyes.

'If you think that then you are seriously deluded.'

The plan he had kept to himself had fallen at the first post. He was going to offer Una a deal. To sign over Woodbourne House to his father in return from not handing her over to the police.

'What's the reason officer? Fraud? Theft or …' He stepped close to Una not heeding the warning from the officer on her left, 'grievous bodily harm? You've no idea the damage you've done to my father have you?'

'Stuart. Let's go.' Fergus tugged his sleeve. 'There's nothing more we can do.'

'Well I hope Dad throws the book at you. Women like you need locking up. It's not surprising the female prison population has risen if your behaviour is anything to go by.' Stuart pushed his face into hers. 'You nearly killed my Dad. I hope you can live with yourself.'

Pulling back his shoulders he asked if he could go into the house to collect some documents. After much argument, Una agreed to fetch him what he wanted.

'There's no money if that's what you're after. We're bust. Broke. Bankrupt. Thanks to your wonderful father.'

Stuart shut his ears to her ranting and throwing the folders into the back of the car told Fergus he wanted to get as far away as possible.

'Hospital?'

'Not until we've gone through this stuff.'

'Your Dad will have to know what's happened. I hope he's up to it.'

'Let's go to the Sack of Taters first. I could use a beer.'

Once Stuart had time to see the financial damage he was able to plan a way forward and package it in a way that Iain would hopefully accept. Una had been right. Debts spewed out of every hole. He pushed the mortgage documents towards Fergus just as he was about to bite into a panini.

'Does that look like my Dad's signature to you?'

Fergus scrambled for his glasses before declaring it didn't.

'Well that's good news too.'

By the time they reached Iain, he was dressed and sitting in the day room. He was chatting animatedly to some patients about their favourite music.

'My son,' he beamed, 'and the man in the luminous green waistcoat featuring a tomato blob is Fergus.'

'Lo. Thank the lord you're taking him 'ome. He's got a right gob on him! Mind 'ow you go. Tra a bit.'

'Straight home Dad?'

'No. I fancy a bit of a wander. Cannon Hill Park. I've not been in the new Arts Centre. Can you believe that? It's on the way isn't it?

Fergus rolled his eyes but was pleased to see Iain had lost his pale listlessness. A pale sun did its best to throw down some warm rays as they wandered around the gardens stopping to give Iain time to regain his balance. Three men joined in quiet solidarity exchanged the odd comment about the gardeners who were having a cigarette break and some litter spilling out of a forgotten bin. Nothing deep, nothing heavy.

When Iain got tired they found a seat and Stuart fetched some coffee into which Fergus poured a few drops of whisky for Iain.

'I'm not supposed to drink with the tablets.'

'There's not even enough in there to wet a gnat's bollocks,' Fergus grinned. 'Don't go wussy on me.'

Stuart bit the edge of his lip as he figured out how to raise some of the difficult issues his father needed to face.

'What is it Stu? I know that look. You used to bite the edge of your thumbnail when you had something on your mind.'

Stuart explained as simply as he could everything he and Fergus had figured out. He waited for Iain's reaction but his face was unreadable. He leaned forward on the stick the hospital had let him borrow and breathed slowly. Then he grinned and began to laugh. He laughed until his ribs screamed in pain and water pooled in his eyes.

Stuart looked at Fergus for help.

'That must be pretty strong whisky,' he said, pouring a drop more into Iain's cup.

'But Dad. This is horrific. She's ruined you. The family. What about the twins? And where is the bloody cello?'

'Ah the cello. I'd almost forgotten. Fergus, you know Steve's cello you borrowed. Well, it had a bit of an accident and I've been fretting about it ever since.'

Both Stuart and Fergus watched bemused as Iain collapsed into more howls of laughter.

'Pass us your cup, son. We could do with a bit of what he's got.'

CHAPTER TWENTY-NINE

Una had been waiting in the interview room for the duty solicitor for over two hours. She shook out the cramp in her left foot, refusing offers of tea or coffee. When the woman finally arrived, her long blonde hair spilling out of a navy blue barrette, she greeted Una with a limp handshake. Laura Bailey was exactly the sort of woman Una disliked. Young, energetic and an air of omniscience. She ordered bottles of water and time to confer with her client.

'At this stage it's best we listen to the charges and you say nothing. I'm not up to speed with the case yet so silence is golden as they say.'

Una wondered whether they trained solicitors in charm schools rather than law colleges but she did as she was advised. After being cautioned and told that the interview would be recorded, Una switched her mind off as the barrage of questions began.

'No comment,' she said, with an approving nod of Miss Bailey.

'Tell me about your marriage to Dr. Millar? Would you say it was happy?'

Una turned her eyes to the top corner of the stuffy room where she saw a broken cobweb. Iain's face passed across her vision but wouldn't stick for long. She remembered him, grey and frail in the hospital but that wasn't what she was looking for. It was an image of him ranting at some unseen voice she needed to recall. As she looked around her the faces seemed as if they'd fallen off a surreal painting. She shouldn't be here, she told herself. She was needed at home with Iain. To help him get better. She felt as if a bucket of ice had been poured over her head. This couldn't be happening.

'Miss Carrington?'

'Is this relevant?' Laura Bailey cut in.

'No comment,' Una said in a voice barely audible.

*****

Five Ways island was jammed with traffic owing to a broken down transit van. Nothing was moving. Frustrated at being a mile from their destination, Tom suggested they pulled into the next side street and walked.

'What with five grand oozing out of our pockets. No. We need the car close by. No telling what this Curtis bloke might do. I'm going to nip down this road.'

'You can't Dad. It's a one way street.'

Fergus was too intent on finding the address that he didn't take any notice. Lost in the shabby streets of inner city Birmingham, it took them an hour to locate the semi derelict building marked 48.

'Are you sure this is it Tom? The door's hanging off its hinges.'

'Like most of them round here,' added Stuart. 'I don't like the look of this.'

'Tom, you stay in the car and I'll go in with Stuart. He's got the documents and ID. You keep on the look out.'

'You mean for potential cello-jackers?'

Fergus sent a text to the number he'd been given to alert Curtis to their arrival. They saw the man's gaunt face appear at the grimy window. Following his instructions to go round the back of the building and through a fire escape to the first floor, Stuart held his nose. The stench of urine was overpowering. They stepped gingerly over the used syringes barely concealed in the long grass. Stuart knocked on the door. Longford's eyes darted into the corridor as he pulled them inside. He looked at Stuart for a long time who, knowing he was expected to cower, squared up to him.

'I'm Stuart Millar. Here's the letter from my father.'

Longford cast his eye over it before handing it back.

'Let's get this over with. Have you got the money?'

'First you tell us the name of the woman who contacted you.'

Stuart pressed the voicemail button on the phone in his pocket.

'Woodbourne. That's all I know. It's her you should be going after. Money. Now.'

Fergus patted his jacket pockets and pulled out a bulging envelope and handed it over. At the moment, Stuart pulled out his phone, scrolled to camera and clicked.

Longford dropped the money as quickly as if it was hot ashes in his hand.

'What the…?'

'Just evidence that you've been paid for something that never belonged to you. Evidence that you are handling stolen goods.'

The control in Stuart's voice belied the sick feeling in his stomach.

Longford tried to grab the camera, falling backwards as Fergus executed a sharp kick to his ankle.

'Delete that picture. We agreed no funny business.'

'I can't see any of us laughing can you? Hand over the cello.'

Fergus was beginning to enjoy himself. It was like being in a film with a very clichéd plot.

Longford pulled himself up, cursing as he caught his sleeve on a nail.

'It's in my car. Follow me.'

Fergus insisted on opening the case and checking it was the right instrument. Satisfied, he put it in the boot of his car.

Longford grabbed him by the collar and towered over him.

'Now listen to me fat man. You're going nowhere until you give me my £5,000. That was the deal.'

Stuart dialled a number and moved away. 'Police?' he said loudly. 'Sorry the line's bad. I want to report a crime.'

Longford threw open the door of his Range Rover and skidded out of the parking bay into the traffic having no idea that his number plate had been photographed by Tom.

'The joys of modern technology, eh Dad?' he sighed happily.

A few days later

'That workshop in Hanbury's done a good job of repairing Steve's cello. You're getting a good sound from it too. You'll be ready to come back into the ensemble. I've planned on a lead role for you.'

Iain ran a cloth over the borrowed instrument, careful not to let it get any more damaged.

'It's good news about Stuart too. That job sounds tailor made for him. Just think how many times you will see each other. And the twins. Do they know?'

Freda pushed open the door with her hip as she edged carefully into the snug with a laden tea tray.

'Sugar and fat free muffins.'

'Oh…'

'Fergus. You are on a diet as from now.'

'Not yet. There's still a lot to sort out.'

Iain picked up his mug and held it out in his right hand. He kept marvelling at how steady it was. Dr. Gordon had been right all along. Stress is a killer. The new tablets were doing their job as Iain felt the rock on top of his head begin to lift.

'No more progress on my cello?'

Freda caught her husband's eye.

'Tricky negotiations but it will be fine. Be patient,' he said peering into one of the muffins as if a hand was about to leap out and chop off his nose.

'It was a bit of a turn up for the books that Una had actually protected my half of the assets. Maybe I've underestimated her.'

Fergus shoved a chunk of cake into his mouth to stop from commenting.

'You did the right thing Iain by reporting the assaults. The courts need to know what sort of person she is. She could turn on the children.'

'She wouldn't do that.'

Iain didn't sound very sure.

An awkward silence fell over the trio as they sipped and indulged their thoughts.

'Well this won't buy the babby a new nappy,' said Fergus, slapping his knees and reaching for a folder of music. 'You need to practice this Cello Concerto, particularly these bars.'

Freda gathered up the mugs and left them to it. She was glad Stuart had decided to come back to the UK to be with his family. It was what Iain needed. Her heart fell a little at the thought of Tom leaving in a couple of months to go travelling then onto university.

A week later

Iain had been out walking in the fresh spring air. His energy levels were returning and along with them a sense of renewed hope. He'd checked his emails in the hope that Una would try to make contact but there was nothing. All he knew was what his solicitor was prepared to tell him. A sadness shadowed him with each day there was no news of his cello. Steve's replacement was perfectly adequate he reasoned and he should be grateful for all the good things in his life, especially Fergus, without whom he knew he would have died. It was Fergus who'd stood by him and hauled him out of the darkness of the well that threatened to drown him. It was Fergus who had told him he was a fecking eejit when he said he wanted to end his life.

As he pushed open the front door, he saw his best friend locking up the boot of his car.

'Get a shower and put something half decent on. We're going out for the afternoon.'

'Where?'

'Just to see some people. Hurry up.'

When Tom was sure Iain was out of sight, he dashed into the garage and loaded the cello into the boot, along with music stands and his Dad's violin.

***

The M5 carried light traffic to Worcester from where they took the exit for Malvern. Finger on the map, Tom directed his father towards Lower Broadheath avoiding the touristy Elgar trail.

'We thought you'd like to visit the Elgar Birthplace Museum,' said Freda reaching inside her bag for some mints.

'Oh lovely. I've always wanted to come here.'

Iain's face lit up as they turned into the car park. He wanted to see for himself the statue of the great man sitting in the garden.

A short woman with a grey bun and lilac jumper approached them.

'Mr O'Neal? Dr. Millar? Welcome to the Elgar Birthplace Museum. I think you'll find everything in order. There's quite a crowd gathering.' She tugged on her beads and led the way into the garden.

Iain frowned and looked at Freda for an explanation as Fergus strode off ahead, leaving Tom to unpack the boot. The scent of English bluebells was sweet in the still air. A bee hummed in some early white hawthorn as Iain looked across the horizon to the hills and understood the strength of inspiration Elgar must have found in this idyllic spot.

He turned round to find music stands being set up, and Fergus fiddling with his bow. Freda tutted as she noticed he'd slipped on his black silk waistcoat with a mark down the front that looked like a snail trail.

'What's going on?' asked Iain, his pulse raising. From the corner of his eye he could see what looked to be a cello case. There was something familiar about it.

'Tom?'

Tom was opening the score to the Elgar Cello Concerto. Behind him was Stuart, carrying the cello case engraved with I.M.

'Dad? This is yours I believe?'

Iain walked towards it, his hands shaking as he unclipped the catches, aware of many pairs of eyes on him. Freda wiped the corner of her eye as she watched him run a loving hand over the fine woodwork, touching the distinguishing mark that set his cello apart from any other. He gently plucked each string, turning the tuning pegs until the pitch was perfect. Pulling out the end pin to settle the cello, Iain adjusted his bow, the special gift from Fergus, and teased out a perfect A. The reunion was complete.

Fergus waited until Iain ran his eyes over the score. The notes swam like tadpoles in murky water but as Iain connected the bars with the music in his head, he began slowly to draw out the primal earthiness of the piece. People were gathering in the warm sunshine, falling into silence as Fergus picked up his violin to blend his unique interpretation of the music, giving Iain a conspiratorial wink as he did so.

Iain looked across to where Edward Elgar was relaxing on a bench and he hoped the great man would approve. Together they lifted their eyes to the distant hills, and Iain felt the music beckoning a brighter future…

Angelena is a graduate of Birmingham University and is a passionate defender of a city which she believes is misunderstood. Originally from the Peak District, she made the city her home for over 30 years from where she ran her very successful international training consultancy specialising in interpersonal skills and conflict resolution. One of her claims to fame was the Bouncer's Charm School in the late 80's which attracted global media attention. She spent 3 years working on the Shankill Road in Belfast training former paramilitaries to acquire new skills for the burgeoning tourism market in Northern Ireland.

Angelena trained as a journalist in British Columbia before returning to the UK to study modern languages. She is the author of 3 business books published by Management Pocketbooks and has a business column with the Isle of Man newspapers.

Angelena has been a chorister since the age of 7 and in midlife was awarded the Archbishop's Certificate in Church Music. Now living in Malvern she indulges her love of Elgar.